IMPUNITY

Rough justice for murder

RAY CLARK

THE
BOOK
FOLKS

Published by The Book Folks

London, 2023

ISBN 978-1-80462-083-0

www.thebookfolks.com

IMPUNITY is the tenth book in a series of mysteries by Ray Clark featuring DI Stewart Gardener. The full list of books is as follows:

Impunity: *Freedom from punishment or from the unpleasant results of something that has been done.*

"God is dead! Heaven is empty —
Weep, children, you no longer have a father."

Gérard de Nerval (1808 – 1855)

Chapter One

The kettle boiled as the clock struck midnight.

In the back room of the Bramfield police station, desk sergeant Maurice Cragg rose up out of his armchair and approached the table. Next to the kettle was his cup, and next to that, his plate, filled with cheese and ham sandwiches. He lifted the kettle and poured the boiling water over the tea bag. He reached over to his right, opened the fridge, and removed the milk.

Placing the bottle on the table, Cragg retreated in the direction of his armchair and increased the volume on the radio, which was on a shelf above his armchair. The BBC was running a series of mystery plays at midnight and he had been waiting in anticipation for tonight's thirty-minute episode – *The House of Death.*

He reflected on what he knew about the play: Aunt Martha and Aunt Louise were sure their nephew, Roger, was trying to kill them for their money, so they had decided to take whatever steps were necessary to prevent his actions. They had been moved out into the country to live with Roger and his wife, Ester. She had made no secret of the fact that she thought the aunts were invalids and too old to live alone. Since moving to the country, however, Martha and Louise had noticed strange things happening. Roger had put their house up for sale, and now, their beloved cat has been poisoned.

With his tea mashed and his sandwiches at the ready, Maurice Cragg took his seat, figuring it wouldn't take him long to work out what was going on and who was responsible.

The town and the station had been quiet all evening. Two constables were out on patrol, and he wasn't going to let anything spoil his break.

Except for a very strange whining sound.

He sat forward, staring at the radio. The presenter was introducing the episode, so he doubted the noise had originated there.

He leaned even further forward, lowering the volume, listening intently for it to return.

Thinking about it, the sound had actually come from the back of the building, which led into Market Place, so it was possible that on a Thursday night in late February, there may be one or two people on the streets, returning from one of the town centre pubs after a lock-in.

He waited patiently, staring at the clock, aware that he may well be missing vital clues if the play was underway.

Deciding it was nothing to concern himself with, he reached out to adjust the volume on the radio, when he heard the sound again. The tone was more urgent. The first time, the noise was low, which could have been anything – an animal possibly. The second time, it had an air of desperation to it, and ended an octave higher than it had started.

Someone could be in trouble.

"Here we go," said Cragg.

The policeman in him could not let it go. He stood up, buttoned up his jacket, put his helmet on and left the sitting room to enter the lobby, which was empty. Cragg lifted the hatch and walked toward the front door.

Out on the street he felt a chill as a cold wind encircled him. Staring up and down and left and right, he saw no one. He studied the row of shops opposite; all the doorways were empty. Further down the street, The Royal Oak was lit up inside, as was the sign outside, but there was no one leaving.

Maurice Cragg set off around the back of the building. A number of cars were in the car park, but most of them had a thin film of frost on the windscreens.

He was pretty miffed now; the play would have started and his tea would be cooling.

All that changed however, when he rounded the corner at the back of the station.

The girl was laid on the ground, close to the wall of the building. And the sound came again as she gasped for breath.

Cragg almost tripped and fell forward, catching himself before he dropped on top of her. He knelt down and asked, "Are you okay?"

She made no reply.

It would have been very easy to see the situation as a prank, or the girl as someone who'd had too much to drink, especially at such a late hour. But a closer examination revealed a grave expression. In the darkness of the street lighting, it was very hard to tell, but Cragg would have said she was ashen. Her mouth was fixed in a grimace and she held her hands tight to her abdomen. She appeared to be sweating and very certainly struggling to breathe.

"What's your name, love?"

She still didn't reply, other than to make a strange wailing sound.

He estimated her age as early twenties. She had short dark hair, with a straight nose and straight white teeth. He couldn't tell the colour of her eyes. From what he could ascertain, she was chunky, not fat but still well built. Her clothing of black dungarees, boots and a large overcoat may have been more suited to a male.

At that point, she screamed out and doubled up, reaching out her right hand for some obvious help.

"It's okay," said Cragg, taking the hand in his own. "I'm here. Where have you come from?"

The girl tried to speak but could form no words, only noises of terrible distress.

Maurice Cragg glanced around but he saw no one in the town at all.

"Is anyone with you?" he asked the girl.

He couldn't be too sure but he thought she shook her head.

"Do you have a mobile phone on you?"

Again, she shook her head.

He couldn't understand that. Everyone had a phone these days. He made a very polite search of her clothing, finding nothing in any of the pockets he could see.

He couldn't actually find anything: no phone, no purse, no money, and no ID of any description. He desperately wanted to reach inside, and felt that under the circumstances, and being a police officer, he would be excused.

He found nothing there either, apart from a damp patch around her abdomen, which was discoloured, and may or may not have been blood, but it was very difficult to tell under the light.

Cragg felt a sense of urgency and asked, "How did you get here?"

No reply.

With both of his hands, he took hers. "If I help you, can you get to your feet?"

"No," she screamed, which was the only word he had made sense of since he had found her.

Decisions needed to be made. It was apparent that she couldn't move. He figured he needed to do something more constructive. She needed an ambulance, and he needed backup from his own officers on patrol. He reached into his pocket, but he didn't have *his* mobile phone either. He quite clearly saw – in his mind's eye – that it was still on the arm of his chair in the station.

"Oh Christ. Isn't that just typical?"

He needed to return to the building, but he didn't want to leave her alone.

He tried once again. "Can you tell me *your* name, or the name of someone I can contact for you?"

At that point, a guardian angel appeared on the scene, behind him, in the form of a female voice.

"Is everything okay?"

Cragg glanced around. The lady was quite short, dressed comfortably in a fur coat, a hat, a dress, and black ankle boots. She was middle-aged and wore tortoiseshell glasses.

"Is there anything I can do to help, Sergeant?"

It was then that he recognized her as Betty Miller. She lived in the town and worked in one of the newsagents.

"Betty, love, would you mind staying here for just one minute while I run into the station and call for an ambulance?"

"What's happened?"

"I have no idea," said Cragg. "But it's serious. I need to get her a warm blanket and an ambulance – now!"

"Can we move her?" asked Betty.

Cragg was halfway down the building when he called back. "Best not to. I'll be two minutes."

Entering the station, he grabbed the phone and called the Bramfield Community Hospital. He then reached for the radio and called his constables, all the time aware that whatever was going on outside, could very well become a crime scene before long.

Chapter Two

Having finished giving out his orders, Maurice Cragg quickly ran upstairs to one of the supply rooms. Opening a wall cupboard, he reached in and found a thick woolly blanket.

Back down the stairs he slipped into the back room where he found another wall cupboard and located a flask and a small torch. He quickly made a coffee with the warm water from the kettle and then ran back through the lobby, out of the front door, and around to the rear of the building.

One glance at the girl on the ground and he feared he was far too late to help her. He turned to Betty Miller.

"What happened?"

The lady shook her head and placed her hand to her mouth. "She just... I'm afraid she just died."

Cragg peered at the girl again. He dropped the blanket on the ground and stood the flask next to it. Kneeling, he reached out a hand to check for a pulse. Betty Miller was right; the girl had gone.

He stood back up to face Betty. "Did she say anything?"

"I'm afraid not. I asked her a couple of questions: her name, and where she lived but she couldn't reply. She seemed to be in far too much pain. I asked her where it hurt and she managed to squeal out the word 'here', and pointed to her stomach."

"And then what?" asked Cragg.

"There was such a sharp intake of breath, and she just left us."

Maurice Cragg could see how upset Betty Miller was. It had really affected her in the short space of time she had spent with the girl.

He turned and knelt down. Grasping a pair of gloves from an inside jacket pocket Cragg slipped them on and inspected the girl's abdomen.

"What's happened to her, has she been stabbed?" asked Betty.

Cragg didn't reply.

"I really don't know what the world is coming to," added Betty.

Cragg fished around in his jacket pocket for the small torch. Luckily the batteries still had some life and he shined the light on to the girl's stomach. As far as he could tell, the damp, dark patch had not grown any larger. He was pretty sure now, with the extra, concentrated light, that it *was* blood.

He pulled back a little. Bramfield was a small town. Stabbings and shootings were not unknown, but they were few and far between. No one had reported anything. To his knowledge, there had been no incidents tonight.

Betty Miller interrupted his thoughts. "No one's safe anymore. Nothing like this has ever happened here."

Cragg would dispute that, especially when he thought of the reasons that Gardener and Reilly had been here previously. One of those occasions still remained a cold case, and he knew an evil man by the name of Robbie Carter to still be on the loose somewhere, but the scene before him was not Carter's style. On that note, he knew he needed to treat it as a crime scene. He had no idea what had happened to the girl, but whatever it was, there was nothing natural about it.

As he stood up, the squad car pulled into the car park next to the police station and PC Evette Mulson, known to everyone as Dulux, and PC Mike Atherton exited.

Atherton was tall, with short dark hair and pinched features: a very dedicated professional. He was the first one over. "What's happened?" he asked Cragg, staring at the girl on the ground.

Cragg explained what he'd found, ending with the fact that it was now a crime scene.

"What do you want us to do?" asked Mulson. She was short and stubby with her dark hair tied up and pushed underneath her peaked cap.

"Go into the station," replied Cragg, "and grab some police cones. Close off this passage." The area Cragg was talking about, behind the police station, was approximately ten feet wide and around thirty feet in length.

Before Mulson made a move Cragg asked if she knew the girl on the floor. After a quick examination, she said she didn't.

She then scooted off to join Atherton to grab some cones.

Cragg turned to Betty Miller. "Where did you come from, Betty, love?"

"Round the back of Princess Road. I've been to see my sister. When I left, I walked here via Greengate and then on to Market Place."

"Have you seen anyone else around?"

"I can't say I have. I generally visit my sister on a Thursday and often walk home late. I remembered thinking how quiet the town was tonight. Never thought I'd run into anything like this. It's terrible. What do you think happened?"

Cragg didn't answer the question – couldn't.

The two constables returned with traffic cones and started closing the area down.

"You didn't happen to see this girl anywhere in the town, did you?" Cragg asked Betty Miller.

"I didn't," she replied. "Like I said, I never saw anyone."

Cragg wondered which direction the girl had come from. But all of that would have to wait. There was only one man he thought capable of sorting out the problem.

His final job for now was to make a call to the Major Investigation Team at Leeds Central.

Chapter Three

Within thirty minutes of the phone call, DS Sean Reilly pulled the pool car into the Market Place car park, stopping next to an ambulance with a flashing blue light. He killed the engine. DI Stewart Gardener jumped out and approached the small crowd that had gathered: Maurice Cragg and two uniformed PCs – one he knew as Mike Atherton, the other a lady he had not seen before. Alongside those, were two medics.

He nodded to Cragg, noticing the area behind the police station had been cordoned off using traffic cones and crime scene tape, which he found a novel idea. In front of those, next to Cragg, was a bin with scene suits.

"Morning, Maurice," said Gardener, tipping his hat.

"Morning, sir, we do seem to be meeting quite a lot lately."

"Proper little hotbed of crime, this place," said Reilly. "For a sleepy little town in the middle of nowhere."

"Not so sleepy," said Atherton, who introduced PC Evette Mulson to the SIO and his partner.

"What do we have, Maurice?" asked Gardener.

The desk sergeant took Gardener through everything that had happened since he heard the sound at the start of his tea break.

"And you don't recall hearing anything before that?"

"No, sir."

Cragg then took the opportunity to introduce Betty Miller and asked her to relay to Gardener the few minutes she had spent with the girl. When she had finished, she stepped back slightly.

"She didn't say anything at all about what had happened to her?" Reilly asked Betty Miller.

Betty shook her head. "I think the girl was in far too much pain to speak, officer."

Gardener turned to his partner. "Let's take a look, Sean."

Dressed in scene suits, the pair of them entered the cordoned off area. The body of the girl had by now been covered with the blanket that Cragg had brought from the station. Gardener noticed a flask next to the body and asked whose it was.

"Mine, sir," said Cragg. "I'm afraid I was too late for it to be of any use to her."

Gardener nodded, turning his attention to the body. He rolled back the blanket. Whatever the girl had gone through, she was at peace now. Her expression was soft and relaxed, as if she was sleeping.

The SIO turned to Cragg. "So you have no idea how she ended up like this?"

"No, but like I said, there is a wound of some description around the area of her abdomen."

Gardener nodded. "I've noticed that."

"But you don't think she's been stabbed or shot?" asked Reilly.

"Doesn't look like it to me," Cragg said.

"Any idea what you think might have caused her death, Maurice?" asked Gardener.

The desk sergeant frowned. "I wouldn't like to say, sir. All I do know is, when I first examined the girl, I noticed that dark stain on her clothing. She passed away a few minutes later but the stain was no bigger, as if whatever had caused it had stopped."

"So it could still be a stab wound?" added Atherton.

"It's not likely, son," replied Reilly. "If she'd been knifed seriously enough to kill her, you'd expect more blood than Maurice is talking about."

"As you would if it were a gunshot wound," added Cragg.

Atherton nodded, with a mystified expression.

"Where have you been tonight, Mike?" Gardener asked Atherton.

"We started in Bursley Bridge and drove back into Bramfield about half an hour ago."

"And you saw nothing untoward going on in the town?"

"No," replied Mulson.

"Which way did you come into the town?" Reilly asked.

Atherton made a show of trying to think. "Came in on Old Bramfield Road, slipped on to Hungate, Southgate and Westgate, and then pretty much circled the outskirts of the town."

"And you can't remember seeing anything that might connect to this?" asked Reilly.

"Nothing that we can recall," said Mulson.

"And I'm sure we would have seen *her*," said Atherton, "especially in the condition she was in."

"Stupid question, Maurice," said Gardener. "Is this exactly how you found her, on the ground? You didn't see her approaching?"

"No, sir."

"So no hint as to the direction she came from?"

Cragg shook his head.

Gardener rose up and studied what he could see of the town. He would have described it as unnaturally quiet. Thursday night into Friday morning was close enough to the weekend for people to be out. If it had been as quiet for the rest of the night, Gardener would have a serious problem with witnesses. But there would have to be someone. Surely a girl couldn't have been staggering around in such a state and no one see her.

He asked Reilly to have a quick peek around the perimeter of the building, see if he could spot anything untoward.

With Reilly gone, Gardener knelt back down to the body, removing the rest of the blanket. His examination revealed no other areas of concern, only the dark stain in the region of her abdomen. He didn't like that. A lack of evidence of a stab wound could open up something seriously nasty.

His partner returned, kneeling to join Gardener.

"Anything?" asked Gardener.

"Nothing as far as I can see. I've not spotted any blood stains anywhere. The only pub on that side is a place called The Golden Lion. That seems empty, all the lights out. I checked the church, it's closed. There's no one in the public toilets, and nothing untoward going on anywhere else."

Reilly turned his attention back to the girl and then asked his partner, "No indication of a knife wound, no holes in her clothing?"

"Nothing," said Gardener.

"I don't like the sound of that."

"So where does that leave us?" asked Gardener.

"Whatever's causing the dark patch has started on the inside?"

"Precisely. And maybe whatever's happened, was done somewhere else, and she's been dumped here."

"That would mean at least one vehicle, possibly two people," replied Reilly. "Judging by the state she was in, she can't possibly have walked very far, so all this must have happened not too long ago, and not very far from here."

"I'm inclined to agree, Sean." Gardener turned to Atherton. "You didn't see any cars trying to make a quick getaway, did you; no one in a car acting odd?"

"Nothing that I can recall, sir," said Atherton.

"There *were* one or two cars," said Mulson. "But they weren't doing anything suspicious, or driving in a manner to arouse our attention."

Gardener turned to his partner when suddenly one of the medics spoke up.

"Oh, God," she said.

Gardener glanced at her. She was tall, approaching six feet, pencil thin, with what appeared to be blonde hair, but difficult to tell in the light. At the moment, she was in fact leaning further over the crime scene line in order to gain a better view.

"What's wrong?" asked Gardener.

"I think I know who the girl is," she replied.

"Okay. What's your name, please?"

"Katie Stones."

"Okay, Katie," said Gardener. "Who do you think she is?"

Katie leaned in a far as the crime scene boundary would allow her and then said, "She looks to me like Chloe Harrington."

"Are you sure?"

"As sure as I can be."

"What do you know about her?" Gardener asked.

"I'm pretty sure she volunteers for one of the charity shops in the town; not sure which one, though. I do know that she's the daughter of a rather eminent surgeon by the name of Sir Michael Harrington."

"Sir?" asked Reilly.

"Yes," replied Katie. "Bit of a legend by all accounts."

"Who?" asked Reilly. "Her, or her father?"

"Her father."

"Do you know where she lives?" asked Gardener.

"Not too sure, Thornton le Dale comes to mind. Her father works all over the world. He may not even be at home."

"Do you know the man, Maurice?" Gardener asked Cragg.

"I know *of* him, but very little about him."

"Okay," said Gardener. "There's nothing further we can do here. I'll call the team, and the Home Office pathologist. The quicker we know what's happened to the young lady, the quicker we can form a plan."

He turned his attention to the desk sergeant. "Maurice, can you take everyone into the station, perhaps make drinks, and take a statement from Mrs Miller here?"

Cragg tipped his helmet. "Will do, sir."

"And can you also gather the CCTV from the police station? There might be something on there that will help us."

Cragg nodded and set off on his mission.

As everyone disappeared, Gardener stared at Chloe Harrington. The fact that her father is a surgeon was an area of concern for him.

Chapter Four

It was approaching six in the morning before Gardener and Reilly finally made it back inside the small rural police station. During that time, the pair of them had overseen the arrival of Dr George Fitzgerald, the Home Office pathologist, otherwise known as Fitz, the SOCOs, and their own team, as they had turned up in twos.

Gardener had spent considerable time with Fitz, explaining what everyone had told him about the girl, and the suspicious circumstances surrounding her death. Following a short examination, Fitz couldn't add anything to the little that Gardener and Reilly already knew. He wouldn't like to guess at what had caused her death, and with that in mind, he wanted to take the body to the mortuary, so he could start work on it immediately.

Maurice Cragg had taken a statement from Betty Miller, before finally allowing her to go home. Atherton and Mulson, with the help of Gardener's own officers, had concentrated on setting up the incident room. The SOCOs were now outside, combing the area for any possible evidence, which, at best, would be scant.

Presently, in the back room of the station, Cragg had brewed and made fresh drinks for the senior officers, and listened to what they had to say, which was basically nothing: they still didn't know how Chloe had died, or where she had come from.

Whilst being particularly mindful that there were two parents out there that may well be missing their daughter, Gardener really had to speak to his team; the quicker they were moving, the better. The fact that no one had called about a missing girl called Chloe Harrington, meant he might still have a small window in which to conduct his investigation, and gather a few facts before imparting some really bad news.

The team was waiting for him in the incident room. Atherton and Mulson, who were technically approaching the end of their nightshift, had agreed to remain to see what help they could offer.

Gardener spent almost another hour bringing everyone up to date on what had been discovered since Maurice Cragg had been about to start his tea break.

"Sounds like this is going to be a tough one," said DC Frank Thornton.

"I suspect you're right, Frank," replied Gardener. "Judging by what we've heard, the town was very quiet last night, probably due to the FA cup match on in Leeds, so we might very well be thin on the ground with witnesses."

"There'll be one somewhere," said DC Bob Anderson, Thornton's partner. "There is always the insomniac. Can't sleep, gets up to go to the toilet ten times a night, and eventually makes some tea."

"Yes," said DC Dave Rawson. "That kind of person is bound to look out of the window at some point. So that's who we need to find."

"Depends if they're willing to come forward," said DC Colin Sharp. "You know what people are like for not getting involved."

"You'd like to think they may have something of a conscience," said Gardener. "Looking at it from the point of view that the girl staggering down the road might be their daughter."

"Our problem there, boss," added Reilly, "is that we might have some busybody who thinks the girl is drunk and should know better."

As Gardener was about to reply, Cragg entered the room with the CCTV evidence taken from the cameras mounted to the wall of the police station. There were four altogether: two gave an almost three-hundred-and-sixty-degree view of Market Place. Another faced Newgate. The fourth concentrated on Finkle Street. They would have to go through them all, because Chloe could have wandered in from any direction. It didn't take long before one of the cameras facing Market Place showed them what they wanted; Chloe suddenly staggered into view from around the corner of the church.

"There's our girl," said Reilly.

"But where's she come from?" asked DS Sarah Gates, one of two female officers on the team.

"Hard to tell," said Cragg, peering closer at the screen. "She could have come from anywhere. Market Place is a bit like a big square, which goes down to the intersection of Newbiggin and Wheelgate, which leads to the hospital."

"You don't think she's been there, do you?" asked Thornton. "And something's gone wrong?"

"It's not likely," said Cragg. "But worth a phone call."

"Can we just play that back?" asked Gardener. "Let's pay very close attention to how far up Market Place the camera actually shows us."

PC Julie Longstaff – the other female member of the team, and one of the PCs that had originated in Bramfield – worked the computer.

She dropped back a few minutes and Chloe was not in sight at that point. The camera angle was good, giving them a clear view until the road bore off to the left, toward a local arts centre known as The Milton Rooms, and a pub called The New Malton.

Studying the footage further they noticed that Chloe's first appearance was when she clumsily rounded the corner near the church. She raised her right arm and placed her hand on the side of the church building to steady herself, whilst holding her stomach with her left, all the time staggering. She continued in the direction of the police station and what would have eventually – if she had continued walking – taken her to Finkle Street, clutching her abdomen with both hands, trying desperately to remain upright.

"Judging by the route she's taking," said PC Paul Benson, "she knows where she is, and where she is heading for."

That was backed up when Chloe veered into the back of the station.

"I'd agree, Paul," said Gardener. "That confirms what Katie Stones indicated, that she is local to the area."

She then disappeared from view, which was obviously when she had turned into the back of the station.

"Stop the frame," shouted Gardener.

Longstaff jumped. "Christ, I nearly passed out."

"Sorry, Julie, but I need you to go back a few seconds, to just before she turned into the back of the station."

As she did so, Gardener asked her to freeze the frame. He pointed to the screen. "Who is the man on the pushbike?"

Each of them had been so engrossed in the footage that they had missed the man at the side of the road; but Gardener hadn't.

"Can you zoom in, Julie?" asked Gardener.

She did. The screen revealed a man who was possibly middle-aged, sitting on a bike, with his right leg outstretched and his foot on the ground, in front of Derek Fox, the local butcher's shop. He was dressed in a long trench coat, with a scarf around his neck, and a baseball cap that was more like a legionnaire's cap as the sides came down around his ears. On his hands he wore gloves.

Gardener noticed the time on the CCTV footage as five minutes to midnight.

"He's certainly noticed her," said Reilly. "Why isn't he doing anything?"

"Understandable," said PC Patrick Edwards, taking notes on a pad. "Probably too bloody scared to approach her at that time of night, a girl on her own."

"Point taken, Patrick," said Gardener.

"No disrespect," said Rawson, "but if you saw her staggering around at that time of night, late in the week, you might think she'd been on a bender. The last thing you'd want to do is approach her."

"And given the way she's dressed," said Gates, "black dungarees and boots and a large overcoat, he's never going to see what we now know to be true."

"Not someone who is drunk," said Longstaff. "But someone who is in fact, injured."

"I take all your points," said Gardener. "Now we've seen him, though, I want to know who he is, what he's doing there, where he's been, and where he was going."

Gardener then glanced at Cragg, whose nickname was 'the oracle'. "Maurice, do you know him?"

Cragg leaned in closer. "It's a bit blurry, sir, what with the cap around his ears and everything, but if I'm not mistaken, I'd say it's Peter Forrester."

"And who's he?" Reilly asked.

"Works at the furniture warehouse a few miles outside the town."

"Does he work nights, Maurice?"

"From what I can remember."

"Well, that might account for where he is at that time of night," said Gardener. "Can we have two of you down there sharpish? He may well still be working. We might be able to catch him coming off his shift."

Benson and Edwards volunteered for that one.

The team continued to watch the footage closely for the next fifteen or twenty minutes but nothing else was of any value.

As that footage came to a finish, Steve Fenton, Head of Scenes of Crime, slipped into the room and left a number of photos of Chloe Harrington in order to help the team with their investigation.

"Have you found anything of importance, Steve?"

"Nothing yet, sir," said Fenton. "It's pretty clear out there."

When Fenton left, Gardener addressed the team with tasks.

"It's going to be very difficult, but when the businesses around the town start to open, I'd like you guys to do the usual: house-to-house calls, but mainly the businesses. Gather every scrap of CCTV footage from those in Finkle Street, Market Place and Newgate, and anywhere else around the town that might give us a picture of Chloe's movements.

"It's very important to work out a time frame of what actually happened, and when, as soon as possible. We need to know any establishments she might have visited."

There was very little else he could add to that at the moment, other than to ask Cragg to call the HOLMES team and have them set up in another room.

A lot had happened in a short space of time, and he figured – because of the time of night it had happened, and a distinct lack of people around the town – it would be tough.

Gardener's mobile chimed. His heart sunk a little when he noticed it was the Home Office pathologist, Fitz.

He doubted it would be good news.

Chapter Five

"Her kidneys?" Gardener asked of Fitz.

"She's had her kidneys removed?" questioned Reilly, as if he couldn't believe it, which Gardener could fully understand.

They were sitting in Fitz's office. Music in the form of an opera played in the background, and Fitz had brewed and poured fresh coffee for them both.

"How the hell do you live without your kidneys?" asked Gardener.

"She didn't," replied Fitz.

"She did for a short while," retorted Gardener.

"I know. Takes some believing, doesn't it?" said Fitz. "I honestly wouldn't have thought it possible."

"What the hell's going on here?" asked Reilly. "Who takes kidneys out and throws someone back on the street? And where do you do it?"

"From what I've seen," said Fitz, "it's someone who has a fair idea of the human anatomy. Which signifies to me that there is an option – however dark – you will have to consider."

"Harvesting and stealing organs?" said Gardener, realising his knowledge on that score was limited.

Fitz nodded.

Gardener's heart sunk. Harvesting organs was a huge minefield, and not one he would have suspected as rearing its ugly head in a small Yorkshire town.

"Organ theft is the most likely option," said Fitz. "The kidneys are the usual organs to be taken. Normally, it's only one that's taken, because you can live with only one. People are either coerced into selling, or they need the money to pay a debt, or feed their family."

"I can understand that happening somewhere in Eastern Europe, or Turkey," said Gardener. "But not here."

"I'm inclined to agree with you, it's very bleak over there," said Fitz. "People generally die because of a botched operation to take only one kidney, although there have been an increasing number of cases where people are killed and both kidneys taken."

"You mentioned that whoever had done this had reasonable anatomical knowledge, Fitz," said Gardener. "What makes you say that? What have you found to come to that conclusion?"

"Whoever removed them knew exactly which cut to make, and exactly where to make it. There was evidence of the correct medication needed, and also evidence of a painkiller. They tied the ends of all the arteries; they didn't miss one."

"Tied them up," repeated Gardener. "What with?"

Fitz pulled out a small plastic bag with what resembled two small plastic tubes. They were around ten millimetres in length, black and incredibly thin.

"What are they?" asked Reilly.

"I have no idea," replied Fitz. "I've never actually seen anything like them before. I can only imagine they're some kind of fusion tube. They couldn't use normal clamps because they're far too big. Whoever did this, needed to clamp off the ends and leave them inside the body."

"What would have happened if they hadn't sealed the arteries?" asked Reilly.

"She would have bled to death almost immediately."

"So we're looking for a professional?" said Gardener.

"I wouldn't like to go so far as to say they are professional, but whoever it is, they have a very good anatomical knowledge. The field could be wide open," replied Fitz.

"What exactly do the kidneys do?" asked Reilly. "Stupid question, but I don't actually know."

"Both the kidneys and the liver deal with disposing of the body's waste products. The symptoms of removal would be much the same for both. Any other organ wouldn't really have either a dramatic effect or a relatively quick effect. Someone who has had one kidney carefully removed by a competent person should make a good recovery and live a healthy life, as long as the remaining kidney stays healthy.

"The thing with kidneys is that they can fail, especially if someone has been poisoned, or they poison themselves, but there are other reasons. When kidneys fail, people need dialysis, or better still a transplanted organ; otherwise they cannot get rid of excess water, and many other waste products, which eventually poisons their bodies, resulting in loss of life.

"There aren't many other organs that are routinely taken because the risk of rejection by the recipient's body makes a transplant too difficult, or even dangerous, the heart for example. Livers are often transplanted but it's not easy and they *are* often rejected by the recipient's body."

"It almost sounds like we have someone who wanted to inflict as much pain and discomfort as possible," said Gardener.

"Definitely sounds like they wanted her to suffer," said Reilly. "Given the short time she was still alive, what symptoms will she have suffered?"

"As we've said, someone who has had both kidneys removed carelessly would bleed to death almost immediately. If done carefully, they could live if given dialysis, but without dialysis, the likely effect would be that she would have probably sunk into a coma, and died very soon afterwards, maybe having convulsions on the way."

"Which is probably what Maurice Cragg saw," said Gardener.

Reilly sighed. "So there's no question of what's been done; what we need to find out is why?"

"This is where organ theft comes in," said Fitz. "Assuming you want to sell the kidneys – why else take them – they would need to be removed carefully in a sterile environment, and properly by someone with surgical experience; a medical student, doctor, vet, possibly a nurse, or someone who has had the most basic surgical training.

"The kidneys would have to be cooled and kept cool, and used as quickly as possible. The tissue starts to degrade as soon as the blood supply is cut and even when properly stored, they would probably only have a viable life of a few hours.

"They could be removed in a makeshift operating theatre, although the risk of contamination is greater. To make the sale of kidneys viable, they would have to be removed, transported and transplanted as part of a carefully timed and organised process. In other words, the recipient would have to be prepped and waiting in an operating theatre too. There would have to be a courier to transport the organs to the recipient quickly, and under the proper cold storage conditions."

"That sounds like a big operation," said Gardener. "One or two people simply couldn't run an illegal transplant business of that magnitude."

"Not at all," replied Fitz. "You would need a lot of things to fall into place for a successful business to work."

Whatever was happening here was growing worse by the minute, thought Gardener. He did not like the sound of a big operation on his patch. But they had to happen somewhere.

"Give me your best guess, Fitz," said Gardener. "How long is she likely to have lived in such a state? What I'm trying to work out here is when was it done?"

"I can't imagine," said Fitz. "Given what you've said, the window of opportunity was limited."

"How limited?" asked Gardener.

"Fifteen or twenty minutes, perhaps thirty at the most."

"As little as that?" said Reilly.

"Maybe even less," offered Fitz. "She would have been in considerable pain and I'm very surprised she could have walked at all, let alone the possible short distance that she did."

"That pretty much ties in with what Maurice said," offered Gardener. "She did appear to be in considerable pain and we know for a fact she was staggering around in Market Place, sometime around midnight, from the police station CCTV."

"Given a half hour time scale at best, that suggests her kidneys were removed on our own doorstep, so to speak," said Reilly.

"Almost certainly," said Fitz.

"Maurice mentioned that the road leading out of Market Place led to the Bramfield Community Hospital," said Gardener. "Is it possible she could have come from there? That something had happened after hours, and somehow she managed to get out of there?"

"I wouldn't have thought so," replied Fitz. "The Bramfield Community is mainly A&E and small accidents. It would be very rare for them to conduct such a specialised operation, and especially out of hours. But I do know the staff there very well, and I will make some inquiries."

"That begs the question of where else it could have happened," said Gardener.

"And just how many are involved," added Reilly.

"And then there's the vehicle involved," said Gardener. "You would need one large enough to transport that person around in."

"I'm not sure large comes into it," replied Fitz. "Fully equipped would be more appropriate."

"Meaning an ambulance," said Gardener.

"A larger version of one, maybe," said Fitz. "If you'd managed to perform such a delicate operation, and you wanted the girl to live long enough to have a dramatic impact, you would need a vehicle equipped to be able to deal with her condition."

"We need all of the CCTV footage from the town," said Gardener to Reilly. "An ambulance – or something like it – wouldn't go unnoticed."

"Not for what we want," said Reilly. "We need to look in a specific place, but an ambulance is an everyday occurrence. How many times do they speed past you and you think nothing of it?"

"Point taken," said Gardener. "And at that time of night, if Bramfield is A&E, you'd expect ambulances in and out of there all the time."

"We should check to see if one has been stolen," said Reilly.

Gardener turned to Fitz, changing the subject. "Does the name Harrington ring a bell?"

Fitz nodded. "Sir Michael Harrington."

"Yes," replied Gardener. "Do you know him?"

"I can't say that I know him," replied Fitz. "We've met on a couple of occasions. I *can* tell you he is a leading heart specialist – probably the very best in his field – and his general knowledge is second to none; a doctor who has been decorated and pretty much given his life to the profession. I have heard that he's performed a number of organ transplants if needed, including liver and kidneys. He travels all over the world and spends most of his time in London."

The comment about a kidney transplant struck a chord with Gardener but he chose not to say anything. "London? Any ideas what he does in London, or where he's based?"

"I'm afraid I don't," said Fitz. "I've heard that he stays in his own penthouse in Notting Hill whilst he's down there, but whether he's actually based in any particular hospital I'm not sure. I think he goes where he's needed. Why do you ask? You haven't found any evidence that he's involved, have you?"

"You could say that, Fitz," replied Gardener. "The girl you've been working on is related to him."

"Oh dear," said Fitz. "This doesn't sound good. Who is she?"

"His daughter," said Reilly.

Fitz ran his hands down his face. "Oh my goodness."

Chapter Six

After leaving the mortuary, Gardener had called Cragg to request a full address and postcode for the Harringtons in Thornton le Dale. He and Reilly pulled up at the house shortly after eleven o'clock, which was located on the A170, Bursley Bridge Road, opposite Green Gate Lane.

Reilly whistled as they left the road and turned into a driveway, through a pair of wrought-iron gates that were already open. The house was large, detached, with extensions; the walls were covered in creeping ivy and the building had dark oak, leaded windows. The roof was thatched. On the right, inside the gate, were a number of barns and outbuildings, one of which could have been a stable. On one of the walls was the largest clock that Gardener had ever seen.

"Wow," said Reilly, driving the car up to the front door.

As Gardener jumped out, he noticed a brand-new black Range Rover parked in front of a garage. He glanced over at the house. It had to be at least a four-bedroom property, if not more.

"Look what being a top-class surgeon can get you," said Reilly.

"As beautiful as this property is, Sean, it's not going to mean anything when we tell him what we've learned."

The door opened before they went any further. The man who came out was tall and skinny, with dark hair, greying at the temples. His skin appeared very healthy and unlined. His smile displayed two rows of white teeth. Wearing glasses, and dressed casually in a blue sweater and grey chinos, with one hand in his right pocket, he slipped down the concrete steps that led up to the front door.

"Can I help you gentlemen?" he asked, clearing his throat loudly, something that they would have to become used to.

Gardener immediately noticed his shoes; they had to be Italian leather, which would likely have cost something in the high hundreds. He moved determinedly and slowly, and appeared to speak the same way, as if he carefully constructed sentences in his head before unleashing them.

Gardener produced his warrant card. "Detective Inspector Stewart Gardener and Detective Sergeant Sean Reilly, MIT, Leeds Central."

"This sounds serious," replied Michael Harrington. "What can I do for you?"

"Is your wife home, Mr Harrington?"

"Yes. She is."

"Is there somewhere we can talk?"

"When I know what it's about, yes, I imagine there is."
Harrington cleared his throat loudly again.

Gardener suspected he would have the usual problems
before long.

"We'd like to speak to you about your daughter," said
Reilly. "Chloe, is it?"

"What's she done now?"

"Can we please go inside, Mr Harrington?" asked
Gardener. "What we have to discuss should be done inside
and in the company of your wife."

Michael Harrington, very likely sensing the
conversation was not going to be pleasant, backed away,
before pointing to the stairs and the front door. "Follow
me."

Once through the door, Gardener and Reilly walked
into a wood-panelled hall with some seriously valuable oil
paintings on the walls – none of which Gardener
recognized. The carpet was dark green and so thick that
they sunk into it. The wallpaper was nearly as thick as the
carpet underfoot.

Harrington motioned them into a room on the right,
which turned out to be a study, with more oil paintings
and another thick carpet, a log burner in an ornate
fireplace, a grandfather clock, a huge dark oak desk and a
number of differently styled chairs.

"Please, take a seat," said Michael Harrington. "I'll give
my wife a shout."

He returned a couple of minutes later, carrying a tray
with coffee on it. "I'm not sure whether you wanted a
drink or not, but I sense it's going to be that kind of
conversation. I would very much like to know what my
daughter has been up to in my absence."

"May I ask where you've been?" asked Gardener.

"I've been in London since Monday. I spend most of
my week there."

"What time did you get back?" asked Reilly.

"Around ten o'clock last night."

"And you were here all the time?" asked Reilly.

"What is this about?" asked Michael, his eyes narrowing.

At that moment, the door to the study opened and a lady walked in that Michael Harrington introduced as his wife, Roxanne. She was dark-skinned, probably in her forties with long dark hair and a slim figure. She was dressed in blue jeans and a lighter blue jumper. Her expression was grim and she was very obviously worried about what the police were going to say.

It was the part of the job that Gardener hated the most. There was simply no easy way of saying it, but he finally broke the news when Roxanne Harrington had taken a seat. He said that Chloe had been involved in a very serious situation. As yet, he was unsure of the cause, but he was so sorry to have to tell them that she had passed away.

Michael Harrington sat stock-still, as if he hadn't actually heard.

Roxanne's expression collapsed. She put her hand to her mouth, rose from the chair, and ran out of the room.

Michael – for some reason – apologized and ran after her.

"Oh, God," said Reilly.

"I know," said Gardener. "We'd best give them a few minutes to digest that information."

Reilly leaned over and poured coffee from the pot.

"I hate this part of the job," said Gardener.

"If it helps, I thought you handled it really well."

The pair of them remained seated for a further ten minutes and, at the point when Gardener was going to see if he could find the Harringtons, they both came back into the room, with the same grave expressions. Roxanne was dabbing her eyes with a tissue.

"I'm afraid you'll have to excuse us," said Michael. "We didn't expect that."

"Are you sure it's Chloe?" asked Roxanne. "Who identified her?"

"We're as sure as we can be, Mrs Harrington," said Gardener. "When the ambulance was called, it was one of the medics who recognized her. She gave us her name, said she worked in a charity shop in the town but didn't know which one, and she even mentioned Mr Harrington and where she believed you lived."

"Where is Chloe now?" asked Michael Harrington.

"She's at the mortuary," said Gardener. "We've just come from there."

"Which one?" he asked.

"The Leeds General Infirmary in Great George Street."

"Which more than likely means she was cared for by Fitz."

Gardener nodded.

"I'm relieved," said Michael. "At least he's the best in the business, and he would have looked after her."

Roxanne broke down again but remained in the seat. "Oh, my God, I can't believe this."

"What happened to my daughter, Mr Gardener?" asked Michael.

Gardener detected a change of tone, sterner. From here on in, he suspected, the going would be tougher.

"If I may, Mr Harrington, I'd like to ask you a few questions first."

"That may be the way *you* want to do things, but this is *my* house and *my* daughter we're talking about, and I want to know what happened; and who, if you know, is responsible," said Harrington.

"Darling, please," said Roxanne. "It's not his fault. He's doing his job, and I'm sure he'll tell us in his own good time what has happened."

With that said, she broke down again.

Gardener continued, feeling it best to try and grab as much information as he could. He suspected that when he finally told Harrington what had gone on, he would raise the roof.

"Mr Harrington, I always try to explain that my questions are going to be necessarily blunt and personal. We are treating this as a murder investigation, and I want to waste no time in catching the person or persons responsible."

"Murder?" shouted Roxanne. "Oh, my God, someone has murdered our daughter, Michael."

Michael Harrington moved to her side, knelt in front of the chair and cupped her hands in his.

Quickly, he turned to face Gardener. "Good God, man, can't you see what this is doing to her?"

"I do understand," said Gardener, "but the quicker we have answers to our questions, the quicker we can start this investigation and find some justice for you."

Michael Harrington nodded, but his expression told Gardener he was far from pleased. He took his seat again, quickly pouring a coffee.

"Can I ask where you both were last night?"

Reilly removed a pad and pen from his jacket pocket.

"As I told you," said Michael, "I was in London, and didn't get home till ten."

Gardener glanced at Roxanne.

"I was at home all evening. I spoke to Michael on the phone around eight o'clock, when he was on a break at one of the service stations. Then I went for a shower, and came down and watched some TV."

"Which service station would that have been, Mr Harrington?" asked Gardener.

"Leicester Forrest on the M1. I feel like I am being interrogated as a criminal here."

"Can you remember what you watched?" asked Reilly, of Roxanne, breaking the tension a little.

"Is this relevant?" asked Michael.

"Please," said Gardener.

"As it was a Thursday night, I watched Emmerdale, and then I found a documentary on Sky about our planet."

"Did you speak to Chloe on the phone at all?"

"No," replied Roxanne, trying desperately to hold herself together. "She was out with friends, one of them was her girlfriend, Anushka Wilson; another friend was with them too, Tina Wells."

"Do you have addresses and contact details for them?" asked Gardener.

Roxanne nodded. "I'll get them before you leave, if that's okay?"

"Sure," Gardener said. "Do you know where they all went?"

"A restaurant in the town, in Bramfield. I think they had a meal booked but I can't tell you what time."

"Do you know which restaurant?"

Roxanne started crying. "I'm sorry, I'm sure she told me, more than once, but it's gone clean out of my head."

"Don't worry," said Gardener. "We can check with her friends. When did you last see Chloe?"

"Monday, for me," said Michael. "Before I left for London."

"Have you spoken to her since?"

He shook his head; no.

"I saw her yesterday afternoon," said Roxanne. "She left work early, said she hadn't been busy, so she had been able to work on her forthcoming placement in Africa – three months starting September. We spent an hour together. We talked about the placement. I was happy for her, because she was following her dreams, doing what she wanted. I knew Michael wasn't too happy about it, but he would come to terms with it. She had no plans to come back home after the night out. She said she was staying with her girlfriend, Anushka."

"She seemed happy, then?" asked Reilly.

"She was fine, excited about going out for a birthday meal and spending time with the girls."

"What time did she leave the house?" asked Gardener.

"Sometime around six, I think. A taxi picked her up."

"Can we have the details of the taxi company?" asked Reilly.

Roxanne nodded.

"How *was* your relationship with Chloe, Mrs Harrington?" asked Gardener.

Roxanne took her time in answering, and when she did, it was strained. "Like any mother and daughter. We got on fine, shared a lot of interests. Never shared clothes because we have different styles and sizes."

"Did she have any problems that you were aware of, or talked about?" asked Reilly.

Roxanne shook her head. "Not that I can think of. She had a good job, volunteering at the Oxfam shop in Bramfield. She had a small but close circle of friends, and Kyle, her younger brother. She was happy." Roxanne shuddered as she said her final statement.

"If she volunteered," said Gardener, "what did she do for money?"

"We looked after her, Mr Gardener," said Michael.

"In what way?"

"Chloe is a bit of a tomboy," he replied. "She is nothing like I wanted her to be. But I love her immeasurably nevertheless, because she is my daughter. It was as if she rebelled all the time. I wanted her to follow in my footsteps, in a well-respected job, but she wasn't having any of it. Instead, she chose to work in the Oxfam charity shop in the town, which was something I could not argue with. I may not like it, but we support her in something that is very worthwhile. And, as you can see, officer, we have enough money to keep her in whatever lifestyle she chooses, until she decides to find a job that would earn her her own money – or even if she never finds a job."

Gardener noticed he was still talking in the present tense. He changed topics after that somewhat lengthy and heartfelt answer.

"We will need access to her bank accounts, and any other accounts she had with money," said Gardener.

Both parents simply nodded.

"Would you say she had a good social life?" Gardener asked.

Michael glanced at Roxanne for the answer.

"I think so," Roxanne said. "She enjoyed her job, the people she worked with. They often met up after work for drinks and meals. She went out once or twice a week, sometimes to the cinema. She's had one or two weekends away with them."

"And she didn't have too many friends?" asked Reilly.

"Not considering how popular she was," replied Roxanne. "But that was her choice. She didn't tolerate fools, and she chose her friends very carefully. Certainly, the two I have just mentioned were as close as anyone to her. I'm sure *they* can tell you more about her social life than I can."

"Did she have a social media presence?" Gardener asked.

"Yes, definitely," said Roxanne. "She understood all that stuff: Facebook, Twitter, Instagram, and a whole host of others I can't remember, or know much about. As you can tell, I'm a bit old school."

Gardener smiled. "That makes two of us."

"Does she have her own transport?" asked Reilly.

"No," said Roxanne. "Michael or I would take her where she wanted to be, and if we couldn't, she was quite happy to take buses or taxis."

"I'd like to ask you a little about her routines," said Gardener. "Was she a same-time-same-place type of girl, or more random?"

"It's a bit difficult," said Roxanne. "I believe she was a bit of both. She had to be routine for work so she wouldn't let them down, but she was random in the fact that she was a volunteer and could be asked in at short notice, or to cover other shops in nearby towns. In her personal life, a lot of the things she did, were done so at the last minute. Often, when I thought she would be home for the night, she would suddenly announce she was meeting friends."

"And you were happy with that?" asked Reilly.

"How do you mean?"

"My impression is that you went along with her plans even though you may have made plans of your own."

Roxanne smiled for the first time. "I suppose I did, really. Parents always come second when their children have grown up, don't you think?"

Both officers nodded.

"How did she get on with her brother, Kyle?" asked Gardener.

Michael Harrington smiled then, before clearing his throat. "They fought like cat and dog most of the time, but they were immensely protective of each other: hurt one, you hurt them both. They could call each other names all day, but they wouldn't let anyone else do so, even though they rarely saw eye to eye on most things. I'd say it was a typical brother/sister relationship."

"Where is Kyle now?"

"He's at work," said Roxanne. "He's training to be an accountant with Porter and Preston in Thornton le Dale."

"Where was he last night?"

"Here with me," said Roxanne.

"You may not like this question, but I have to ask it," said Gardener. "Does she have any enemies?"

It was the straw that broke the camel's back for Roxanne. She broke down again. Michael said he knew of none. Eventually, Roxanne agreed. She might have had some, but if she had, Chloe never said anything.

"Did she seem worried about anything?" asked Reilly.

"Not that we knew of," Roxanne replied. "She was certainly very careful with food and drink, because of her condition."

"What condition would that be?" asked Gardener.

"Two years ago, she had a kidney transplant," said Harrington. "Since then, she's had to pay attention to her diet and her lifestyle."

Gardener and Reilly glanced at each other.

Michael Harrington picked up on it. "What are you not telling us?"

Gardener hesitated.

"Does this have something to do with her kidneys?" asked Michael.

"Have they suddenly packed up?" asked Roxanne.

"They can't have done," said Michael. "She was regularly checked and not less than a month ago they said her kidneys were fine. No problems. So what are you not telling us, Mr Gardener?"

"I'm really sorry to have to inform you, Mr and Mrs Harrington, but when we found her, Chloe had had her kidneys removed."

Chapter Seven

The room felt as if it had plunged into an abyss, like all the air and any atmosphere had suddenly been sucked out.

"Let me just make sure I'm understanding this absolutely correctly," said Michael Harrington, clearing his throat once again. "Chloe has had her kidneys removed?"

"Yes, Mr Harrington," said Gardener. "I'm afraid so."

"And not just one, but both?"

Gardener nodded but remained silent.

"And not replaced?"

"No," said Reilly.

Gardener explained the details as he knew them, and the Harringtons remained silent. Gardener suspected that Roxanne was on the verge of collapse. She was trembling, crying, and had paled.

From his expression, Gardener could sense that Michael was seething. His face was tight, his expression a grimace. Finally, he said, "Removed – well there's irony for you."

"Did she suffer?" asked Roxanne.

Gardener hesitated. To be perfectly honest, he had only seen Chloe after she had died, so he had no first-hand knowledge. According to Cragg however, she most certainly had.

"Michael?" asked Roxanne, turning to her husband. "Would she have suffered? I need to know."

His expression told Gardener that he was choosing his words incredibly carefully. "I can't imagine for one second that whoever did this actually cared. They will have had to anaesthetise her in order to perform the operation. I suspect however, that some pain medication will have been used – perhaps not enough."

"So she did suffer," pushed Roxanne.

Michael stared at his wife without answering. He turned to Gardener. "This smacks of organ harvesting. I've seen it too many times. Those people don't care, it's all about the money for them."

"Mr Harrington," said Gardener, "can you please tell me the circumstances in which Chloe had to have a kidney transplant?"

Michael was slowly shaking his head. "It seems like such a waste."

He stood up and left the room. Roxanne remained where she was. No one spoke.

When he returned, he had with him a glass of brandy.

"Don't you think it's a bit early, Michael?" asked Roxanne.

"I wouldn't normally argue with you." He glanced at Gardener. "Would you both like one, or are you on duty?"

"On duty, I'm afraid, sir," replied Gardener.

Michael Harrington sat down, without actually taking a sip, and started to talk. "Chloe had something we call FMD."

"What is that?" asked Gardener.

"Fibromuscular dysplasia," said Michael, "is a rare blood vessel disorder. Basically, some of the strong, flexible cells of the arteries end up being replaced with cells that are more fibrous. Fibrous cells are weak, less flexible. This change in the composition of the arteries leads to their becoming stiffer and more prone to damage.

"It's different from most other vascular diseases because it does not involve inflammation or plaque. Many vascular problems are caused by atherosclerosis, which is a build-up of fatty plaque inside the arteries that eventually hardens and narrows them, which in turn reduces blood flow. It can sometimes lead to aneurysm or dissection. FMD, on the other hand, is a disease of the artery walls that can exist even when there is no plaque build-up."

Michael did then take a small sip of brandy, and though Gardener wanted to ask questions, he thought it best to allow him to continue.

"In fibromuscular dysplasia, the muscle in the artery wall doesn't grow as it should. It often begins in childhood, which was what happened to Chloe. It was first detected when she was about six or seven. The renal artery can have narrow sections alternating with wider sections, giving a bead-like appearance in images of the artery.

"It can narrow so much that the kidney is basically starved of blood. I'm not sure how much you know about anatomy, Mr Gardener, but that kind of starvation can lead to high blood pressure, even at a young age. Strangely enough, it can happen in either one kidney, or both."

"What causes it?" asked Reilly.

Harrington snorted. "I'm afraid the experts don't actually know the cause. It appears that the condition is more common in women, and may be something that's present at birth, in other words, congenital. Narrowed kidney arteries and FMD can affect other arteries in your body, as well as your kidney arteries, and cause even further complications.

"You see, a healthy, elastic artery responds to the rhythmic movement of blood by expanding and contracting as blood pulses through it. An artery affected by FMD may be too stiff – or not stiff enough. If it's too stiff, the artery will be unable to expand as the blood rushes through it. That leads to high blood pressure. If it's not stiff enough, it can balloon or dilate, leading to an aneurysm."

"Are there any symptoms?" asked Gardener, his interest piqued.

Harrington puffed up his cheeks and blew out air. "There may not be any. If there are, they vary. One of the symptoms is tinnitus; a ringing or swishing sound in the ears that occurs with the heartbeat. Neck pain, in the case of carotid artery dissection. High blood pressure. Sudden onset of hypertension, or a sharp rise in blood pressure when it was previously well controlled."

"What happened with Chloe?" asked Reilly.

"It started with splitting headaches out of nowhere. She had dizzy spells and she was generally red in the face," said Harrington. "I checked her blood pressure, which was too high. I immediately took her into hospital, where she was put under the care of a specialist called Edward White. Between us we asked for a number of tests: a CTA, which is a computed tomography angiography, and as many others I could think of, but I won't bore you with them."

"Was that when Chloe had a kidney transplant?" asked Gardener.

"No," said Michael Harrington. "The FMD was treated with medication. She made some lifestyle changes, and she managed it very well. The young often take to changes much quicker than adults."

"So when and where did she have the transplant?" asked Reilly.

"Two years ago," said Roxanne. "She was having a night out with her girlfriend, Anushka. What we didn't know, because Chloe never told us, was that she had been suffering constant headaches and migraines for some time."

Michael then took over. "Given that she had been spending a lot of time with Anushka, I was unaware of this. Anushka had been on at Chloe that it needed sorting out. Chloe, as usual, had ignored her, and kept taking tablets – what, she had no idea. Apparently, Anushka had been under the impression that I was a party to it and that I had prescribed the tablets."

"But you hadn't?" asked Gardener when Michael had grown silent.

"No. Chloe had bought something from the Internet in order to curb Anushka's questions. Turns out they were nothing more than placebos. Anyway, this particular night, they were in Giorgio's Italian in Headingley. Chloe was suffering another headache, feeling unwell and, finally, she fainted with the pain and the pressure."

"Anushka was brilliant," said Roxanne. "She called an ambulance immediately, told them who her father was, and Chloe was taken to St James's Hospital."

"As soon as I found out, because I was in London," said Harrington, "I made a call to St James's and asked that she be taken directly to LGI, the Leeds General Infirmary, and placed under the care of Edward White. As I've already mentioned, he knew of her condition. I then immediately called Edward, explained what had happened and, to his credit, he ordered every test under the sun.

"The result showed that the FMD had advanced. The kidneys had been damaged, almost beyond repair. There was no cure and, at best, the condition was managed with medication until replacements could be found. But that could have been some time."

"Was it?" asked Reilly.

"As it happens, no," said Michael. "Within a week, a girl in London had met her death in a fatal traffic accident. I received a call from St Bartholomew's Hospital, they told me the girl was a perfect match. We had to move heaven and Earth so that my daughter's life could be saved."

When Harrington grew silent, Gardener figured he had everything he needed for the moment, and he felt that the Harringtons had coped considerably well under the pressure, but needed time on their own to adjust.

Before leaving, Gardener and Reilly arranged for a family liaison officer to pay a visit, and took down the details of the people they needed to speak to in order to follow up the investigation. Gardener asked for a recent photo.

He also asked, and was granted, some considerable time to search Chloe's room. Gardener wanted her electronic devices, including her computer, phone – which appeared to have been lost somewhere along her journey – iPad or tablet, and any diaries. With all of those he could check and contact her friends, acquaintances, work colleagues, and her girlfriend; in particular, he wanted Gates and Longstaff on Chloe's social media pages.

If he could collate all of that with CCTV, he may well be able to trace her final movements, which might eventually give them a break.

Chapter Eight

The following morning – mid-morning – Gardener and Reilly had called the team together to pass on all the information they themselves had collected from the previous day: starting with what Fitz had told them and moving on to the Harringtons; the latter being the reason they had not made it back in time for an incident room meeting yesterday.

Gardener also told them that he had checked with the taxi firm, TLD Cabs. They had collected Chloe from home at six and dropped her off in Newbiggin, outside Mamma Mia's grill house, which is opposite The New Malton.

There were a number of shocked expressions from the team.

"Her old man's a surgeon and she's had her kidneys removed?" said Frank Thornton; the expression of disbelief on his face said it all.

"And not just any surgeon," said Cragg. "A man who's been decorated; he's even been knighted."

"I bet he took that well," said Bob Anderson.

"Surprisingly well," replied Gardener. "If you must know."

"To your face, maybe," said Dave Rawson.

"What do you mean?" asked Reilly.

"Let's be honest here," continued Rawson, "he's in the right game to find out what's going on, isn't he?"

"You'd think so," said Colin Sharp. "If there is a gang harvesting organs, he's bound to find out before we do."

"And then what's he going to do?" asked Sarah Gates.

"Hopefully nothing," replied Gardener. "He'll leave it to us."

"Are you serious?" asked Julie Longstaff. "If *he* finds the person responsible for this, I bet *we* won't."

"Too right," said Rawson. "I reckon he could make someone disappear without even trying."

"He could probably dissect them and dispose of them all over the place," said Paul Benson. "We'd never know."

"Sounds to me like we're going down a similar route to the one we had a while back," offered Patrick Edwards. "You know, that bloke who was inserting Bluetooth chips into everyone and killing them by remote control."

Gardener nodded, but chose to address Benson's comment. "Let's hope he doesn't, for his own sake."

"If it was your daughter, what would you do?" asked Rawson.

"Try my best to keep her away from you," said Reilly. His comment lightened the mood a little.

"I can see where you're coming from," said Gardener. "And yes, I'd be very angry, but I'd like to think I'd have enough common sense to let the police deal with it."

"It's not us, though, is it?" said Thornton. "I'm sure we'll catch whoever is responsible, but it's what happens when it goes to court. They always have smarmy bastard lawyers these days that get them off easily."

"Yes," said Anderson. "Look at that case recently. Bloke was attacked on a bus in Armley; had his throat cut with a kitchen knife. When it went to court, they spent three days arguing whether a kitchen knife should be considered a weapon or not. Lawyer took them all to pieces and the scroat ended up with eighteen months."

"Months!" shouted Reilly.

"Yes, months, not years."

"How the hell did that happen?" asked Rawson.

"Don't ask me," Anderson replied. "But that's the point I'm making. I've no doubt we *will* catch who's responsible, but the sentence may not suit her old man.

But if Harrington finds the person responsible before we do, he can make sure that justice is served."

"We'll just have to hope that doesn't happen," said Gardener.

"I can't get my head around this," said Longstaff. "I know Chloe died from her injuries, but somehow or other she managed to live for a short while. How? I mean, how do you remove someone's kidneys and they can still live?"

"That's what I was thinking," said Gates. "We've all seen these medical programs. Whenever they're doing stuff like that, they tie up the ends of the arteries with these bloody great metal clips. What's this bloke used?"

"These," said Gardener. He reached down on to the table and held up the clear evidence bag containing the tubes Fitz had given him.

"What the hell are those?" asked Rawson.

"Some kind of strips, or tubes. When they were in place, they acted as a fusing device, closing the artery off."

"And where do you get them?" asked Sharp, as if he was in the middle of a medical conference, not a murder investigation.

"I don't know," said Gardener. "Because Fitz has never seen anything like them, but I do have an idea for a follow-up that I'd like to come back to."

"Did Fitz indicate how long she might have lived?" asked Cragg, before adding, "After the op?"

"It's very difficult to pin that one down," said Gardener. "I think we have a window of around twenty to thirty minutes."

"That doesn't give them much time," replied Cragg. "If you get a map and draw a radius of possibly twenty minutes from here, that wouldn't stretch very far."

"True," said Gardener. "We'll have to try it."

"So when was she taken?" asked Gates. "It could have been any time?"

"May not even have been yesterday," offered Longstaff.

"It was," said Gardener, relaying the timings of what he'd so far discovered from the Harringtons. "There are people we need to speak to about that, friends who were with her in one of the town's restaurants. I need to come back to that, and I will, very shortly. What I *can* tell you is that we have been through Chloe's room and we are now in possession of her electronic devices and diaries, but we are still looking for her phone, so we should be able to work out some kind of timeline that pretty much counts down the last hours of her life."

"And who exactly are we looking for?" asked Sharp. "If this is part of some huge operation to harvest organs and sell them on, that's pretty specialised. The chances are her kidneys will be in someone else by now."

"Didn't her old man offer anything about that?" asked Rawson. "He must know what goes on."

"I think there will come a time and place when we should speak to him about it," said Gardener, "but right now he's coming to terms with his daughter's death. However, Fitz has arranged for someone to come and see us very shortly." Gardener checked his watch. "He's based at St James's Hospital. He's coming to talk to us about organ theft, and the areas we need to be investigating."

Organ theft was a field Gardener knew very little about. He knew it went on but he had never been caught up in anything of that nature. He doubted any of his team had either, so an expert would be most welcome.

"However, before he comes in, I'd like to set some tasks for us to be going on with. Firstly, after checking with Fitz, I discovered that there are three different hospitals in the area where Harrington is known as a consultant. I'd like us to pay a visit to those places. You can ask about organ harvesting, see if any of the people there know of anything that's happening in the area. Although if it was, I'm sure we'd have heard by now. The main thing I'd like you to do is inquire about Harrington himself."

"Harrington?" asked Thornton.

"You don't think he's involved, do you?" asked Anderson.

"I don't know, Bob," replied Gardener. "Gut feeling is no, but I'd still like to get an idea of his character. Let's find out what kind of a person he really is. As some of you have already put forward, he's in the right field to conduct his own investigation, and he's the right man to take revenge if he feels fit. He could also be the right man to orchestrate something of this nature for whatever reason he feels fit..

"Sean and I will go to the Leeds General Infirmary. They specialise in cardiology, as does Harrington. Frank and Bob, I'd like you guys to go to the Leeds Children's Hospital; their specialty is hepatology. And Colin and Dave, can you go to the St James's Hospital; they specialise in nephrology. See if you can get a lot more detail than we managed. Maybe when we have all that information, we may have another avenue to look into here."

"Are you sure you don't suspect her father of something untoward?" asked Thornton.

"Like I said, Frank, we just need to dot all the i's and cross all the t's."

"It wouldn't be the first time, would it?" said Reilly. "The first rule of thumb in any murder is look at the family."

"Judging by what you've told us about him and where he lives," said Gates, "it doesn't sound like he would have done it for some big insurance payout, and I can't think of any other reason."

"Probably not, Sarah," said Gardener. "But we wouldn't be doing our job properly if we didn't consider every possibility. For the record, I don't think he is involved, but we have to be seen to be doing our job.

"Further tasks," continued Gardener, "are a list of people to speak to. Dave and Colin, perhaps you can speak to Kyle Harrington, Chloe's brother. The parents said they fought like cat and dog but were also very protective of each other. Sounds very much like a normal sibling relationship, but it's possible he might know something about Chloe's relationships that the parents don't."

"Yes," said Longstaff. "It's possible he would know if she was upset about something, or if anyone was giving her a hard time."

Gardener nodded. "Bob, Frank, can you speak to the mother, Roxanne? I'm particularly anxious that we speak to these people independently. There may have been a little tension in the relationship at some point, and Roxanne may have something to add to what she told us, but wouldn't do so in front of her husband for fear of upsetting him."

Gardener turned his attention to Cragg to see if there was anything at all on the town's CCTV cameras.

"Two CCTV cameras that we've accessed show that there *was* an ambulance in the town at the right time and the right place," said Cragg, something that excited the team a little.

"I made inquiries with the hospital about them, and they had been on a genuine call-out. They'd been to see old Mrs Charterhouse on Peasey Hills Road; she's ninety if she's a day. Anyway, they sorted it without the old dear having to go back to the hospital. Once done, it seems that their policy is to have a ride round, make sure no one else needs them."

"Were there any other ambulances in the town?" asked Gardener. "Did they report seeing any unusual activity?"

"No to unusual activity," said Cragg. "Yes to another two, both on official business. Neither of those were actually picked up on the CCTV. But we know the ambulances and the drivers. I've left a message for the drivers to contact us so we can ask more questions."

"Which begs the question," said Gardener. "Was there another, also not picked up on CCTV?"

"Well, we'll just have to hope that as we go through the CCTV – because we haven't covered it all, yet – we pick up on it."

"There hasn't been any mention of an ambulance having been stolen, has there?" asked Gardener.

"Nothing that I know of," said Cragg. "But I'll do a bit of digging. One further thing I did was to inquire about any major operations having been performed at Bramfield last night."

"And?"

"Negative, sir. As we've mentioned before, they're A&E."

Chapter Nine

That wasn't what Gardener wanted to hear. Nothing may well have been performed on the record, but that didn't mean something off the record after hours wasn't going on. Though he figured that would be one very significant risk to take, judging by the money they made, it might be one they felt was worth taking.

Moving on, he turned his attention to Benson and Edwards and the man they had seen on the pushbike when Chloe was wandering around the town in a very distressed state.

They had caught up with him at the factory as he had finished his nightshift. Benson confirmed what Maurice Cragg had said; the man *was* called Peter Forrester.

"What did he have to say?" asked Gardener.

"He admitted seeing the girl, near the police station," said Benson.

"So what was he doing there?" asked Reilly.

"He'd actually stopped for a break because his right leg was giving him some real aggravation," replied Edwards.

"How come?" asked Gardener.

"Apparently he'd been fixing some guttering on his house earlier in the day and he'd slipped off the bloody ladder."

"He won't be the first," said Reilly.

"There talks a man with experience," added Rawson.

"You carry on, lad, you'll get the benefit of my experience," said Reilly, smiling.

Benson continued with Forrester's information. "He didn't approach her because he thought she might have had a little too much to drink. He thought that seeing as she was near the police station, she might very likely be seen by one of us."

"You see, that's the problem nowadays," said Gates. "Because of the media, people daren't approach a single woman on her own, whether she's in trouble or not."

"I *can* understand," said Longstaff. "Still, you'd think common sense would prevail. It doesn't take a minute to ask if she's okay. And if it turns out that she is drunk, you'd back off."

"We know that he works shifts," said Gardener, "but why was he actually in the town at that time? Surely most night shifts start at ten."

"He'd had a prior appointment and couldn't start at ten o'clock," said Edwards.

"What appointment?" asked Reilly.

"Well to be honest, he had two," said Edwards. "Firstly, he was down the A&E having his leg checked out. They said it was nothing more than bruising, and to rest it."

"And secondly," added Benson, "he volunteers for the local homeless shelter, and they had particularly requested his time from ten till midnight."

"He'd previously notified the company and they were fine with it," said Edwards. "Mainly because he's close to retiring age, and because he works part-time on a zero-hours contract."

"Okay," said Gardener. "Doesn't help a great deal but at least he had a reason for being there. Have we checked his story out?"

"Yes," said Edwards, "and it fits."

"Did he see which direction Chloe had come from?" asked Reilly.

"He only noticed her on the Old Bramfield Road," said Benson. "He hadn't passed her anywhere else in the town. When he stopped, he was stretching his leg, rubbing it, and heard a noise; looked behind him and there she was."

"Stupid question but how did she seem at the time?" asked Gardener.

"Difficult to say. He said he couldn't see her face. She was staggering and holding on to the wall with one hand, and clutching her side with the other."

"But he didn't think to ask if she was okay?" questioned Reilly.

"It's like we've said, sir," said Benson. "Single girl, close to midnight, on her own, staggering around. He *could* have stopped and asked, but for all he knew she might have shouted 'rape' and he'd have had all sorts of problems."

Disappointed though he was, Gardener had to accept what had happened. He couldn't change it.

He turned his attention to Gates and Longstaff. "I need you ladies to do what you do best. Can you check out Chloe's computer, and her iPad or tablet? From those we can probably see who her closest friends are, what they might all have been planning and where she was going on the night in question. It's imperative that we find out exactly where she was when she was taken. Her mother believes she was in the town at a restaurant but doesn't know which one. We need to check if that story is true, and which one they went to.

"We need to speak to all of her friends, any acquaintances, and her work colleagues. Let's try to get to know Chloe as well as she knew herself. What type of person was she? What was she like at work? What did she do in her spare time, and what did she do with friends? At least one of those people will know if she had any enemies, or of any recent disagreements with anyone that could have sparked off what's happened."

"Christ," said Rawson. "It would have to be some disagreement to end up losing your kidneys."

"I'm inclined to agree, Dave," said Gardener, "but it takes all sorts."

Turning his attention back to the girls, Gardener said, "In particular, I'd like you all over her social media pages; there will be stuff on there that her parents will probably know nothing about. Roxanne said she didn't understand social media, but Chloe did, and apart from the main sites, she was on a whole host of others that her mother didn't know about.

"If we can collate all of that information with the CCTV in the town, we will have a very good chance of tracking her last movements."

Gardener spent a few minutes updating the whiteboard before turning and adding some more tasks.

"Two people we really need to talk to: one of them is a girl called Tina Wells. We have all her contact details so I'd like you two ladies on that one, please? The other girl we need to see is called Anushka Wilson, Chloe's girlfriend and partner. They spent a lot of time together and when Chloe had her kidney incident, the Harringtons said Anushka handled the situation brilliantly. Sean and I have her details so we will pay her a visit."

"Once we have all of that information, I'd like you all to update Maurice as soon as possible so that he – along with Mike Atherton and Evette Mulson – can collaborate with HOLMES."

Cragg nodded his approval.

"Finally," said Gardener, "we need to put out a press appeal, using a photo that Roxanne has given us. We have very little to go on, so I feel it's important to concentrate on what Chloe did in the final hours or minutes of her life, and build up a picture of her movements, which is something they will almost certainly be able to help with."

He glanced at Gates and Longstaff. "The restaurant will be important, I'm sure there will be something in her diary. If it's not Mamma Mia's grill house, we need to find out which one it is. All the girls could have met up there for a drink and gone on somewhere else. Once we know where it is, can someone call in and talk to them? We need to find out what time the girls entered, and when they left. Did anyone see what happened outside the restaurant when they left? Did they all leave together?"

"You'd probably say not, sir," said Bob Anderson. "Otherwise, her friends would surely have known what happened to her."

"And so far," said Thornton, "we have not had anyone call us to say she's missing."

"Good points," said Gardener. "So, if she was alone, had any transport been sorted out for her to get home? Did she stay where she was supposed to have stayed? Can the staff at the restaurant offer any information? Can anyone remember seeing her, standing in the doorway? Can anyone remember seeing her move away, or talking to someone? Patrick and Paul, can you coordinate that line of attack, try to find out what happened?"

As they nodded, a knock on the door interrupted the meeting.

Chapter Ten

Gardener strolled over to the left side of the incident room. When he opened the door, he saw a stocky, middle-aged, well-dressed gentleman in a blue suit, white shirt and blue tie. The man had thinning grey hair with a round face, wearing glasses. He presented a card with his credentials and Gardener asked him to join them.

Once both men were in front of the whiteboard, Gardener introduced the surgeon as Mr – not doctor – Brian Chesterton. Gardener then took the opportunity to update the man on the case so far, explaining that one of the avenues they were thinking about was organ theft. He then asked Chesterton to tell them what he knew about organised crime organ theft, and the possible uphill struggle that they might be facing.

Before he tackled the question, Chesterton mentioned that he did in fact know of Michael Harrington, and he found what had happened very disturbing.

"Sounds like you have a very interesting problem," said Chesterton, who was very softly spoken. "The fact that the girl was missing her kidneys opens up a lot of possibilities. Is Chloe your first victim, the only one?"

"That we know of," said Gardener. "Should we find more, organ theft will be a route we need to explore more deeply. I personally don't know too much about it, and I thought it might be a good idea to perhaps draft in an expert to explain some of the difficulties facing us."

Chesterton nodded. "With organised crime groups, sometimes known as OCGs, think about the *why* and it starts to give you the *how*, and eventually the *who*. One thing I will tell you is that one or two people can't run an illegal transplant business. It's simply not possible."

"Too big?" asked Gardener.

"Yes," said Chesterton. "You need a number of things to fall into place for a successful business to work. One of the first is being able to identify your customer base. There are lots of people out there who need organs; I think the kidneys would perhaps be the most popular. Some are willing to pay big money to get hold of them."

"How big?" asked Bob Anderson.

"It can run into the millions," said Chesterton.

Frank Thornton whistled through his teeth. "That's big."

"Which is when it becomes very big business," said Chesterton. "It's not without its problems. For example, how do you work out who needs them? It's not as if you can open a newspaper and find something in the wanted ads. People do not generally advertise the fact that they need organs."

"There's always the dark web," said Longstaff.

The comment amused Gardener – if anyone was going to start with the Net it would be Julie Longstaff.

Chesterton nodded. "I will come back to that. But to continue, you also have to be able to work out who can afford to buy them. And perhaps most importantly, who do you trust? In other words, how do you work out who won't grass you up to the police?"

"Which brings us back to the dark web?" asked Reilly.

"Most certainly," nodded Chesterton. "When identifying your donors, the most important thing is that they will have to be fit, healthy people. The OCGs need easy access to them. It's very unlikely the donors will belong to any of the rare blood groups. Secondly, there has to be no known contamination issues. That's very important. If the organ is not a perfect match, it will be rejected by the recipient's body."

Chesterton asked for a drink of water. Cragg left the room and returned almost immediately, probably in case he missed anything, but there had been no need, Chesterton had waited for him.

Following a drink, he continued. "One thing you do need is someone with considerable medical knowledge, and the skill to remove and properly store viable organs. You simply can't have anyone. That will of course cost the OCGs heavily, but it will be factored into everything."

Gardener told him what Fitz had found. He lifted the evidence bag from the table containing the tubes and passed it over to Chesterton.

"Have you ever seen anything like these?" he asked.

Following a good examination, Chesterton shook his head. "Whatever these are, they could be home-made, or possibly foreign. May I take them with me so I can do some research for you?"

Gardener nodded. "We'll sign them out for you."

The doctor placed them back on the table and continued with his explanation. "The OCGs need a place to perform the transplant operation. You need somewhere large enough, because it will be filled with expensive equipment; it needs to be sterile, and the procedure would involve a number of specialists: at least a surgeon, an anaesthetist, and possibly a nurse. They will need access to anti-rejection drugs, and a recovery location for ongoing care and recuperation. So you can see how wide they have to cast their net, and why I mentioned that two or three people could not run it on their own."

Gardener could see the kind of headache they may be facing if what Chesterton was saying was true.

"One very important thing you also need is a method to transfer money without raising suspicion," said Chesterton. "And don't forget the logistics of moving people, and organs, and equipment around and ordering the drugs needed, without raising suspicion. All this points to a high-end OCG, which is where I think you would need to start.

"From what I have researched, there are not that many of them that could successfully pull off something like this on a large scale without tripping over some wires and alerting the police, as may now be the point in case with you people."

"So, of the groups to investigate, you'd certainly be looking at surgeons," said Colin Sharp, obviously intending to continue, judging by his expression, but Chesterton nodded enthusiastically and took over.

"Definitely, particularly ones who had been struck off. Another area to concentrate on are those that are in the UK illegally; that number will be quite high. Maybe you should study any medical people who are unable to work for any number of reasons, such as a hospital or doctor's surgery closing down, leaving them unable to gain another position. Just like the OCGs, some people get desperate when they can't find employment and need to feed their families.

"Have a look at the drugs: who has access to them; who is ordering them? The equipment – as we've already mentioned – is also very specialised. Consider, outside of a hospital, who has, or needs, this type of machinery?"

"One thing that ran through my mind," said Gardener, "was a hospital out of hours."

Chesterton shook his head. "Very unlikely, Mr Gardener. If you've ever been to one – there are no after hours for organ transplants. I actually have a friend who drives organs all over the country. He's a retired policeman; doesn't live far from me. Last week he was called out at four in the morning to drive to Durham, pick up a heart, and run it down to Cornwall. They were actually waiting for him at the door – both sides."

"So basically it would be impossible to run an operation of that size from a hospital and not be detected?" asked Gardener.

"Definitely," replied Chesterton. "It's a lot of people, and a lot of moving parts. People get greedy, they talk. Do you remember when coronavirus hit and there was a national shortage of ventilators?"

"Do we?" said Rawson.

"The BBC donated all they had in the props department from *Holby City*."

"You're joking," said Gates.

"No," said Chesterton. "They are actually real, live fully functional machines."

"Oh my God," said Longstaff. "I've watched that a few times. I often wondered if the equipment was real."

"Now you know," said Gates.

There was a short silence before Chesterton added something else of serious interest. "If I were running an enterprise such as this, that's the kind of thing I'd do. Set up a bogus film production company, buy all the equipment in from abroad, because it is harder to trace. I would rent a remote warehouse, and build an operating theatre inside it.

"I'd find a disgraced surgeon, and other staff who need money; bring them in from the Far East – after all, why do they need to speak English? Make sure there is some muscle around to keep everyone in check. The easiest way to identify your clients, as we've already discussed, would be to advertise on the dark web, which is very risky, because there are undercover policemen on there as well as people who might not have the necessary funds."

Gardener figured that investigating something of such magnitude could be a living nightmare: chasing down hundreds of leads from imports, people trafficking, cybercrime and dark web investigations. They would have to consider money laundering, drugs, OCGs, medical experts; the list was endless.

Not to mention very sobering.

Chapter Eleven

Reilly drove the pool car through the centre of Leeds, before finally steering it into Great George Street. They were visiting the LGI to see a man called Edward White. Also known as the Leeds General Infirmary, the LGI is a large teaching hospital based in the centre of the city, and part of the Leeds Teaching Hospitals NHS Trust. Its previous name The General Infirmary at Leeds is still sometimes used.

"Are we also dropping in on the big man?" Reilly asked Gardener.

"Unannounced?" asked Gardener, with a shocked expression. "You want to go and see Fitz unannounced?"

"Well, this bloke might not give us any coffee," said Reilly, parking the car outside the entrance.

"His might be better."

"That's a point. He might have better chocolate bars as well."

Gardener laughed as they exited the car. Once through the entrance doors, he inquired about Edward White and was given directions to his office on the third floor. Like all hospitals, the doctors, nurses and porters dashed around all over the place, and a clinical smell ran through the building as a constant reminder of why people didn't like visiting.

As they reached the third floor, a middle-aged, blonde secretary, dressed in a navy skirt and white top met them from the lift and took them to White's office. They were shown into a room with a lot of dark wood and leather, thick Persian rugs, more books than they could count, and an overbearing smell of beeswax.

Edward White rose from a chair behind a large mahogany desk that was probably as neat and as clean as the one Fitz had in his office. A laptop perched on one side, with a couple of cardboard files on the other. There were also a number of photo frames but Gardener could not see what they were pictures of. The office was warm and incredibly silent. The view from the window was of Leeds city centre.

White was a tall man, overweight, with dark hair, a ruddy complexion and a red nose. He had a bushy beard and moustache. For a physician, Gardener didn't think he was a good advert for the profession. He wore small, steel-rimmed spectacles perched on the bridge of his nose and when he introduced himself the SIO detected a Scottish lilt in his accent, but not too strong.

When they were all seated, the secretary popped in with a tray containing tea and coffee; as if she had read Reilly's mind, there were biscuits too.

"I wasn't sure what you wanted so I asked Doreen to prepare both."

The men helped themselves to a drink before Gardener asked, "What do you do here?"

"We're a specialist centre for a number of services, Mr Gardener, including the major trauma centre and hand transplants. We also provide many general acute services like A&E, intensive care and high dependency units, maternity, and we have state-of-the-art operating theatres.

"Did you know that the Leeds Infirmary was opened in 1771 on what is now the site of the former Yorkshire Bank in Infirmary Street off City Square? Notably, the five founding physicians at the infirmary were all graduates of the University of Edinburgh Medical School. Construction of the building we're now sitting in was started in 1863 to the designs of Sir George Gilbert Scott."

White seemed proud of the building's heritage. Gardener asked about cardiology.

"Most definitely," said White. "That is definitely an area we specialise in. I believe you are friends with our Home Office pathologist."

"Love him like a brother," said Reilly.

All three men laughed and though Gardener was interested in the history, he was very keen to move things on to the reason for their visit. "We'd like to ask you about someone a lot younger than Sir George Gilbert Scott."

"Michael Harrington, I believe," said White, nodding. "What about him?"

White's telephone rang. He glanced at the display and pressed a button which ceased the ringtone immediately.

Gardener went on to explain the dire circumstances in which he'd had to meet Harrington for the first time.

"Yes, a terrible, terrible business," said White, shaking his head. "It must be awful to lose a loved one, but when it's your child as well." After pausing, he added, "They do say you shouldn't outlive your children. He came to see me, you know?"

"Came to see you?" asked Gardener. "When?"

"Yesterday, around lunchtime."

"Do you mind me asking what about?"

"As a matter of fact I do, that was between Michael and myself." The surgeon's mood and tone flipped like a coin.

Gardener wasn't sure how to treat the answer but felt he needed to assert his presence. "Are you saying you were treating him as a patient, and therefore bound by the laws of confidentiality?"

White sipped his tea. "I can't imagine a doctor competent enough to treat Michael; he's above us all. What is it in particular you would like to know?"

"A little bit about the man: his life and his character?"

The defensive mood was still present. "Can I just point out that a lot of what I know about him and his family is confidential? So there will be things I am not prepared to discuss."

"We're not asking for trade secrets," said Reilly. "But can *I* just point out that this is a murder investigation, so we do expect cooperation."

White was about to speak when Gardener stopped him. "Look, Mr White, all we want is to be allowed to do our job. And to do that, we need to know everything about everyone. That way, we will catch the person responsible. We don't want to get heavy and start turning up mob handed with warrants. That puts everyone on edge. We'd like to keep it civilised."

White nodded. "Where would you like me to start?"

"From what we hear, he is a very dedicated surgeon," replied Gardener. "Maybe you could furnish us with a bit of background."

"Michael Harrington is a transplant surgeon, who specialises in cardiology, but he has expert knowledge of how everything else in the human body works. He performs operations in hospitals all over the UK; even Bramfield when needed."

Gardener nodded, satisfied they were making progress.

"If you train to be a doctor, the route is pretty standard. It was no different for Michael. He attended medical school for five years, followed by another two at Foundation. He went on to core surgical training for a further two years, before he was then allowed speciality training at the highest level, which lasted a further six years."

"That's a long time," said Reilly.

"Shows you the kind of man you're dealing with, but you haven't heard the half of it. He graduated from Dundee University in the year of the millennium, and following surgical training in the North West, he became a member of the Royal College of Surgeons of England two years later. Two years after that he completed a fellowship in Extracorporeal Membrane Oxygenation (ECMO) in

Leicester, followed by specialist higher surgical training in adult cardiothoracic surgery in Sheffield, St George's Hospital in London and Harefield Hospital."

"How old is he?" asked Reilly. "A hundred and fifty?"

Even White smiled. "You'd think so, wouldn't you? It would take me all day to go through his list of achievements."

"I gather he's been decorated," said Gardener.

"Over the years, yes. He's won countless awards for his research in cardiac surgery."

"Sounds like he's definitely the man you'd want on your side if you had a dodgy ticker," said Reilly.

"He's certainly the man you'd want on your side in a crisis."

"Apart from hearts, I believe he has transplanted other organs as well?" asked Gardener.

"Yes," said White. "He's pretty much done everything."

"Forgive me for asking this," said Gardener, feigning ignorance and knowing otherwise. "Did he perform Chloe's kidney transplant?"

"Not at all. Apart from anything else it's unethical. I operated on Chloe."

"When was that?"

"About two years ago now."

Gardener was satisfied that White corroborated the information Harrington had given them.

"Are you able to give us the details; where the kidneys came from, for example?" asked Gardener.

White sighed. "I don't really suppose it will do any harm now. The kidneys came from a young girl in London, about the same age as Chloe. I believe she was from Acton. Her and her boyfriend were in Whitechapel, on a Jack the Ripper tour, I think. Anyway, she was knocked down in a hit and run. Poor girl was dragged about twenty yards and ended up in a bus stop. When the group reached her, she was still alive but badly injured.

One of them phoned for an ambulance and she was taken to the hospital. However, she died a few minutes after she had been admitted.

"The girl carried a donor card and her parents gave permission for the staff to use any organs they wanted. They couldn't save their daughter's life, but they felt obliged to help save someone else's. She was a perfect match for Chloe."

"How does that work?" asked Gardener. "Is there a list of people; are some a higher priority than others?"

"Basically, that is how it works. There is a national database and it is regularly checked by all."

"And Chloe was at the top of the list?" asked Reilly.

White paused, but then said, "She must have been."

"You didn't know?" asked Reilly.

"I don't really have that kind of access," said White. "It isn't relevant that I know who has priority over anyone else. It's my job to perform the operation, not get involved in the logistics."

"Are we able to have all the details?" asked Gardener.

White nodded, reluctantly. "I can't imagine there being a problem, but if you'd like to have your chief constable contact my secretary, I'm sure it can be arranged."

Gardener nodded, but wanted to change topics. "You obviously know Mr Harrington very well. He seems nice enough as a person, and very competent as a physician. Is he likely to have any enemies?"

"Michael? Enemies?" White seemed surprised. "I wouldn't have thought so; he saves lives, he doesn't take them."

"You'd be surprised how many people we come across who have enemies," said Reilly. "Even doctors."

"Well, I'm certainly not aware of any that Michael has."

"Are you aware of any OCGs operating illegally in the area, particularly involved in organ theft?" Gardener asked.

"That was one of the things Michael asked me."

"So he is conducting a private investigation?" said Reilly.

"He's quite within his rights, I would have thought."

"Of course he is, Mr White," said Gardener. "But we are professionals. And it isn't our right, it's our job. Perhaps if your friend continues to conduct his own investigation you might politely ask him to stop."

"You don't tell a man like Michael anything," said White, sternly.

"What does that mean?" asked Gardener.

"It means," replied White, "that he's very strong-willed and knows his own mind. He knows what he wants. And like all successful men, he usually gets it. Now, if that's all, gentlemen, I do have another appointment."

Chapter Twelve

An hour after leaving LGI, they were sitting in the 21 Co. café in Headingley central on Otley Road. Both Gardener and Reilly loved the place because the café was run for and by people with Down syndrome, to offer training and work experience with the aim of creating job opportunities. It was part of the Sunshine & Smiles group, which provides a support network in Leeds for children and young people with Down syndrome, and their families, providing a vital role in the community.

They had taken a table near the window and Gardener had chosen lemon and ginger fruit tea; despite being a healthy eater, he had a weakness for their home-made cheese scones with butter.

Reilly on the other hand, true to form, had ordered a flat white, toast and jam and a piece of carrot cake, and was still eyeing up other treats in the glass cabinet that formed part of the counter.

Glancing around, Gardener noticed that all the tables but one had been taken, which said a lot for the standards.

Once they were seated and their food had been served, Gardener started with the questions. "What do you think, Sean?"

"I think we're going to have to watch Harrington carefully."

"Do you think there is any connection with him and Chloe's missing kidneys?" asked Gardener, taking a sip of his tea.

"You can't rule anything out, boss, but what possible motive could he have?"

"I've no idea, Sean, although there is one thing that sprung to mind."

"What's that?" asked his partner, demolishing his toast and jam, with his eyes fixed on the carrot cake.

"That maybe Chloe isn't his biological daughter."

That finally slowed the Irishman down. He sat back in his chair. "What makes you say that?"

"I realize everyone reacts differently to news like that but there was a distinct difference between the two of them. Roxanne was distraught. She asked questions; she wanted to know if Chloe suffered. She was in bits."

"And you felt he was taking it better than expected?"

"Either that, or he's made of much stronger stuff and he's able to hide his feelings better than her. But take today, we find out that he's already been making his own inquiries."

Gardener had finished one half of his scone. He wiped his hands and face with his napkin.

"I'm in two minds with that one," said Reilly. "I figured he'd do that, him being a doctor. They seem more used to that side of life. But not straight away."

Gardener took a sip of tea. "What bothers me is not that he made the inquiries, but he didn't do so by phone. He left his wife alone, within twenty-four hours of hearing the news, and drove into Leeds to speak to Edward White."

"I'm not so sure about him either," said Reilly, taking a sip of his coffee and picking up the fork with which to attack his cake.

"You think he's covering something; hiding behind the patient confidentiality rule?"

"He made it pretty obvious that there were certain things he wasn't going to speak about. So you start to wonder what they were."

"I wondered as well," said Gardener. "I wonder if they're both involved?"

"Running an OCG themselves, you mean?"

Gardener sipped more tea, thinking about the implication. "It's a bit of a stretch, but why not? If anyone would know how to go about it, they would."

"Okay, but if we open that can of worms, what the hell are we going to find? Yesterday, Chesterton told us that one or two people could not run an operation as big as that."

"I don't think one or two people will be running it," replied Gardener. "What do we actually know about Harrington? Everyone speaks highly of him. White told us his background. He's away in London most of the week, he travels all over the country to perform operations. All of that, to me, sounds like a perfect cover for something like this."

"It would take some doing," said Reilly, finishing the carrot cake and pushing his plate to one side.

"Agreed, but if he's away all week, how does anyone know what he's really doing? Perfect cover."

"What is it they always say in our game, suspect family first?"

"It's the general rule of thumb, Sean. I say we have a much closer look at him, and White."

"Yes, but we're talking about his daughter. Why the hell would he do that after all the trouble he'd gone to in order to get the kidney for her?"

"Once again, you have a good point. The way that White put it, suggested nepotism to me. When we asked him about lists and priorities, he explained it all to us. But we asked about Chloe possibly being at the top of the list and he replied, 'she must have been'; he hesitated."

"I noticed that," said Reilly. "For what it's worth, boss, I don't think Harrington's involved. Look at his life, it's picture-perfect. Would he risk all that for… for what? What else could life offer him?"

"Not to mention what his wife would do to him if it came out."

"Assuming Chloe is his daughter," said Reilly. "If she's not, that means Roxanne has been hiding quite a lot from him and she'll have some explaining of her own to do."

"What's happened might make sense if it's something he's only recently found out, but it's still a hell of a risk to take," said Gardener.

"Maybe Anushka Wilson might let something slip. It sounds like she knows Chloe as well as anyone."

"I'm inclined to agree. Hopefully, Gates and Longstaff will learn something from Tina Wells too. There's still a long way to go here, Sean. So far, we don't have much: a girl missing her kidneys and virtually the only thing we know is her name. We don't know what happened, where she came from in the town; and as yet, we have no witnesses."

"At least we have the press release," offered his partner, finishing his coffee. "I think if anyone lets anything slip, it will be the brother; they fought quite often but they were very protective of each other. Isn't that what he said?"

Gardener nodded, finishing his tea. "Michael Harrington's bothering me, Sean, even this early into the investigation. He has the knowledge, he has the network, he has places he can do it. If it isn't him, all of those apply to the fact that he can deal with whoever is responsible, and we might not even know."

"Which brings us back to White's parting comment," said Reilly. "That you don't tell Michael anything."

Gardener nodded, rising from the table to ask for the bill. "And that he always gets what he wants?"

Chapter Thirteen

For a late February morning, the weather was surprisingly good as Julie Longstaff parked in the Morrisons supermarket car park in Bramfield, which was around the corner from where they needed to be.

Exiting the car, Longstaff said, "I just need to nip in here and pick up a couple of things for tonight."

"No problem," said Sarah Gates, checking her phone for messages. As there were none, she glanced around surveying the area.

They were here to talk to Tina Wells, one of Chloe's closest friends. Tina owned a hairdressing salon in Castlegate, called Hair Today, Gone Tomorrow. Gates noticed a fish and chip shop to the left of the salon. Due to a previous phone call, she knew that Tina lived next door to her shop, around the corner, where two large houses had been converted into flats. All the local amenities were very handy.

Longstaff returned, dropped a carrier bag into the boot, and locked the car before the pair of them set off towards Tina's shop. Once inside, the heat was welcoming. It wasn't particularly big, but like most salons it was all mirrors and dryers and chrome adjustable chairs. A comfy sofa was perched along one wall. In front of that was a table with magazines. On top of a cupboard, a radio played at a level that allowed conversation between customers, of which there were three; one was under a dryer, and the other two were in the chairs receiving whatever treatment they had booked.

A chubby, dark-haired girl in uniform turned to greet them, all lipstick and make-up. "Can I help you?"

"We're here to see Tina Wells," said Gates.

"I'm sorry, she's not in today," replied the girl.

"We know," said Longstaff. "But we're here to speak to her personally."

The girl appeared to be ready to put up a fight until Gates showed her warrant card. The customer in the chair was staring fiercely into the mirror, trying to pick up on what was happening.

"Oh, I'm sorry, I didn't realize. She's at home but she must be expecting you. Do you know where she lives?"

"Is it around the corner?" asked Gates, pointing.

"Yes," replied the girl. "You go round. I'll let her know you're here."

As they were leaving, the girl rushed after them. "Tell her we hope she's okay, and not to rush back. She's had a right shock."

"We will," said Gates, eager to leave.

Outside, around the corner, Gates rang the bell and waited.

"This is handy, isn't it?" said Longstaff. "You've got everything you want right here."

As Gates was about to reply, a voice came over the intercom. "Come on up."

The buzzer sounded, a latch on the door clicked and the pair of them climbed a staircase to the top-floor flat.

Tina was waiting with the door open. She let them into the living room, which had good views of the town.

"Would you like some coffee?"

"If you don't mind," said Gates.

When the coffee was poured and placed on a small table, all of them took a seat. Tina was twenty-four: slim, brunette, with dark, almond-shaped eyes, and a normally bright personality. Gates noticed plenty of colour in the room. A deep lemon emulsion adorned the walls, with a number of equally loud paintings. The suite was white leather, the table glass and chrome. A radio played at a low volume somewhere in the flat.

They asked about the flat and how long she had lived there. Tina explained it had two bedrooms, and that she liked to fill her life with bright colours and lots of flowers. She had hoped the salon would have been big enough to live in but there were only two small rooms and she'd had to use them for stock. She'd lived in the flat as long as she'd had the business, which was three years.

She said she was single, but had an on/off relationship with a man called Craig White, who was a technician at JB Motors, the local Vauxhall dealer. She had a reasonable social life, liked to go out clubbing and dancing, and loved to relax with weekends away, particularly the spa town of Harrogate.

"We're sorry we have to meet you in such bad circumstances," said Gates. "It must have been a shock."

"You're telling me," replied Tina. Her bright expression changed immediately. "I still can't believe it. Have you found anyone for it yet?"

"I'm afraid not," said Longstaff. "We're just trying to build up a picture of what happened, and we know you must have been one of the last people to have seen her."

"How are her parents coping?" asked Tina. "They must be in bits. How the hell do you manage to go on after hearing something like this?"

Gates didn't know whether Tina Wells was a chatterbox by nature, or it was simply shock. She suspected the former, because that's one thing hairdressers were good at – talking. She couldn't begin to think how much they heard in one day.

"It will be hard for them," said Gates. "If I can just ask you, Tina, how long have you known Chloe, and how did you two meet?"

Tina took a sip of coffee. "I think it was about two years ago now."

"Was that before or after her kidney incident?" asked Longstaff.

"After she'd had the kidney transplant," said Tina. "She'd been in recovery for quite a while; you know what that can be like, everyone telling you not to do this, or that, don't overtax yourself. It can be a nightmare. Anyway, in an effort to cheer herself up, Chloe came into the salon for a bit of a makeover."

Tina's eyes glazed over. She was obviously thinking about her friend. Gates had the impression they were very close despite only meeting a couple of years ago. Sometimes it can be like that.

"We hit it off immediately," said Tina. "Mainly because we had something in common."

"What was that?" asked Gates.

"The fact that my brother had also had a kidney transplant, a few years previously."

"Really?" said Longstaff. "It must be more common than you realize."

"I was able to pass on everything I knew about it," continued Tina. "That was an amazing help to Chloe's recovery. Up until that point, Chloe had felt that her father, Michael, was being an old washerwoman, telling her what she could and couldn't do, like I mentioned a few minutes ago. She was getting really fed up with it.

"To be honest, I put her right," continued Tina. "I told her that Michael had been talking a lot of sense. How could she possibly ignore a surgeon?"

"How did you get on with her parents?" asked Longstaff. "I assume you've met them."

"I have, I saw them quite often," said Tina. "Michael and Roxanne were lovely, and they really took to me when we first met. I remember Michael saying that he really appreciated all the help I had been to Chloe. I didn't think I had, but he told me that she had actually listened to the things I'd said. He thought, up to that point, that he wasn't getting through to Chloe. He felt she wasn't really taking in what he was saying, but he was only doing it for her own good."

"How was Chloe afterwards?" asked Gates. "After the recovery period?"

"She was fine. She was eating the right stuff, taking the right medication, exercising. She had a good job in the Oxfam shop in the town. She talked about a placement in Africa. God, she was excited about that."

Tina finished her coffee and stared at them. "Chloe liked people. She liked helping them. She seemed to care about them. I always thought she would have made a good nurse. I never really heard a bad word from her about anyone."

"How was Chloe on the night itself?" asked Longstaff.

"Pretty much like I'd just mentioned. Bubbly. She'd had a good day at work. Finished early, went home to see her mum for an hour. She caught a taxi, turned up at The New Malton. She had a new outfit on, well, not new, someone had brought it into the shop the weekend before. Chloe loved it. It was her style, some kind of boiler suit-cum-dungarees with a thick top. They matched and they suited her. She was a bit of a tomboy."

"Is that where you stayed, The New Malton?" asked Gates.

"No," said Tina. "We started there and moved on after about half an hour."

"Where did you go next?" asked Longstaff.

Tina had to think. "We moved on to The Blue Ball Inn in Market Place. We met up with three more girls and had another drink. Finally, we went to the La Trattoria restaurant on Wheelgate for a meal. The table had been booked for seven-thirty. The meal lasted until nine."

"Can you let me have the details of the other girls, please?" asked Gates.

"Yes, no problem. I'll write them down before you leave."

"What happened at nine?"

"We all left the restaurant. One of us had decided during the meal that we should go clubbing in Leeds. Not sure who decided it, but we all thought it was a good idea. It was my birthday. It wasn't what Chloe wanted to do. We ordered a taxi. When it came, and we were outside, Anushka and Chloe spent a few minutes together at one side of the shop, we were all at the other, so I don't know what they were talking about, or planning. Anyway, the taxi turned up, we all said goodbye to Chloe, but only after we'd arranged for another taxi to take her home."

"Was it the same company?" asked Gates.

"Yes. The driver who picked us up messaged the office to send another car for Chloe. She said she would wait outside the restaurant."

"Is that the last time you saw her?"

Tina's eyes misted over. "Yes."

"I know this is a stupid question," said Longstaff, "but did any of you call to see if she got home okay?"

"No," said Tina. "I wish we had, or that she'd come with us, or maybe even jumped in our taxi and we'd dropped her off at home. None of this would have happened. Problem was, we'd all had a drink, we were all in the party mood and none of us gave it a second thought. You don't think anything like this will happen, do you?"

"True," said Gates. "Look, don't beat yourself up about it. You could have offered any one of those solutions, and Chloe might have had other ideas. She may not have taken you up on them."

"When had you last seen Chloe before the night out?" asked Longstaff.

"Maybe a week before that. We didn't see each other a lot because we were both busy, especially me with the salon. I think we'd met up in one of the cafés in town for a quick sandwich, but I'm not sure exactly when, or which one."

"Was she okay?" asked Gates.

"She was fine, same old Chloe."

"Nothing bothering her?" asked Longstaff.

"If there was, she never said."

"No health problems?"

"None that I knew of," said Tina. "Like I said, eating all the right stuff and taking the medication. She had regular check-ups."

"What about your brother?" asked Longstaff. "How is he doing?"

"Pretty much the same. He's well."

"How did Chloe get on with her parents?" asked Gates, throwing in an oddball question. Tina had already mentioned that Chloe did not seem to take her father's advice all that seriously.

"Pretty well from what I saw. Her mother was lovely. Michael could be a bit domineering but that's only because he loved her. They clashed, though. He wanted the best for her, but she wanted to do what she wanted. She could be headstrong. But for all that she seemed happy with life. Her health didn't bother *her* as much as it bothered him; I guess that's because she was young and he knew what he was talking about."

"With Michael," said Longstaff, "was it only the usual teenage daughter and parent problems, or did you ever sense anything more serious?"

"There was nothing serious that I could see, but you have to remember, he was in London quite a lot, so I never really saw much of him at all."

"We know that she was a volunteer in the charity shop, and that her parents kept her. Did he ever threaten her with anything; like cutting off her money supply?" asked Longstaff.

"No," said Tina. "But he wasn't keen on the trip to Africa. I think he still saw her as his little girl, and after what she'd been through, he was maybe more protective."

"And her relationship with her mother was a good one?" asked Gates.

"Very," said Tina. "They were more like sisters. She was much more understanding, maybe because she was at home all the time. She saw a lot more of Chloe, and probably how well she was coping with it all."

"What about Kyle?" asked Longstaff.

"Strangely enough," said Tina, "I don't know him. In all the time I've known Chloe, I met him only once. They lived different lives and moved in totally different circles, so I can't comment on him."

"Did Chloe ever mention him?" asked Longstaff.

"On and off. From what I can gather they were typical brother and sister. Loved each other, but argued frequently, but I really can't tell you any more than that because I never saw them together."

"Do you know of any conflicts she might have had with anyone recently?"

Tina thought about the question but shook her head. "Nothing that I know of. Like I said, she was a caring person. She didn't like arguing with anyone, apart from her dad, maybe."

"Did she have any enemies?" asked Longstaff.

"No, not that I know of. She had her fair share of admirers, but they were all of the same age and mostly the same sex."

"Mostly?"

"Well, I'm sure you're aware that Chloe liked girls, not boys. She had a girlfriend, Anushka. She did have some male friends, but that's all they were, friends."

"And there is no one you can think of that would do anything like what happened to Chloe?"

Tina seemed startled by the question, and took her time in answering. "None of them would know how to remove body parts, if that's what you're thinking. Except for possibly one."

Gates and Longstaff glanced at each other, before Gates said, "And who might that be?"

"Look, I'm not sure I should be saying anything here. The person I'm thinking of could be completely innocent, and probably is. I really don't think he would do anything like that."

"Maybe not, Tina," said Longstaff, "but it's possible he might know someone who would, and for any number of reasons. So for that reason alone, we need to know who he is and we need to speak to him, if only to rule him out."

Tina relented. "His name is Sam Sheppardson. He's a medical student. If I'm going to be completely honest, he is a little strange."

"In what way?" asked Gates.

"I really don't think he would have hurt Chloe, but he really liked her. He sometimes bought her small gifts. But Chloe didn't like *him* in the same way, only as a friend; she did try to politely discourage Sam – even to the point of their last meeting where she had to admit to her sexuality."

"How did he take that?" asked Gates.

"From what I know, he was a little shocked, but I have no real idea how he took it because I wasn't there. But as I said, I don't think he would hurt Chloe, would he?"

No one spoke.

"You need to speak to Anushka Wilson, her partner," added Tina. "She was way closer to Chloe than I was. If anyone knows how Sam took that news, and how he dealt with it, it would be Anushka. I'm still not sure I should have said anything about Sam. I don't think it is right to judge someone when you don't know them."

"Don't worry about that, Tina," said Gates. "You've done the right thing. If you don't tell us everything, no matter how small, we can't do our job properly. And I'm sure you want Chloe's killer caught as much as we do."

As they were leaving, Longstaff mentioned she could do with a good cut and maybe a new style. Tina invited her to try out the salon, and said she would do the job personally.

Chapter Fourteen

After leaving 21 Co., Gardener and Reilly headed over to see Anushka Wilson, Chloe's girlfriend and partner.

From the details they had been given, Anushka lived in a two-bedroomed flat/apartment in an area of student accommodation in Leeds, called Devonshire Hall in Headingley.

As Reilly turned the car into the street, Gardener noticed Headingley Hill Congregational Church, a redundant Unitarian church that stood at the corner of Headingley Lane and Cumberland Road. Devonshire Hall was further down. Reilly drove through an arched gateway, and the first thing they saw was a large clock tower as the centrepiece.

"Christ," said Reilly. "That's big enough."

"No excuse for being late, is there?" replied Gardener.

After speaking to one or two of the students, they found the girl they were looking for. She was early twenties, slim, dark-skinned, with olive eyes and sleek black shoulder-length hair. Gardener fixed on a set of beautiful white teeth. She was dressed casually in jeans and a T-shirt, but they were very smart, trendy.

"Please, come in."

They walked through to a sitting room and Gardener immediately clocked her as a minimalist; nothing was out of place, the room was spotless, fresh; he caught the odour of incense, and noticed in the corner, near the television, a candle burning. Indian music played in the background.

She asked them both to sit and if they wanted refreshments. After where they had recently been, both men declined, explaining why.

"Oh, I love it there, they're so friendly."

"We just like the fact that we can put something back into the community," said Reilly.

"And good on you. I wish there were more people like that. Chloe and I used to love the place."

As soon as she said that, her eyes misted over. Gardener could see how popular Chloe must have been by the effect her death was having on people.

To put her at her ease, Gardener asked her a little about herself. She said her father was English, and her mother was Indian. They had been warned about mixed-race marriages but they were still happily together thirty years on. And they were very good to Anushka because they helped with her accommodation.

Anushka told them she was a health care assistant, based at the Kirkstall Lane Medical Centre. Her duties were quite intense, including sterilising equipment, carrying out health checks, restocking consulting rooms, processing lab samples, and taking blood samples. There were also occasions when she spent time on the road going to people's houses to offer care.

"That must really keep you busy," said Gardener.

"It's not a nine-to-five job, that is for sure."

"You should have ours," said Reilly.

"Oh, I don't think I could do yours, not with the kind of people you must meet."

"It has its drawbacks," said Gardener.

Anushka smiled. "So, you want to know all about Chloe?"

It was here that Gardener realized they were dealing with a very smart young woman, a no-nonsense talker who usually said what she meant.

"How well did you know Chloe?"

"As well as anyone," replied Anushka. "After we'd been together a while, I loved the fact that Chloe was never one for studying. I remember her telling me she didn't care much for school. Not because she didn't like the teachers, or what it stood for, but she felt it was a waste of time."

"How come?" asked Reilly.

"She was very intelligent. She had an almost eidetic memory, soaked up knowledge like a sponge, and retained it. Her father was really disappointed."

"By what?" asked Reilly.

"Because with that kind of brain power, he felt she could do much better for herself. He figured she could have been anything she wanted. And he really wanted her to follow in his footsteps."

"Did he say as much?" asked Gardener.

"All the time."

"In what way?"

"He constantly harped on about it, wanted her to change her mind. Not to work or volunteer for a charity, but to do something where she could change people's lives."

"How did she counter that?" asked Gardener.

"Oh, she was Michael's daughter alright. She was just as headstrong. She said that she *was* helping people; people who really needed it. If they butted horns, they were equally as stubborn as each other. A discussion could sometimes become really heated, which would only end in a stalemate when one of them left the room. But at the end of the day, a parent's wish is mainly to see their child happy and healthy. Often, it was Michael that let it go."

"And did these arguments happen often?" asked Gardener.

"To be fair, no. I only ever saw it a couple of times, but Chloe did mention it on other occasions."

"What was Chloe like?" Gardener figured Anushka would probably give him a more honest answer than anyone else.

Anushka's expression became distant. Gardener had to remember that what had happened to Chloe was still very fresh in her mind.

"She was good fun. She wasn't a big drinker, but she still enjoyed going out on the town for the night. She liked people because she cared about them; liked meeting and making new friends. You're probably aware that her sexual preference was girls, and that was not aimed at her father."

"Why would it be?" asked Reilly.

"Did he look down on that sort of relationship, because it wasn't following the normal pattern?" asked Gardener.

"*He* didn't," replied Anushka. "Wish I could say the same about her brother."

Gardener found the comment very interesting but he wanted to return to the subject, so he left Anushka to continue talking about Chloe.

"It was simply how she was, and she regularly fought her corner and stood up for what she believed in. Her father respected that. To be honest, I think it filled him with admiration. Her mother was happy about it as well. We all regularly met for meals."

Anushka stood up and left the room and returned with a photo in a frame, showing the pair of them on what Gardener suspected was a day out.

"Where was this?" he asked.

"It was taken about six months ago. We went out for the day to the Ryedale Folk Museum. If you haven't been, you should; teaches you a lot about the past."

Gardener nodded and made a note, passing the photo to Reilly.

"You both look really happy," said Reilly.

"We were. We bonded really well. Deep down, Chloe was really cultured. She could be happy with a cosy night in around the fire, watching rom-coms, or a day out at a museum. Alternatively, she liked music and dancing; we used to visit clubs regularly."

At that point, Anushka simply fell back on the chair and started crying. Gardener noticed a box of tissues and passed her one.

"Who the hell would do something like this?" shouted Anushka. "Not only have they robbed Chloe of her life, they've just about ruined mine, not to mention others."

"It's okay, Anushka, love," said Reilly. "Let it out, you'll feel better."

"I doubt it."

"Ms Wilson," said Gardener. "If it helps, you're doing really well. We don't expect miracles, knowing what's happened. We do realise how bad this must be for you, but the things you're telling us are just what we need to hear. We need to build up a picture and we need to find who did this, and you're really helping us."

"And we will find who did it," added Reilly.

Anushka sniffed and smiled and said she would do her best to tell them everything.

"Chloe spent most of her spare time involved in some charity project or other," Anushka continued. "She had pretty much been that way since she nearly lost her life with kidney problems. You know what she did recently?"

"From what we've heard," said Gardener, "signed up for a project in Africa."

"Yes, but not just herself. Me as well."

"Oh," said Gardener. "We didn't know that."

"It was probably the only reason that Michael was letting her go. He knew I'd be there to look after her."

"I must admit," said Gardener, "that both of her parents have said how brilliant you were about the kidney incident; what do you actually remember of the night?"

She pretty much told them word for word what Michael had told them about the incident, which pleased Gardener. At least some things were falling into place.

"Where and when did you guys meet?" asked Reilly.

"It happened about four years ago. Chloe was eighteen and she was out celebrating her birthday at a club in Leeds. I can't remember which one. Anyway, we met at the bar, both trying to order a drink, and both looking for somewhere quiet to chill out. We eventually found the quiet room, slipped inside for a drink and a talk, and hit it off immediately."

"If you've been seeing each other for four years, you must know Chloe's routine quite well?" said Gardener.

"She didn't really have a routine sort of life, only where her medication was concerned. That was something that had to happen religiously. That's why I was so annoyed when she started taking that crap off the Internet when she was having FMD problems."

As Gardener knew all about that, he continued with his line of questioning. "When did you last see Chloe alive?"

Anushka didn't fare too well with that one. "It was outside La Trattoria in Bramfield. We met up earlier just after six, near one of the grill houses."

Anushka told them where they went afterwards, and which places they visited before telling them the last time she saw Chloe was nine o'clock outside the Italian restaurant.

"When we left the restaurant, me and the girls took a taxi into Leeds to a club. Chloe wasn't too bothered. I think, to be honest, she was tired. Me and Chloe spent a few minutes together outside the restaurant before the taxi came. I arranged to meet Chloe on the Saturday for a shopping day. We also arranged her taxi home with the driver who picked us up. He messaged the office to send another car for Chloe. She said she would stay outside the restaurant until it arrived."

"And that was the last you saw of her?" asked Reilly.

Anushka nodded. "By that time she was being approached by someone we both knew – Sam."

"How was she?" asked Gardener.

"Like I said, tired but still in a good mood."

"How was Chloe on the night itself?" he asked.

"She was fine. Upbeat, talking about Africa."

"When had you last seen Chloe before the night in question?"

"The Tuesday night. She stayed here, and we had a night in, by the fire, watching a film." That was another straw that broke the camel's back, as Anushka reached for the tissues again. "I just can't believe I'm never going to see her again."

After the tears subsided and Gardener felt Anushka was okay, he pushed on. "Was anything bothering her that you know of?"

"No, she would have said. We're both a bit like that. If we have something to say, we say it."

"No health problems, then?" asked Reilly.

Anushka shook her head.

"Moving on to Kyle, her brother," said Gardener. "I have the impression you didn't really like him for some reason."

"I don't," replied Anushka. "He'll say one thing to your face, and another behind your back. Sometimes, he'll be equally as nasty to your face."

"In what way?" asked Reilly.

"He hates same-sex relationships. He thinks they should be outlawed. He's so old-fashioned. He never liked the fact that I was Chloe's partner. It took him a long time to say as much. When we first got together it was mainly down to his dark expressions. He looked at me as if I was something he'd stepped in."

"How did that make you feel?" asked Gardener.

"I didn't care. I had it out with him one day. Took him right by surprise. He stuttered and stammered and eventually left the room. Didn't look like he could deal with it. I have to say, it never really happened again."

"How was he with Chloe?"

"To be fair, he was good with her. Very protective, always had her back. Didn't like anyone calling her names, despite them two arguing like cat and dog. And our relationship was the cause of most of their arguments, but Chloe gave as good as she got."

"Did it leave you with the impression that he might do more than disagree with just words?" asked Gardener.

"Are you asking me if I think he did this?"

"I suppose we are," said Reilly, never one for dressing things up.

"No," replied Anushka. "Apart from the fact that he wouldn't have a clue, he's a numbers man – an accountant. He doesn't have the bottle. He's basically a coward. He'll fight battles with words, when he can string a sentence together, and if he's losing, he'll bail out. No, Kyle Harrington is not your man for this."

"Can you think of any conflicts that Chloe had with anyone else recently?"

"None that I know of. She wasn't that type of person. Oh, don't get me wrong, she wasn't frightened of having a confrontation, and she would lock horns, but she didn't like it; really used to upset her, and she could be quiet for a few hours afterwards, sometimes all night."

"Did she have any enemies?"

Anushka shook her head. "Not Chloe."

"I suppose this is a big ask," said Gardener, "but can you think of anyone capable of doing something like this?"

Anushka made no bones about dropping a name.

"Only one. There is definitely something strange about him, and if anyone is capable, it's him. He has the knowledge."

"Who are we talking about?" asked Gardener.

"The man I mentioned earlier, Sam Sheppardson."

Chapter Fifteen

Monday morning was pretty much the first opportunity Gardener had to call the full team in for an incident room meeting. It was down to the sheer pressure of work, and the fact that they could not always make appointments with people as quickly as they would have liked; but that was police work for you.

"I appreciate you guys have all been busy with your own follow-ups. This is the first chance we've had for a briefing, which means we have a lot to talk about," said Gardener. "I'd like to start with the three hospital visits so we can confirm what we've discovered about Michael Harrington."

Gardener told the team what Edward White had said. He added that they were not happy with the lack of information because they felt he was choosing to hide behind the rules of patient confidentiality.

"Confidential?" questioned Bob Anderson. "Is he treating him for something?"

"That's what we wondered," said Reilly. "He said not; he also said that he didn't think anyone was more qualified."

"That good, is he?" asked Thornton.

"Apparently," said Gardener, reading out Harrington's list of achievements from a notebook.

"So why exactly did he go and see this White character?" asked Colin Sharp.

"Has he been snooping around himself?" asked Rawson. "Is he trying to do our job?"

"It looks like it," added Reilly.

"That's not a very good idea, is it?" offered Sharp. "One mistake and he could undo everything we're trying to do."

"Someone needs to have a word, sir," said Cragg.

"According to White," said Reilly, "you don't tell Michael Harrington what to do."

Gardener nodded. "Also according to White, what Michael wants, Michael usually gets. Anyway, before we get into that, what do you guys have from the other hospitals?"

Anderson responded first, reporting that they had been to Leeds Children's Hospital. "Sounds like we have a difference of opinion on the man."

"In what way?" asked Gardener.

"A couple of the people we spoke to, didn't seem to like him," said Thornton.

"Not that they actually *said* as much," added Anderson.

"It was more what they didn't say – a bit like your White character. What we picked up on was the odd expressions they gave us to support the things they *were* saying."

"Go on," said Gardener. "Enlighten us. Why don't they like him?"

"A couple of the surgeons think he is arrogant," said Bob Anderson.

"They believed he uses his position in life to get what he wants," said Thornton.

"Can you give me an example?" asked Gardener.

"Although no one would directly accuse him of it," said Anderson, "they think Chloe's operation was bumped up the list, and it's likely that money changed hands in order for that to happen."

"That's a serious accusation," said Cragg.

"That's what *we* said," added Anderson. "The thing is, as they pointed out, it was only opinion, but you'd be very hard pressed to actually prove it."

"I thought that lot usually stuck together," said Longstaff. "They might call each other in-house, but surely they'd protect each other on the outside."

Anderson smiled. "Like I said. No one actually accused him. They simply pointed out that the rumours were rife amongst some of the staff around the time of Chloe's operation, and that was the basis of them. Some people had their noses put out of joint, speculating that if it hadn't been Michael Harrington's daughter, it wouldn't have happened."

Gardener took in what had been said, particularly the fact that it would be next to impossible to prove, especially if they were talking about cash. Checking the man's financial status would likely prove nothing.

He turned to Rawson and Sharp. "How did you get on at St James's?"

"No one had a bad word for him," said Sharp. "They reckon he's worked wonders for the place. He's performed operations for them at short notice. He's recommended people for jobs who have turned out top-notch, and they are still there."

"No one can think of anyone who would have a grudge against him – certainly not to that degree," said Rawson. "Everyone spoke highly of the family."

"But they *were* shocked about what had happened to Chloe, and what caused her death," said Sharp.

"The people at St James's simply couldn't accept that you could have your kidneys removed and still live," Rawson said.

"They said she shouldn't have been able to *walk* after such an event, never mind live and breathe and stagger around for half an hour," said Sharp.

"Well, we're still not sure of that precise window, not yet," said Gardener.

"We did ask them about illegal organ trafficking," said Rawson.

"Are they aware of anything?" asked Gardener.

"Nothing locally they know of," said Sharp.

"Is it something they're *likely* to know about?" asked Reilly.

"I'm sure they'd get to hear something," said Rawson.

"Which begs the question, where *was* it done?" asked Gardener. "The window we're working with appears to be so small that it had to have been done locally."

"If it wasn't," added Reilly, "why had she been brought back home? Bodies are usually dumped; discarded in out-of-the-way places, so they might not be found for days."

"There's something else we should mention connected to this subject," said Gardener. "When Harrington went to see White, that was one of the things he was interested in, illegal organ trafficking."

"You mean he was asking White if he knew anything about it?" asked Sharp.

Gardener nodded.

"What did White say?" asked Rawson.

Gardener thought about the question, and then glanced at his partner, before saying to Rawson, "To be honest, I don't think he actually answered the question."

"And you let him get away with that?" asked Anderson.

"You must be slipping in your old age, sir," said Thornton.

Gardener appreciated the humour but felt embarrassed that he had not pursued the answer. That was a black hole in his book, and one that could cost them.

"Maybe he skilfully dodged it because they're both involved," offered Cragg, bringing the room to a silent standstill.

"What, White *and* Harrington?" asked Reilly.

"Stranger things have happened," replied Cragg. "Perhaps that hasty, unscheduled meeting was to figure what to do next, now that we're involved."

"But we're talking about his daughter," said Gardener. "Surely to God he wouldn't do that to her. Even if he did, he wouldn't have done something so stupid as to leave her wandering the streets."

"Maybe that wasn't part of the plan," said Rawson. "Even the best laid ones go wrong."

"He couldn't have done it," said Reilly. "He was in London all day; didn't come home till ten o'clock."

"That's an alibi I think we'll have to confirm, Sean," said Gardener. "We need to check his movements for the day. According to Roxanne she spoke to him at eight o'clock on the motorway services at Leicester Forrest, and it was still another two hours before he arrived home."

"We could triangulate his phone service," said Longstaff. "That would probably give us a rough idea where he was."

"Okay," said Gardener. "Let's just make sure."

"He could still have been involved," said Gates. "Depending on exactly what time Chloe was taken."

"He may not have performed the operation," said Cragg. "Doesn't mean he wasn't involved. It could all have been arranged and left to White."

"I'm really struggling with that one, Maurice," said Gardener. "If we come back to something Chesterton said, one or two people could simply not handle an operation of that size."

"Maybe not normal people," said Cragg.

"What do you mean?" asked Longstaff.

"They're both doctors," said Cragg. "Perfectly placed. They have the knowledge, probably the contacts, certainly the recipients."

"That's a massive operation, Maurice," said Gardener. "Takes a lot of people."

"I know," said Cragg. "But all of them belong to the medical profession. They'd all know what they were doing."

"It's a lot of people to keep quiet," added Reilly.

"Especially when you consider something else Chesterton said," added Gardener. "People get greedy. What if one of them wanted more?"

"You'd have to get rid of them," said Rawson.

"Yes," said Benson, "and we're not talking about sacking someone."

"No," said Cragg. "You'd have to make them disappear. And once again, they're all in the right place to make it happen."

Gardener puffed up his cheeks and blew out some air, and then asked, "Is anyone else thinking the same thing?"

"We hadn't," said Anderson, "until now."

Gardener waited but nothing else came. "Okay, I won't rule it out. I do think it's a stretch, but why don't a couple of you look into missing doctors at any of these places? Has anyone left under a cloud, or just simply disappeared, as if they have walked out? If people *have* left, maybe we could find out where they are now."

"Trouble is," said Cragg, "once you go down that route and you start making a list, it could be a serious amount of work."

Gardener smiled. "Come on, Maurice, it *was* your suggestion."

"Me and my big mouth," laughed Cragg.

Gardener made notes on the whiteboard before turning back. "Okay, I'm going to move on and change subjects."

He asked Thornton and Anderson about their interview with Roxanne.

"She looked terrible," said Anderson. "She was really nice, made us tea, but I noticed that when she brought the tea, she slipped a couple of tablets down."

"We asked if she was coping okay," said Thornton. "She said she'd have to."

"Did you ask about the tablets?" asked Gardener.

Anderson nodded. "She said it was a previous condition she was taking them for, not depression, or anything like that."

"But she didn't say what?" asked Reilly.

"No," said Thornton. "But we did learn something interesting that no one mentioned when you went to see them."

"What?" asked Gardener.

"An argument between father and daughter."

"We have now heard about their arguments," said Gardener.

"So have we," said Longstaff. "Tina Wells mentioned it."

"As did Anushka Wilson," said Gardener. "Let's come back to them." He asked Thornton and Anderson if they knew what the disagreement was about.

"Turns out it was a regular thing," said Anderson. "He was trying to dissuade her from going to Africa, said it wasn't safe, even though Anushka was going with her."

"Anushka told us he was okay with that," said Reilly.

"Didn't sound like he was," said Thornton. "He said he would pay Chloe more money in her allowance to keep her at home."

Anderson continued. "He had other arguments against it: managing to get a regular supply of the correct medication would be a problem where she was going; the right food; the proper time for exercise."

"Sounds like he was flexing his muscles," said Reilly.

91

"How did it end?" asked Gardener. "From what we've heard, one of them usually left the room."

"That's how this one ended," said Thornton. "With Chloe shouting and leaving the room. But she threw out a parting shot."

"Which was?" asked Gardener.

"Before slamming the door, she shouted at him that if he didn't change his mind, she might go out there and bloody well stay out," added Anderson.

"When was this?"

"The weekend before she died," Anderson replied. "On the Sunday, before he left for London."

"Was anything more said?" asked Gardener.

"Not between them two," answered Thornton.

"But there was a little more conversation between man and wife," said Anderson. "Roxanne reckoned Michael was getting frustrated with Chloe's attitude, at the end of his tether. *His* parting shot was that someone needed to teach the girl a lesson."

Chapter Sixteen

"Interesting comment," said Gardener. "Still, it's a far cry from saying something, to actually doing anything, even in view of what we have so far talked about."

"Is that how it was left?" asked Reilly.

Thornton shook his head. "No, according to Roxanne he did apologise to Chloe before leaving for London."

Gardener turned to Rawson and Sharp for another angle on the family, asking how they fared with Kyle Harrington.

"He's an interesting character," said Sharp. "Pretty much chalk and cheese as far as brother and sister are concerned."

"Aren't most of them?" said Reilly.

"In what way?" asked Gardener.

"Mainly their interests," said Rawson. "He's a couple of years younger than his sister; training to be an accountant with a local company called Porter and Preston in Thornton le Dale."

"They're almost complete opposites from what we've gathered," said Sharp. "He's a nice-looking lad: short dark hair, brown eyes, good skin."

"There's nothing on him," said Rawson. "A proper slim Jim. We ribbed him a little bit about that, to see how he reacted."

"Apparently he's quite picky about his food. Years ago, he read a number of disturbing articles, accompanied by videos, all online. Not sure what they were but it turned him vegetarian," said Sharp.

"Oh, God," said Longstaff, "not another one."

"You can't beat a decent piece of meat," said Gates.

Rawson sniggered. "I had you down as that type of girl."

The comment raised a laugh; even Gates saw the funny side and then mentioned something about sexual harassment.

Gardener motioned for Sharp to continue. "His parents thought it would be a phase, but they were wrong. He was pretty adamant about it; now he's almost a vegan."

"How were they opposites?" asked Gardener.

"The impression we had of Chloe was that she was a bit of a tomboy," said Rawson. "In the way that she looked and dressed. She was more than happy to get stuck in around the house, get her hands dirty. Kyle is a numbers boy; gained the top grades in school in every subject. Then stayed on, but instead of training to become a doctor, he followed his instincts of being excellent with numbers and secured a job as a trainee accountant."

"I don't suppose his father was trying to influence him into being a doctor, was he?" asked Cragg.

"It did come up," said Sharp. "Kyle wasn't having any of it."

"Did his father treat him the same way as Chloe?" asked Gardener. "Did he keep harping on about it, try to get him to change his mind?"

"Apparently not," said Rawson. "He did mention that, though. Even *he* thought Michael was a bit hard on Chloe, but he never really bothered Kyle."

"Did he say why?" asked Reilly.

"Not really," said Sharp. "I don't suppose he actually knew. He was probably just pleased he was being left alone."

"His parents said that he was at home on Thursday night, with them," said Gardener. "Did he confirm that?"

"Yes," said Rawson. "But so did his boss."

"His boss?" questioned Gardener.

"Apparently he had to work late on Thursday to sort out some accounts; Porter, his boss, vouched for that. He said the pair of them were in the office till around eight and then he dropped Kyle off at home."

"In which case, Kyle can't really add anything to what we already know," said Gardener. "Did he mention any recent disagreements that his sister might have had; or any enemies?"

Sharp shook his head. "Other than the usual spats with his dad, there was nothing he could think of. He's said pretty much the same as everyone else; she was one of life's happy people, got on with everyone."

"It's beginning to sound like Chloe was the perfect person who simply happened to be in the wrong place at the wrong time," said Thornton.

Gardener shook his head. "I'm not sure, Frank. What happened to her cannot be a chance thing. The window was too tight, and let's face it, how did they know she was the right donor; had the right kidneys? Whoever did this had to have been following Chloe, knew her routine, knew *her* very well."

"Which might come back to a hospital or a doctor being involved," said Reilly. "Who else would have had that sort of information?"

Gardener glanced at Gates and Longstaff. "How about Tina Wells, did *she* say anything that might have caught our attention?"

Gates and Longstaff filled the team in on the meeting with the hairdresser.

"*She* must have known Kyle. Did she say anything about him?" asked Gardener, wondering if Tina Wells shared the same views as Anushka Wilson.

"Not a lot," said Gates.

"She said that she didn't really know him," added Longstaff, consulting a notepad. "In all the time she'd known Chloe, Tina Wells said that she had met Kyle only once."

"She said pretty much the same as we've just heard from Colin and Dave," said Gates. "They lived different lives, moved in different circles; apparently he's big into cars, vintage and modern; loves to visit car shows, take photos. Given the little contact, Tina couldn't comment on him."

"But she reckoned they were typical brother and sister," said Longstaff. "Loved each other, argued frequently, but she never saw enough of them together to comment any further."

"That's the impression we had," said Rawson. "He'd do anything for Chloe but didn't always agree with the things she said and did."

"If you're looking for a possible suspect here, sir," said Longstaff, "I don't think it would be Kyle, or perhaps any of the family."

"Has Tina Wells mentioned someone else that might be in the picture?" asked Gardener.

"Yes," said Longstaff. "The name that cropped up was Sam Sheppardson."

"Sheppardson?" said Gardener.

"Yes," said Gates. "Why? Do you know him?"

"Let's just say we've heard of him," said Gardener. "Tell me what you know."

Gates told them what Tina Wells had said about Sam Sheppardson, before finishing with, "But I have to admit, she wasn't sure she was doing the right thing talking about him."

"Why?" asked Reilly.

"She didn't think it was right to judge someone when you don't know them."

"Sounds like she knew him enough to point the finger," said Rawson.

"She wasn't the only one," said Reilly.

"Why?" asked Longstaff. "Who else has mentioned him?"

Gardener told them about his meeting with Anushka Wilson. The one common but alarmingly frightening subject now *was* Sam Sheppardson. "The thing is, she didn't hold back."

"Why? What did she say?" asked Longstaff.

"That there was definitely something strange about him. He would always manage to be in the right place at the right time where Chloe was concerned. He regularly used to buy her gifts. She said, if anyone was capable, it was him. He had the knowledge."

"That's pretty damning stuff," said Cragg. "But why? What would be his motive?"

"Maybe she's had some sort of run-in with him," said Rawson. "That no one else knew about."

"She certainly didn't seem to trust him," said Gardener. "The one thing we found refreshing about Anushka Wilson was that she wasn't frightened to speak her mind.

Anushka felt he was a bit of a pest, as did Tina Wells, and eventually Chloe had to tell him she was interested in girls, not boys."

"A possible motive," said Cragg. "How did he take it?"

"On the surface, quite well," replied Gardener. "He didn't kick off. Appeared a little embarrassed but handled it well. He said they could still be friends."

"Anushka didn't like Kyle either," said Reilly.

"Why not?" asked Gates.

"Reckoned he was a bit of misogynist; he made no secret of the fact that he didn't like same-sex relationships."

"That's interesting," said Rawson. "When we mentioned his sister's relationship, he grew very defensive. He has a stammer, which is quite prominent if he feels he's under pressure."

"Yes," said Sharp. "When we asked him about Chloe, and whether or not he had seen her on the day she died, he said he hadn't. She had spent the night with '*that* girl' – his words."

"'*That* girl'," said Benson. "Is that how he said it?"

"Yes," said Sharp. "In fact, I can't recall him mentioning her name once."

"It's all interesting stuff," said Gardener, "but he has a rock-solid alibi for the night in question, as does his father."

"But Sam Sheppardson doesn't," said Reilly.

"How do you know?" asked Cragg.

"Anushka Wilson told us she saw him outside the restaurant when they were in the taxi on the way to Leeds," said Gardener.

"Tina Wells never mentioned that," said Gates.

"She may not have seen him," said Gardener. "She could have been facing a different way in the taxi, or she might have been on her phone."

Before anyone could ask, Longstaff was on *her* phone to Tina Wells, who confirmed she had not seen him on the

Thursday night. She also said that Anushka never actually mentioned it in the taxi.

"You don't think Anushka was just saying that, do you?" asked Anderson. "It's clear she didn't like him."

"Either way, we need to speak to him, find out his version of events," said Gardener. "His name has come up twice, so I would like all his details and I'd like someone on his case."

"We've discovered something even more interesting about the night of Chloe's death as well," said Gates. "Something else that puts Sam Sheppardson in a bad light."

The room descended into silence.

"Go on," said Gardener.

"We checked up on the other taxi that was supposed to have picked up Chloe from the restaurant. It never happened. When that taxi got to the restaurant, she had already gone."

Chapter Seventeen

"She'd gone," repeated Gardener.

Gates nodded.

"What time did the taxi arrive?" he asked.

"According to our records," said Gates, "around nine-thirty, due to traffic problems."

Longstaff took over. "There had been an accident a few miles away on the main A64, which caused a bit of a tailback. He called the office to let them know but there wasn't another driver available."

"So let's just work our way through that window," said Gardener. "The girls left the restaurant at nine o'clock. From the taxi, Anushka saw Sheppardson walking toward the restaurant."

"If that was the case," said Reilly, "he must have been with Chloe by ten minutes past – maybe quicker – depending on how close he was."

"Giving him a twenty-minute window. Would that have been long enough?"

"It might have been long enough to coax her to go somewhere with him," said Anderson.

"Maybe," said Gardener. "But according to Anushka, Chloe didn't see him as boyfriend material; she liked girls. She'd already told him about her sexuality, which should have driven home the message. That's why she might have been less likely to go anywhere with him on her own. And she was tired."

"All the more reason to accept a lift if the taxi hadn't shown," said Cragg. "Assuming he had a car hidden somewhere."

"Good point," said Gardener. "Is it possible that Sheppardson had pre-planned the situation?"

"If he was as struck on her as we've heard," said Longstaff. "Perhaps he *couldn't* accept her sexual preferences. Maybe he thought he still had a chance."

"And maybe, if he realized he didn't," said Rawson, "he might have decided that if *he* couldn't have her, no one could."

"I understand the way you're thinking," said Gardener. "But it does sound a little extreme."

Gardener turned to Cragg. "Can you search our system for Sheppardson; see if he has a record for anything? Either way, I want him picked up and brought to the station for questioning."

He then addressed the team. "It looks like we have a better understanding of events as they happened. We know for a fact that Chloe was outside the restaurant at nine; and she had disappeared by nine-thirty. But whatever happened in the meantime, someone only had just over two hours to perform the operation and get her back on the street. I have another question; is that possible?"

"How do you mean, sir?" asked Cragg.

"I'm wondering exactly how long it takes to transplant a pair of kidneys." Gardener glanced at Reilly. "Sean, would you call Brian Chesterton for me, please? Ask him that question?"

Reilly grabbed his phone and retreated to the corner of the room. He must have connected with Chesterton immediately because he was back after a minute or so.

"It's not an exact science but Chesterton figured if everything was in place and prepped and ready, it could be done in around ninety minutes, maybe a touch longer."

Gardener thought about it. "Okay, so if it is Sheppardson, he managed to get her away from the restaurant at nine-thirty, into a vehicle, which had to have been very close by. Taken her somewhere, which also had to have been very close by, removed her kidneys, and had her back on the streets of Bramfield by around eleven-thirty, maybe a little later. Does that sound plausible?"

"Well, it could to us," said Sharp. "We're not doctors, so we don't really know."

"Good point," said Gardener.

"There's another reason why it might be plausible," said Anderson.

Gardener nodded, to let him speak.

"Our man wasn't doing a transplant," Anderson said. "All he did was remove the kidneys, so maybe the time taken *was* less. And judging by those little plastic tube things, whoever it was, they were certainly prepped and ready."

"Still leaves the question of where he took her," asked Gardener. "It has to be somewhere close. Do we know where Sheppardson lives?"

Most of the team shook their heads.

"I'll get onto it, sir," said Cragg.

"Unless…" offered Reilly.

"Unless what?" questioned Gardener.

"Unless he abducted her, drove off and parked up somewhere, and performed the operation in an ambulance."

The team descended into silence, perhaps doing the same as Gardener: working out what kind of a person they were dealing with if he or she ran a mobile operating theatre from an ambulance.

"It's definitely one explanation for why it was done so quickly," said Thornton.

"Would that even be possible?" asked Benson.

"You can make anything possible if you want it bad enough," said Rawson.

"If that was the case," said Gardener. "It doesn't do us any favours. We are working on the fact that it's someone living locally. If they have a mobile operating theatre, they could live anywhere."

"And given that Harrington works in London a lot, it could even be someone from there," said Reilly.

Gardener stood back against the wall. "I don't like the sound of that."

He turned to Benson and Edwards and asked if there was any news from the restaurant; could they throw any light on what had happened?

"The girl on front of house remembers seeing Chloe outside for some time," said Benson.

"Did she say how long?"

"Not really," said Benson. "Being front of house she was greeting people coming through the door and seeing them to a table."

"Were they that busy?" asked Gardener.

"Even if they weren't, sir," said Benson, "she will have had other things to do."

"All she remembers," said Edwards, "was that Chloe was talking to a young man."

"Did she give a description?" asked Gardener.

"She managed something but it was a bit vague," said Benson. "Tall, thin, wearing wire-rimmed glasses. He had short dark hair, dressed in jeans and T-shirt."

"Not a bad description," said Gardener, "but we don't actually know what Sheppardson looks like so it may or may not be him."

Longstaff was on her phone to Tina Wells. When she'd finished the quick call, she said, "It sounds like Sheppardson from that description."

"Not looking good for him," said Reilly.

"Not now, anyway," said Longstaff.

"Why?" asked Gardener.

"Tina Wells has just told me where he lives."

Gardener smiled. "Go on."

"In student accommodation in a building called The Tannery," said Longstaff, "but she isn't quite sure where that is."

"Won't matter," said Gardener. "I'm sure the oracle will let us know soon enough." He was staring at Cragg when he said the words.

"Pass me the details, Julie, love, I'll get onto it when we finish here."

"I do have one question about all of this," said Gardener.

"Only one?" asked Reilly.

"My question is; if he was the last person to see her alive, and he has nothing whatsoever to do with this, why did he not come forward when we appealed for witnesses?"

"Maybe he's not so innocent," said Anderson.

"If he isn't, he won't want us to know," added Thornton. "We might never find him."

Gardener turned to Benson again. "Did the restaurant see anything of the taxi that was supposed to have picked her up?"

"It was there by nine-thirty," said Benson. "Obviously, the driver couldn't see anything of Chloe so he went inside and asked."

"One of the waiting staff confirmed the five girls leaving," said Edwards. "And we know the front of house lady said Chloe had been talking to someone outside, but no one remembered seeing anything after that. Whoever spoke to the driver said they couldn't help him."

"No one saw her leave that spot," said Gardener. "So she could have gone anywhere or done anything. What did the driver do then? Have we spoken to him?"

"We have," said Gates. "The driver called the office and updated them, and they sent him on another job."

A knock on the door silenced the room. All eyes turned when PC Evette Mulson popped in and gave Cragg a file. He nodded. She left. Cragg opened it, glancing at the contents.

Gardener continued. "Okay, still some work to do here. It's a small town and it appears that whatever happened did so between nine o'clock and midnight. It's Thursday, close to the weekend, so there must have been people around.

"Chloe Harrington had to have been taken somewhere for all of this to happen, and she had to have been dropped off somewhere in the town. We know where she was taken from. What we don't know is where she was taken to."

"We don't really know *how* she was taken," said Reilly.

"We need another press release for witnesses; see what else we can pick up now we've narrowed things down a little. Was she abducted in a car, or a van, and by how many people?" Gardener suddenly stopped. "Talking of which, have we done any good with the first press appeal?"

Cragg nodded. "I have something here."

He worked his way through the transcripts, dragging out a couple that he felt were promising.

"No one spotted anything unusual earlier in the evening. Traffic was light, few pedestrians. A number of taxis were dropping off and picking up. However, a middle-aged couple by the name of George and Elsie Ravenscroft, who live on Old Bramfield Road, were on their way home from The Blue Ball Inn on Market Place after a drink and a bite to eat when they noticed a girl, fitting Chloe's description, standing in the doorway of La Trattoria restaurant on Wheelgate."

"Finally," said Gardener. "Was she alone?"

"No," replied Cragg. "She was talking to a young man. It all sounded friendly enough, suggesting they knew each other well."

"Is this Sam Sheppardson, or someone else?" asked Gardener. "Did they give a description?"

Cragg nodded. "Very similar to the one we've just heard."

"Do you have another eyewitness sighting there, Maurice?" asked Gardener.

"Yes, and this one you might find very interesting; a young couple, name of Jessica Southgate and Martin Wood. They were out for a night on the town, said they saw something strange around eleven-thirty.

"An old-fashioned ambulance, a bit like something out of a *Carry On* film drove past them on the Old Bramfield Road going toward the centre. They knew it were old-fashioned by the shape of the thing – built like a block of cheese, bell on the front, split windscreen. They figured it must have been going to the Bramfield Community Hospital but couldn't think why. There was no one else around."

"Old-fashioned ambulance?" asked Gardener. "What colour?"

"White," according to Martin Wood.

"Registration?"

"No," said Cragg. "Looking at what we've got, they'd had a few in the pubs, came out of one of them a bit worse for wear and straight into a kebab house. They only really saw it through the window."

"Did we see anything on CCTV?" asked Gardener.

Cragg shook his head. "Nothing answering that description."

Gardener grew concerned. "This might be the one thing we're looking for. Do we have the CCTV from that part of town?"

"I thought we'd been through it all," said Cragg. "If we have, nothing answering that description has been seen."

Gardener couldn't leave it. "I need two people on it, now, please!"

Chapter Eighteen

Gardener had left the incident room, and walked through the lobby and into the back room, where he found Evette Mulson and Mike Atherton, each with a cup of tea and biscuits. Dulux appeared shocked and placed her tea on the table, as if she'd been caught doing something illegal.

"I have a small job for you two guys," said Gardener, before correcting the statement. "Well, to be honest, it's not that small."

"What can we do?" said Atherton.

"I'd like you both to go through all the local CCTV on the night Chloe Harrington was killed."

"What are we looking for?" asked Dulux.

"An ambulance," said Gardener. "But it's no ordinary ambulance. This one appears to be very old, white. Might be the kind of thing you see in a *Carry On* film."

"A what?" asked Dulux.

Gardener realized he was showing his age. He thought everyone knew what *Carry On* films were. Atherton said *he* knew, and would explain to Mulson. They would google what they were searching for and come back to him.

Gardener nodded before slipping back into the incident room. He would have preferred Gates and Longstaff for that job but they had yet to report on the things they had discovered during the last three days. So, he started with them.

Gates informed them that they had been through as much of Chloe's personal belongings as they could. Her PC hadn't contained anything out of the ordinary, or anything they had not expected to see. She had saved articles on kidney transplants, and what to do following one. She had saved a lot of photos of Anushka and her, and others of Tina Wells with Chloe, or all three of them, but that was about it.

Longstaff had listed all of her friends on social media and had in fact contacted many of them to ask about Chloe, asking them to report to the police station in Bramfield if they thought they could help.

"Well done," said Gardener. "That must have been a big job."

"Not really," said Longstaff. "She didn't have that many friends, perhaps only about twenty to thirty, so I suspected they were true friends."

"Have we heard from any of them?"

"About ten. I've made a shorter list. I thought maybe we could contact them and have a word."

Gardener nodded.

"Didn't she have a diary?" asked Reilly.

"Yes," said Gates. "There was some personal stuff about her and Anushka. She also seemed to keep a record of where she had been and who with. Again, there's nothing out of the ordinary."

"Nothing about Sam Sheppardson?" asked Gardener.

"We haven't come across anything," said Longstaff.

"Was he one of her Facebook friends?" asked Gardener.

"No."

"Interesting," said Reilly.

Gardener glanced at his partner. "Do you remember what her mother said? That she *didn't* really have many friends. She was careful with them, so those she did have were very close."

Reilly nodded.

Gardener asked about Chloe's bank accounts.

"Nothing untoward," said Gates. "Her father paid money into the account on the first of every month."

"How much?"

"Certainly enough to live on," said Longstaff. "Around a thousand pounds."

"Bloody hell," said Anderson. "He wasn't stingy, was he?"

"I wish my father had done that when I was twenty," said Thornton.

"Well, he can't be short of a bob or two, can he?" said Rawson.

"Did she have money coming in from anywhere else?" asked Gardener.

"Oxfam paid her a little bit," said Gates. "Even though she was a volunteer, they gave her something."

"No unusual activity?" asked Gardener.

"No," said Gates. "Looked to me like she saved most of it. She was very frugal."

"The chances are, because she was living at home, her parents picked up most of the cost," said Reilly. "She probably didn't pay board or bills, or for food."

"She was probably saving for the forthcoming adventure in Africa," said Longstaff.

"Anyway," said Gates, "the upshot is, there was nothing out of the ordinary and nothing for us to go on."

Gardener couldn't help feeling disappointed. He tasked Benson and Edwards to chase down the list Longstaff had made, asking if they could arrange interviews; and hopefully, to call some of them into the station if they could. He wanted Gates and Longstaff to help Atherton and Mulson with the CCTV.

Gardener doubted by now that there would be anything of use, but people often remember things later on. It was always possible some of her friends had been on holiday, and either not heard, or not be in a position to do anything about it.

He moved on to Cragg, asking if the ambulance drivers who had been in town but were not picked up on CCTV had anything to report.

"Sorry, sir," said Cragg. "Both of them have been to see me say they did not see anything unusual, or notice any vehicles that shouldn't have been there, or any vehicles they didn't recognize."

"Didn't recognize?" asked Gardener.

"Well," said Cragg. "It occurred to me that we may have had an ambulance that wasn't from the area."

"Why might that happen?" asked Colin Sharp.

"Oldest trick in the book," said Cragg. "Steal one from somewhere else to do your dirty work in a different area. We had that happen a few years ago. Some lads from Birmingham stole an ambulance and came up here on the rob. No one questions an ambulance when they see it, do they?"

"That's a good point, Maurice," said Gardener. "Let's keep checking, especially now we have the old white one to look for. In fact, Maurice, can you run a check and see if any have been stolen recently?"

Cragg nodded.

"Okay, guys. Thank you for coming, and for everything you've done. We finally appear to have a timeframe of Chloe's last movements, but we're still struggling to make sense of it all. I believe the person we need to speak to most is Sam Sheppardson; he's right at the top of our list.

Frank, Bob, can you make that a priority, please? Find out everything you can and bring him in?"

Anderson nodded. "Leave it with us, boss."

As Gardener was about to speak, Evette Mulson slipped into the room to have a word with Cragg. When she'd finished, he turned to Gardener.

"The Harringtons, sir."

"What about them?" asked Gardener.

"They are in the lobby, asking to speak to you."

Gardener nodded. Once he'd made sure everyone had follow-up tasks, he slipped into the private room they had been shown to with Reilly.

Both of the Harringtons didn't appear to have slept since he'd last seen them: Roxanne more than her husband. She had dark circles under her eyes, with a pale complexion.

He knew all too well why. He couldn't count the number of sleepless nights he'd had following his wife's death, and the odd ones he was still having if truth be told.

Roxanne was dressed in blue jeans and a dark blue padded jacket: Michael wore a chunky cappuccino-coloured jumper and white chinos. Both had a hot drink in front of them.

Gardener and Reilly took a seat and thanked them for keeping in touch.

Michael Harrington took the bull by the horns, asking if they had found out anything at all.

"We do have something," said Gardener. "We feel it's very positive, but you may not."

"Anything will help," said Roxanne.

"We are able to tell you where Chloe was between six and nine thirty," said Gardener. He glanced at Roxanne. "We know she left your house in a taxi at six. Once she landed in Bramfield, we know which pubs she went to with her friends, Anushka and Tina. At seven thirty they went to La Trattoria in Bramfield."

"Oh, God," said Roxanne. "She had told me a couple of times but I just couldn't think of the name."

Gardener nodded. "That's okay."

"What happened after that?" asked Harrington.

"The group of friends decided to go into Leeds. Chloe was tired, so she said she was going home. A taxi came for the five friends at nine."

"What?" said Michael. "They just left her?"

"No," said Gardener. "They made sure a follow-up taxi was on its way to take Chloe home. She said she would wait in the doorway of the restaurant."

"And then what?" asked Michael.

"Here is where information is a bit thin on the ground," said Gardener. "She was seen by a couple shortly afterwards talking to someone she knew."

"Who?" asked Michael.

"Do you know a young man called Sam Sheppardson?"

Roxanne's expression said she didn't, and she confirmed as much.

"His name rings a bell," said Michael. "Who is he?"

"A medical student," said Reilly.

"That'll be where I've heard it," said Michael. "Then what?"

"From that point, we're not sure," said Gardener. "We know she was alive at ten minutes past nine, but at nine-thirty, when the taxi appeared for her, she had gone."

"Gone?" said Roxanne. "Gone where?"

"We don't know," said Reilly.

"Don't know?" questioned Harrington. "She must have gone somewhere. She was obviously abducted. Was this Sheppardson man responsible? Have you spoken to him?"

"We do have all his details and we are going to speak to him," said Gardener.

"Well, you'd better get on with it, then, hadn't you? Find out what he's done with my daughter."

"He may not have done anything," said Gardener.

"Well, it's obvious he's done something."

"It isn't obvious," said Reilly. "But we're anxious to speak to him because he just might tell us something about that twenty-minute window that we don't know."

"Do the police know *where* it happened, yet? Where he did what he did?"

"We don't, Mr Harrington." Gardener was becoming concerned that Michael Harrington was fixated on Sheppardson since they had mentioned the name, but he'd been caught between a rock and a hard place; he had to mention the name, they may have known him.

Michael stood up, displaying signs of agitation by clenching and unclenching his fists, grinding his teeth. He cleared his throat loudly. "You don't know much, do you? How are we supposed to get justice when we're nearly a week into this and you haven't found out anything?"

Gardener asked Michael Harrington to sit down. When he did, Gardener continued. "We have spoken to your colleague, Edward White."

"At least you've done something."

"Michael," admonished Roxanne. "Will you please calm down and let this officer explain to us what he has done? I for one, am very grateful for everything that he *has* found out."

There was a silence, in which Gardener felt Michael had actually been told off.

"He's quite concerned that you had been to see him," said Gardener.

Roxanne stared at her husband. "You haven't told me you went to see him."

"It was a spur-of-the-moment decision."

"Nevertheless, you should have told me."

Gardener wondered about that exchange; why hadn't he told Roxanne about it? Was he hiding something?

Gardener continued, "He mentioned you were asking about OCGs."

Gardener chose to say nothing else. He allowed Michael Harrington to stew in his own juices, under his wife's further stern expressions. Eventually, he added that neither of them knew of any gangs operating in the area, removing and selling organs.

"I apologize, Mr Gardener," said Michael. "I'm just very frustrated at not being able to do anything – at losing control."

"I understand, Mr Harrington," replied Gardener. "But can I please ask that you don't try to find who is responsible by yourself? Leave it to us, that's our job; it's what we're paid for. By all means inform us if you hear or remember anything."

Michael nodded, like a petulant schoolchild who had been scolded.

"Before you go, Mr Harrington," said Gardener. "There is one thing we'd like to ask you about."

"What?"

"Can you tell us about the argument you had with Chloe on the Sunday, before you went to London?"

Harrington's expression darkened and Gardener figured he was prone to mood swings. "What argument?"

Glances were suddenly exchanged between him and Roxanne.

"I didn't mean any harm, Michael," said Roxanne. "It just came out when the other officers came to see me."

Michael didn't reply.

"What did you mean about teaching her a lesson?" asked Gardener.

For a moment, he didn't think Michael was going to answer.

"I didn't *mean* anything by it. What are you trying to imply?"

"I'm not implying anything," said Gardener. "I'm asking a question because I'd like to get to the bottom of something I don't quite understand."

Michael stood up. "There's nothing *to* understand. It was a spat between father and daughter."

"It sounded a little more than that," said Gardener.

"How dare you?" said Michael. "Are you accusing me of murdering my own daughter? I'm the criminal here? I'll have your badge for this, Officer. What the hell do you mean by accusing me of murdering my own daughter? What kind of policemen are you?"

"Like I said, I'm trying to establish all the facts so I can get both of you some justice for the loss of your daughter."

Reilly stood up. "To answer you, Michael, old son. We are decent, honest policemen. Only, sometimes, *we* get a little frustrated, and we might say things we don't mean."

Chapter Nineteen

Kerry Bolton was staring intently down her nose, concentrating on filing her nails. Every so often she would stop filing and blow the dust all over the place, and then start again. She must make an appointment with Tina at Hair Today Gone Tomorrow, treat herself and her nails to a good manicure.

The clock was fast approaching one-thirty and the dinnertime rush appeared to be over. She could never quite understand why a newsagent would have a dinnertime rush, but they did.

Shortly after twelve all the office workers and bank staff would fly through the front door, grab a newspaper first, which Kerry was pretty sure was at the bottom of the list, considering the time they spent studying chocolate bars and crisps.

Some of them appeared to do a weekly shop. You couldn't possibly eat all of that in a dinnertime sitting. The shop had a chiller section. The basket appeared, which would miraculously be filled at warp speed with sausage rolls and pork pies, salad and pasta bowls for the weight-watchers. A few bought ready meals, bags of chips, and pizza. They only had an hour for God's sake; where would they put it all? That said, judging by the size of some of them, Kerry figured she knew. She wondered if they would keep that up now that the cost-of-living crisis had reared its ugly head.

Kerry heard the rattle of cups and saucers from the back stock room. Sheila was making them both a nice cup of tea. Why do people always say that? she wondered. You'd never actually ask anyone if they would like a shit cup of tea, would you? And then add, by the way, I made a Victoria sponge this morning but there's fuck all spongey about it: in fact, it's as rubbery as out of date pasta, but would you like a piece all the same?

She laughed out loud at that thought, trying to imagine it. She was one of three people who worked regularly in the shop, probably because they couldn't find anyone else. How did that work? How was it that you had millions of people out of work, but there were actually millions more jobs that you couldn't fill? Didn't people want to work? Well, why should they, when the government was willing to keep them, spending money they don't have? The good old taxpayer. She wondered what would happen if we all called it a day and went on benefits?

Kerry was twenty-six years old and had worked constantly since pretty much leaving school: Saturday jobs, working on market stalls, as a courier, a barmaid; you name it, she'd done it. She'd been at the newsagent for a couple of years.

There was a rustling sound near the front door as an old man shuffled through the doors. He was quite laden down with carrier bags already. Judging by the bags, he shopped locally. She liked that. Poor old soul probably didn't have transport; she doubted he could actually ride a bike, given his lean, slightly bent frame.

He was pretty scruffily dressed, wearing an old, faded macintosh. Kerry remembered her parents watching a TV detective who wore one, but she couldn't for the life of her think what he was called. Underneath, his trousers, whilst not stained or dirty, appeared old and possibly unwashed. He probably didn't have a washing machine; Kerry figured that he probably lived in a house on the bank of a river, and every Sunday morning he took his scratchboard down to the water.

He smiled as he glanced her way, before slipping down the first aisle. She smiled back but was totally appalled with his choice of footwear – open sandals with, of all things, socks. His hair was mostly black, uncombed, not to mention uncut, hanging at shoulder length, curling upwards. Tina would have a field day with him.

From what Kerry saw, he had dark brown, piercing eyes and a thin straight nose. But his smile revealed perfectly white teeth. Obviously false, she thought. Who had perfect teeth and left everything else to chance? He was definitely on the undernourished side. Maybe he didn't have a wife, and couldn't cook. But that shouldn't really be an excuse nowadays. Ready meals for one were all the rage if you couldn't cook.

"Here's your tea, love," said Sheila Carlisle.

"Thanks, Sheila, love," said Kerry. "How was your holiday?"

"Lovely, thanks. We only went to Bournemouth. One of those coach tours. You know what it's like when you get to our age."

Something else old people always said, thought Kerry. How the hell would she know, she was only in her twenties. Nevertheless, she liked Sheila, who was one of two part-time staff for the shop, the other being Betty Miller.

"When our Bert was younger, we'd think nothing of driving down there," continued Sheila. "Anyway, since his spell in the hospital, he only drives short distances now. Still, it's nice to sit back and watch the world go by while someone else does all the driving."

"Of course it is, Sheila, love. Did you get some nice food while you were down there?"

"Usual stuff. I love a bit of seafood, but my Bert's not the same since his episode. He sticks to what he knows."

Kerry avoided asking Sheila about her love life. Bert hadn't been the same since his operation; fuck knows what he'd had done, she never talked about it. Which could only lead Kerry to think it was something personal, something the older generation only talked about in whispers – or mimed. Sheila being the age she was, Kerry doubted her love life was up to much even *before* Bert's operation.

On that note she decided to change the subject. "Did you read about that awful incident in the market square?"

"Oh, dear, don't remind me."

A banging noise down the first aisle distracted Sheila's attention. She turned back to Kerry. "I didn't know we had someone in."

"It's only an old gentleman. He's probably dropped his guts."

Sheila smiled. "Don't be so crude. I wonder if I ought to go and see if he's okay?"

"I'm sure he would have shouted if he wasn't," said Kerry. At that point, they heard him shuffling through to the next aisle.

"You were saying," said Kerry.

"Wasn't it awful?" continued Sheila. "Such a young girl. I've no idea what happened to her. According to the newspaper she'd been stabbed to death. Still, what can you expect? It's getting terrible these days. You can't go about your business without your life being at stake."

"It *was* past midnight," retorted Kerry. "What decent person is out on their own past midnight? They reckoned she was drunk. Well, you're just asking for trouble being drunk on your own at that time of night."

"I'm not sure what her situation was," said Sheila. "Didn't you read the article in the paper? She came from a very well-to-do family. Her father is a doctor, and her brother is an accountant."

"Probably the worst sort," said Kerry. "The more money they have, the more they think they can get away with."

"I'm sure it's not like that, Kerry. She used to work in the Oxfam shop. Everybody who knew her speaks very highly of her. They say she was lovely, well-spoken, well-mannered, do anything for you."

"Seems like not everyone thought the same," said Kerry.

"What do you mean?" asked Sheila. "Have you heard something?"

"No, what I meant was, someone must have thought differently, because someone killed her, didn't they?"

The old man finally shuffled into view. Both counter assistants placed their tea under the counter. He lifted his basket up, removing the items: *The Guardian* newspaper, a magazine that Kerry could only see the back of – that was okay because that was where the barcode was – and two bottles of spirits: one a single malt whisky, the other a bottle of Havana Club rum.

"Hello, love," said Kerry. "Find everything you wanted?"

The old man bent forward and nodded. "Thank you."

As she scanned the first item through the machine, she couldn't help but notice he winced. She couldn't think why. He did the same again with the second item, raising his hand slightly toward his right ear.

Perhaps some people really don't like the sound, thought Kerry. Good job he didn't work here; he'd be off his tits after an hour, especially if it was dinnertime.

The old man reached inside the macintosh and Kerry noticed he wore a jacket underneath. He pulled out his wallet, selecting a few twenty-pound notes.

"You should be careful, love," said Kerry. "You shouldn't be carrying that kind of money around with you. Didn't you see what happened to that young girl the other night?"

"Terrible," said the old man, still trying to keep to himself.

Kerry glanced at Sheila, whose expression would have stopped a tsunami. Her friend was standing stock-still, staring at the old man.

When Kerry had finished scanning all the items, she placed them in a carrier bag for him – like he needed another. She told him the price and he passed over the notes. She gave him his change and passed over the carrier bag, the rustling sound causing him to flinch again.

He stepped backwards after taking the bag, nodded at them both and bowed slightly. "Thank you, and good day to you."

With that, he left the shop.

Kerry picked up her cup, took a sip of tea and turned to Sheila. "What's up with you? You look like you've seen a ghost."

"I think I just have," she replied. "I haven't seen him in years. I didn't know he was still alive."

"Who is he?"

"He's called Edgar. Can't remember his surname."

"Well, what happened to him?" asked Kerry. "Something has. Did you see the way he flinched when the machine beeped every time I scanned something?"

"Can't say as I did, love."

"Well, anyway," said Kerry. "What's his story?"

"Not a very nice one."

"Well go on, you obviously know."

"It must be nigh on fifteen years since it happened," said Sheila. "And maybe as long since I've actually seen him. I genuinely thought he were dead."

"Well, what the bloody hell happened?" said Kerry, eyes as wide as saucers. "You're worse than them bloody ghost stories on the telly; drop something horrible in and then take an age to tell what's happening."

"He lost his wife, poor bugger."

"Oh, that's a shame."

"It were more than a shame, Kerry, love."

"How did he lose her?"

"I'm really not sure. She were rushed into the hospital one night; never came out. That's all I really know. I think the poor sod went to pieces after that."

"Oh, poor love," said Kerry. "He must have took it real bad. Were they together long?"

"Since school, I heard," replied Sheila. "And if that wasn't bad enough, then he lost his job."

"Oh, Christ," said Kerry. "No wonder he's gone to pieces. Did you see his clothes? They weren't dirty, but they were so old and faded, and starting to fall apart. His hair needed washing and cutting, and he obviously misses out on a few meals. Poor bugger's frame was so thin."

"They say he never left the house," said Sheila, as if she hadn't even heard what Kerry was saying.

"Mind you," said Kerry. "He likes a drink. Two big bottles of spirits in his basket. I bet he's drinking instead of eating."

"They reckon he never left the house, it hit him so bad." Sheila repeated. "Some even said he were dead, that he'd died shortly after she did."

"Well, he obviously isn't," said Kerry.

"No, but he might as well be," replied Sheila. "Looking at the state of him."

"If he lost his wife and then he lost his job, it's no wonder he looks like that. How the hell did he manage to live, especially if he never left the house?"

"I've no idea."

"*Where* does he live?"

"I don't know that either," said Sheila.

"I wonder where the hell he's been all this time," said Kerry.

"Like I said, love, I've no idea," replied Sheila. "I genuinely thought he were dead."

Chapter Twenty

Another day had passed before Gardener and Reilly had actually managed to pin down Sam Sheppardson. Anderson and Thornton had finally caught up with him at home earlier in the day. Sheppardson was quite shocked to hear that his presence at the police station in Bramfield was required to answer a few questions.

His first had been whether or not he needed a solicitor. Anderson had informed him that he was entitled to one if he wished, but the young man said he would wait and see what happened.

Thornton informed Gardener that he was now sitting, waiting patiently in an interview room.

Gardener opened the door and strolled in, followed closely by Reilly. The SIO placed the folder on the table in front of them. Both detectives took a seat.

Sheppardson went on the attack. "Do I need a solicitor?"

"We can call one if you'd like," replied Gardener.

"That isn't what I asked," replied Sheppardson. "I said do I *need* one?"

"Carry on like that and you might," said Reilly. "You might also need a doctor."

"Is that a threat?"

Gardener broke the tension. "You're only here to help us with our inquiries."

"About what?"

Sheppardson was how Tina Wells had described him: tall, thin, with wire-rimmed glasses. His teeth were white, but bucked. His hair down the sides of his head was cut short, but thicker on top, like a bird's nest. He was dressed casually in jeans and T-shirt.

Gardener switched on the recording device and introduced himself and his partner.

"How old are you, Mr Sheppardson?"

"Nineteen."

"Where do you live?"

"In The Tannery, student accommodation."

"And where *is* that?"

"I thought you'd have known. *You* picked *me* up."

"*We* didn't," replied Reilly. "So now we're asking."

"Cavendish Street," replied Sheppardson. "Behind Sentinel Towers."

"Which is a short walk from the Leeds General Infirmary," said Gardener.

Sheppardson nodded. "Popular with us – students."

"Do you have transport, Mr Sheppardson?" asked Gardener.

"Leeds railway station is close by. We have a bus service runs from right outside the residence, to and from campus."

"So you have no transport problems?" asked Reilly.

"Can't afford a car, so I have to use trains and buses."

Reilly changed topics. "Do you have any brothers or sisters?"

"No."

"Where do your parents live?" asked Reilly.

Sheppardson's expression appeared confused but he answered all the same. "Alwoodley in Leeds." He supplied them with an address.

"How is your relationship with them?" asked Gardener.

"Why are you asking about my parents? And what is this all about?"

"Just answer the question," said Reilly.

Sheppardson tutted but did as asked. "Very good: a little more strained with my father than my mother."

"Why?" asked Reilly.

"My father is a big man, likes sports and anything else physical; he's an engineer by trade. I think he expected that of me, but I'm just not built the same way, and that's all there is to it."

"Has he accepted it now?"

"Must have," replied Sheppardson, raising his wrist and glancing at his watch. "He can't do anything about it."

"What are you studying?" asked Gardener.

"Anatomy."

"And what is that, exactly?" asked Reilly. "Just so we know."

"It's a branch of biology, really," replied the medical student. "We study the structures of the human body, and the position of organs; that includes bones, glands, muscles."

"Any physical work in there?"

"It's a bit full-on," replied Sheppardson. "Even in your first year you get to dissect someone who has decided to donate their body to training medical students. That means picking up a scalpel and getting stuck in; can be a bit unpleasant."

"How do you find it?" asked Gardener.

"I don't mind it; others are not so keen. Not a good start if you're training to be a doctor."

"What happens with those people?" asked Gardener.

"It's not really a problem," said Sheppardson. "Some universities use pre-prepared dissections – 'prosections' they call them. You'll still have to learn structures and examine the bodies, but you don't get your hands dirty."

"Does it include physiology as well?" asked Gardener, showing Sheppardson that he wasn't really dealing with a novice, which meant he had to be careful with his answers.

"Not really. Some medical schools teach them together, but physiology is separate."

"Explain the difference," said Reilly. "For me, I'm not as educated as my partner."

Sheppardson laughed. The trick had worked; put him further at ease. "Anatomy studies the structure of the parts of an organism, physiology looks more at the way those parts work and function together."

"Can you give us an example?" asked Gardener.

"The heart's anatomy means the heart's structure: valves, veins, chambers, arteries, that sort of thing. The physiology of the heart means how the heart pumps the blood."

"Judging by your knowledge, Mr Sheppardson, you seem to be doing well," said Gardener.

"I'm doing okay."

"How long does it take to become a doctor, and how long have *you* been doing it?" asked Gardener, though he had a fairly good idea from what Edward White had told him.

"Takes about five or six years if you're serious. I've been doing it for a year."

"So you have a pretty good knowledge of where things are and how to remove them?" asked Reilly.

"You could say that."

"Which hospital are you based in?" asked Gardener.

"Mostly the Leeds General Infirmary on Great George Street, but I do spend some time at the St James's Hospital on Beckett Street."

Gardener wondered if Fitz knew him and then decided that now was the time to ask him the questions to which they really needed answers.

"How well did you know Chloe Harrington?"

"As well as most of her friends." Sheppardson's expression changed, as if it had clicked as to why he was really here.

"Do you know where she lived?" asked Reilly.

"Of course I do, I'm a close friend."

"Do you know where she worked?"

"In the Oxfam charity shop in Bramfield. I know that she was well placed because she was very keen to go and grab some experience in Africa."

"Did that bother you, her going off to Africa?" asked Gardener.

"It did actually," replied Sheppardson. "It's a long way and it's a big place, and I've no idea how safe she would be."

"Why would you worry about her safety?" asked Reilly.

Sheppardson's expression changed again, as if he was angry at the question. "Because she's my friend."

"Do you worry about the safety of all your friends?" asked Reilly.

"Not in the same way."

"So why her?"

"Isn't it obvious?" replied Sheppardson.

"Not to us," said Reilly.

"You must have done your homework before dragging me in for an interview. I dare say you know a lot about me already. What have the others been saying?"

"How did you meet Chloe?" asked Gardener, ignoring his question.

"I knew of her from school, although she was a couple of years older than me. I also saw her in the charity shop on more than one occasion."

"It's been mentioned that you seemed to spend a lot of time in her company, and that you'd show up when she was on nights out with friends," said Gardener. "Did she always tell you where they were going?"

"Not always."

"So how did you find out?" asked Reilly.

"Usual places. Facebook, Twitter, Instagram. There are lots of social media platforms that people use on a regular basis. But a lot of people are stupid. They put too much information on about themselves, and then they wonder why they have their identity stolen."

Gardener found that interesting, considering they had heard that Sheppardson was not listed as one of Chloe's friends on Facebook. "You sound as if you might have some experience?"

"Of what?"

"Identity theft," added Reilly.

"I haven't personally," said Sheppardson, "but I know a lot of people who have."

"Funny that," retorted Reilly. "You know a lot of people who have had their identity stolen, as if you're the common denominator."

"Are you trying to say that I did it?"

"Did you?" asked Reilly.

"No, I didn't. That's not why I use social media."

"Why *do* you use it?"

"To keep in touch with my friends. Do I need a solicitor?"

"Do *you* think you need one?" asked Reilly.

"Well, I haven't done anything wrong, have I?" said Sheppardson. "Anyway, I thought we were here to talk about Chloe. Perhaps you should be out looking for who killed her instead of questioning innocent people."

"We don't know that you *are* innocent yet," said Reilly.

"You soon will."

"Do you know Kyle, her brother?" asked Gardener.

"Yes, we've hung around together sometimes."

"Where do you know him from?" asked Reilly.

"Same place as Chloe, school."

"Do you get on with him?" asked Gardener.

"Strange question."

"We'd still like you to answer it," said Reilly.

"Of course I did, he's nice enough. He's really interested in cars but I don't know anything about them."

"So how were you compatible?" asked Gardener.

"We were both good at maths in school, often ended up competing in the exams. We used to have a tutor who would give you a point for your name. He said people were so engrossed in the test that they often forgot to write their name down. Anyway, one year, one and a half points separated the top three students: eighty-eight and a half, eighty-nine, and ninety."

"Which one were you?" asked Gardener.

"Eighty-eight and a half."

"And Kyle?" asked Reilly.

"If you knew him, you'd know; he came top with ninety."

"Coming back to the Harringtons," said Reilly. "Have you been to their house?"

"A couple of times."

"How did you find them?" asked Gardener.

"They're a nice family."

"Who invited you: Kyle or Chloe?" asked Reilly.

"Kyle."

"Did you see Chloe while you were there?" asked Reilly.

"Only on one occasion."

"What was she doing?"

"I'm not sure, she had one of her friends over and they spent a lot of time in her bedroom."

"Did that make you jealous?" asked Reilly.

"What?" asked Sheppardson. "That she was with her friend?"

"No," said Reilly. "The fact that her friend was in the bedroom and not you?"

"It wasn't like that. I respected her."

"So much that you stalked her?"

"Stalked? Who says I stalked her? I never stalked her. I liked her. There's no harm in liking people."

"Chloe's friends say you bought her presents," said Gardener. "What sort of presents?"

"Small things really, the type of stuff girls like: bracelets, bits of jewellery."

"How did you feel when she told you about her sexuality?" asked Reilly.

Sam never answered the question.

"Have we hit a nerve there, Sam, old son?"

"No," he replied. "Just that it's not the done thing to talk about sex."

"We weren't," said Gardener. "We were asking how you felt about her sexuality? The fact that you had chased her for quite some time, and maybe the fact that she wasn't honest with you about how she felt."

"Did it bother you, Sam?" asked Reilly. "Did you feel that she had led you on?"

"No, not at all."

His expression said otherwise. He felt his collar a couple of times and he was starting to redden.

"But you'd chased her for quite some time, spent nights out with her and her friends, bought her presents, yet at no point did she tell you to stop," said Reilly. "In fact, she let it go on for a while before she corrected you on her sexual preferences – that sort of thing can really wind a man up."

"Not me," said Sheppardson. "Like I said, I respected her."

"So you were not jealous?" asked Gardener.

"I wouldn't say that. I'm human, so it's only right that I'd feel something."

"Something being strong enough to kill for?" asked Reilly.

"No," shouted Sheppardson.

"Did you see her on the night she was killed?" asked Gardener.

Once again, Sam remained silent.

"Were you talking to her on the night she was killed?" asked Gardener.

He hesitated before answering. "Yes."

"Where?" asked Reilly.

"Outside La Trattoria restaurant."

"How did she seem?" asked Gardener.

"She was fine, but she wanted to go home, and not clubbing with them."

Gardener was pleased that he confirmed what had been said by her friends but decided to turn up the heat. "We put out a press appeal for witnesses to come forward; why didn't you?"

"I never saw it."

"Even if you didn't see it, did it not strike you as odd that something had happened to her so close after you'd spoken to her?" asked Reilly. "Something that you felt you ought to mention to us? Did it not occur to you that we *would* put out an appeal for witnesses; that we would be questioning everyone who knew her?"

After a short silence, Sheppardson answered. "I found it very upsetting. I struggled to come to terms with it."

"Where were *you* when you saw her?"

"I've told you. Just passing the restaurant."

"Did you see her friends?"

"No, they'd already left."

"How come you were in the area?" asked Reilly. "It's not as if you live there."

"I see," said Sheppardson.

"You see what?" asked Reilly.

"You're still trying to pin this on me. It's a free country; do I not have the right to be anywhere I please?"

"That would depend on what you're up to," said Reilly. "So, answer the question."

"My uncle lives in Bramfield," said Sheppardson.

"Where?" asked Gardener.

"He runs the betting shop on Yorkersgate."

"And you were there for what reason?"

"We hadn't seen each other for a while. I went to see him and we had a bite to eat. You can check it out with him. I'm telling the truth."

"We will," said Reilly. "What did you talk to Chloe about?"

"Not a lot," replied Sheppardson.

"You'll have to do better than that, son," said Reilly.

"I said I was surprised to see her. Asked her what she had been doing. She told me, and she said she was tired, and that given she wasn't far from her parents' place, she was going back there instead of to Leeds to see that girl she was with."

"*That* girl?" questioned Reilly.

"Yes, her partner."

"You don't like saying her name?" asked Gardener.

"Don't have to, do I?" said Sheppardson. "You know who she is."

"Sounds to me like jealousy is rearing its ugly head," said Reilly. "You were jealous."

"Like I said, I'm human. I'm allowed to have feelings."

"Did you see anyone else talking to her?" asked Gardener.

"No."

"What time did you see her?" asked Gardener.

"I can't remember," said Sheppardson. "About nine o'clock."

"Did you leave before she did?"

"Yes."

"Where were you going?" asked Reilly.

"To catch the last bus, get back home."

"So you didn't see the taxi that was supposed to pick her up?" asked Gardener.

"No."

"And you didn't offer to stay with her while she waited?" asked Reilly.

"Didn't think I needed to."

"Really?" said Reilly. "With all that respect you had for her, you didn't think to stay with her and make sure she was safe? I find that odd, especially as you were worried for her safety if she was going to Africa."

"Bramfield isn't London," said Sheppardson. "She wasn't going to come to any harm."

"But she did, though, Sam, didn't she?" said Reilly.

"Look," said Sheppardson. "I'm telling the truth here. I really liked her. I was in Bramfield on the same night as she was because I knew from her Facebook page where she was going. Haven't you liked someone before? But I'm telling you now, I did not kill her, and I have no idea who did. If I did, I'd probably go after them myself."

Sheppardson was close to tears.

Gardener rose from the table and asked his partner to see him outside.

"What do you think, Sean?"

"I don't think he's our man, boss. He's got a bit of an attitude, but I don't think he has what it takes."

Gardener appreciated the answer. "I think I'm with you. He may be a little strange, but my gut instinct tells me that Sheppardson does not come across as a killer."

"Are we letting him go?" asked Reilly.

"For now," replied Gardener.

Chapter Twenty-one

A little over a week had passed since Chloe Harrington's demise. During those seven days, the police had had a turbulent time, with information still pretty thin on the ground. Gardener had assembled the team in the incident room in the hope that someone would have something positive for him.

An evening meeting meant that a table had been set up across the back wall, with tea urns and snacks that Cragg had managed to procure from the local bakery. Most of the team were seated, with something to eat, which left only Reilly still scouring the area and filling his plate with enough food to accommodate two people.

Once he was seated, Gardener sipped from a bottle of water and asked Thornton and Anderson if they had made any headway with doctors that may have gone missing or could not be accounted for.

"Nothing, chief," said Anderson. "We covered the three hospitals and asked if we could have a list."

"They weren't too happy," said Thornton.

"We told them it was a murder investigation and *we* weren't happy," said Anderson. "But we were trying to track down the person who had killed Chloe Harrington."

"Did that go down well?" asked Gardener.

"Very well," said Anderson. "They said to call back within a few hours. We did. Once we finally had all the lists, we managed to get some help from operational support officers."

"And?" asked Reilly, halfway through a sausage roll.

"All accounted for," said Anderson.

"Those that we've done, anyway," added Thornton. "A number had left to go to other areas but they are all still alive and practising."

"Do you have more to check?" asked Gardener.

"A few," said Anderson.

"Okay," said Gardener. "Keep checking. I really don't think we're going to find any of them are missing without reason, but you never know."

Gardener added some notes to a new whiteboard before addressing the team.

"As you all know, Sean and I spoke to Sam Sheppardson." Gardener went on to tell them that he and his partner had given the medical student a real grilling. Although he was still under suspicion, there appeared to be very little on which to hold him.

"His story about visiting his uncle checks out," said Reilly. "They hadn't seen each other for quite some time, so his uncle invited him over, treated him to a meal in one of the pubs, and Sheppardson left around eight-thirty."

"We also spoke to Fitz," said Gardener. "He pointed us in the right direction as far as tutors were concerned. *They* all spoke very highly of Sheppardson; found him an amiable, intelligent person who was probably guilty of nothing more than having a crush on the girl."

"But all that praise doesn't mean he isn't a killer," said Rawson.

Sharp agreed. "Wouldn't be the first time. Look how many times in history we've had serial killers on the loose, who all appear to be the perfect neighbour; wouldn't hurt a fly. Next thing you know they're being lifted for the deaths of women all over the place."

"I agree with you, Colin," said Gardener. "But we also tracked down the bus and the driver that left Bramfield, the one Sheppardson claimed to be on."

"Don't tell me," said Gates. "It all checks out."

Gardener nodded. "The driver confirmed he was on it."

"What time did it leave, and where from?" asked Longstaff.

Reilly consulted his notebook. "Bottom side of Market Square at nine-thirty. So he had to have left Chloe after about ten or fifteen minutes in order to get there and catch his bus."

The team grew silent, before Longstaff added. "That doesn't mean that he didn't help bundle Chloe into a vehicle, and return later to finish the job."

Gardener smiled. "I take your point, Julie, but I really think that might be stretching things. However, there is no one else in the frame at the moment. So that's something else we have to keep checking."

Gardener realised it was pretty soul destroying, going backwards and forwards over old ground, repeating the same questions, walking the same beat, but it had to be done. One day, you might come across the one person who gives you a gold nugget, a piece of advice that turns the case on its head.

He glanced at Gates and Longstaff, his eyes virtually pleading with them for something.

Gates shook her head. "Sorry, boss. Michael Harrington has a rock-solid alibi, as does Edward White."

The news deflated Gardener. He was yet to hear what the alibis were, but he knew the ladies well enough to know they would have followed it through.

"If there is an OCG, it has nothing to do with either of them," said Longstaff. "Everything he told us about his movements is true. The London hospitals have confirmed where Harrington was. He spent the first half of the day at the Royal Brompton and Harefield Hospital in Uxbridge."

"The second half of the day he was at St Bartholomew's Hospital in West Smithfield," said Gates. "He didn't leave London until around six o'clock."

"Christ," said Reilly. "Every avenue is covered."

"Worse still," said Longstaff. "The mobile signals put him where he said he was at eight – Leicester Forrest services. And what's more, we have CCTV footage of him in the services."

In one sense, Gardener was disappointed, because they were no further on. On the other hand, he hadn't suspected Harrington, and felt relieved that he appeared to have nothing to do with his daughter's death.

"I suppose there could still be an involvement somewhere," said Cragg, clutching at straws. "But it's not looking likely, is it?"

"What about White?" asked Gardener.

"White and his wife were in Harrogate for the day," said Gates. "They had a meal at the Cattleman's Steakhouse, table booked for seven-thirty; and they stayed overnight at The Old Swan – about ten minutes' walk from the restaurant."

"Isn't that where they found Agatha Christie?" said Cragg.

"Yes," said Reilly. "But not this weekend."

A little levity never hurt the proceedings, thought Gardener, but they were heading up the road to nowhere, pretty fast.

Gardener reached down to a table and opened a manila file, extracting sheets of paper. "Chesterton has come back to us. He does not recognize the plastic tubes that were used to seal up Chloe's arteries. He's never seen them before, and they have no markings whatsoever."

"Has he asked anyone else about them?" asked Thornton.

"He has," replied Gardener. "They know nothing either. They're all of the same opinion; they're either something foreign, or they're home-made."

"That doesn't sound good," said Rawson. "Whoever has done this, they're well ahead of the game."

"It might support OCGs," said Patrick Edwards. "A lot of the time, the people who do this – steal organs – are foreign."

"That could make them really hard to catch," said Sharp. "They may only slip into the country for a short while, before hotfooting it back abroad."

"Such a ray of sunshine, Colin," said Reilly, forcing chocolate fudge cake down his throat.

More notes on the whiteboard. Gardener turned to Cragg to ask if anything at all had come up on the strange white ambulance.

"No, sir, not yet. Nothing on CCTV. There is still some more to go through, and I've had the support officers back around the shops, checking for any we might have missed; also asking about the vehicle."

"They have to be connected," said Gardener.

"I agree, sir," said Cragg. "Trouble is, we still don't know whether it's a local, or someone from out of town with a mobile theatre."

"Begging the question," said Gardener. "Is that actually possible?" He turned and asked his partner to call Brian Chesterton again – ask the question.

Reilly put the unit on to speakerphone and everyone heard Chesterton's reply. He figured it *was* possible if they had spent enough on equipment for the vehicle, which would run into literally thousands.

"And it wouldn't be a small vehicle," added Chesterton.

"What size are we talking?" asked Gardener.

"About the size of a National Express coach."

Gardener thanked him for his time and returned to the team. "Should that be the case, it would rule out our little white ambulance."

"Well, if that is the case, sir," said Cragg. "We'll just have to go back to the CCTV and track down every coach in the town. See what we come up with."

"I'm afraid so, Maurice," said Gardener. "I'm still of the mind that it's not someone from out of town. Whoever is responsible is local."

"I'll go with that," said Reilly, now washing the mountain of food down with a coffee. "Because it sounds like he or she knew the route to take in order to avoid the cameras."

"Which would also mean that he or she had the time to scour the area properly," said Anderson.

"All of which points to the fact that he or she knew Chloe Harrington, her routine, and details of her medical history," said Gardener. "This was planned. We're dealing with someone here who plans everything down to the very last detail."

"I know it contradicts what we've been thinking, but it just might also be someone who works on their own," said Cragg. "If you plan that carefully, I doubt you'd trust anyone else."

Gardener had to agree. "Okay. More of the same boring routine work to do. CCTV needs checking more closely for the things we've just talked about. Does anyone show up on any of the routes that could have been taken on a regular basis? Has anyone been asking questions in the shops on those routes on a regular basis? We need to really pull out all the stops. And I'm not having a go at you guys. I know how hard you work, and for what it's worth, I couldn't ask for a better team. But the problem we have now is, time is running out; the case is going cold, and our options are becoming limited."

Chapter Twenty-two

A little over a month had passed since Chloe Harrington's demise. Shortly before lunchtime, following a fraught morning with his team, Gardener and Reilly were sitting in DCI Alan Briggs' office in Leeds Central, a relatively new station on Park Street, behind the Leeds Magistrates' Court.

Gardener had a bottle of water. Reilly had a coffee, and Briggs was nursing a cup of tea. After he'd signed his paperwork, Briggs took a sip of the tea and glanced at Gardener. "It doesn't sound like there's any good news here, Stewart."

Gardener, rather disappointingly, had to concede that their lines of inquiry have not led them anywhere.

Following a solid month of work, chasing up everything, they had no suspects, and nothing in the way of witness statements that had given them anything concrete.

"I can't remember the last time we had a case as tough as this," said Briggs.

"Neither can I," said Gardener, and he genuinely didn't. What concerned him most was he knew where the conversation with the DCI would lead him.

"And there's still nothing on this old white ambulance despite witness sightings?" asked Briggs.

"To be fair, sir, there was only one," replied Gardener.

"Still," said Briggs. "Something as old as that wouldn't surely go unnoticed."

"You wouldn't think so," said Reilly. "That area is steeped in classic cars, God knows how many car shows they have a year."

"Isn't that garage around there somewhere?" asked Briggs. "It's always on the telly."

"You mean Bangers & Cash," said Reilly.

"That's it," said Briggs.

"We did go and have a word with him," said Gardener. "But without knowing exactly what it was, he couldn't help. He remembered having one in about twelve years ago, but he couldn't remember whom he sold it to, or much about it."

"Doesn't he have records?"

"He does," replied Reilly. "But the chances are, it was on paper and when everything went digital a lot of that stuff was scrapped, but he said he'd have a look when he had time."

"And he hasn't come back to us," said Briggs.

Gardener shook his head.

"And you've found no evidence of an OCG, or anything connected to organ trafficking?"

"Nothing as yet," said Gardener.

Briggs sat in silence for a minute or so, tapping his keyboard, staring at his screen.

"As a general rule of thumb – once all current lines of enquiry have been completed and there is, effectively, nothing else that can be done to further the investigation, we have to consider the case cold."

There it was, thought Gardener, the one thing he had been dreading since the summons.

"I hate doing this, Stewart, but there are a number of cases here that need your attention. I really can't have you two chasing down dead ends in the sticks."

"I'm not sure Michael Harrington will see it like that," said Gardener.

"I know," said Briggs. "But we'll have to break the news to him. I'll send everything to the closing officer. She'll make sure there is a case summary, and that all the exhibits are stored correctly with forensic advancements in mind."

"That sounds so final, sir," said Gardener.

"I know, but you know as well as I do, stuff could come up at any point, and if it's a lead worth chasing, we'll get back on it," said Briggs. "But I just can't have the team spending any more time and money on something that has hit a dead end."

"When shall we set the periodic review?" asked Gardener.

"Usually it's a year," said Briggs. "However, what happened here is pretty severe, so we'll cut it down to three months."

Gardener glanced at Reilly, and then at Briggs. "I don't relish another meeting with Harrington."

"I'm sure you don't, Stewart, from what I've heard," said Briggs. "But we need to explain the lack of evidence to him, and to press upon him that for the time being there are other cases that need our attention. He's never going to see it like that because it's his daughter. As far as he's concerned there is only one case."

Gardener nodded, rising from his seat.

"When are you going to see him?" asked Briggs.

"No time like the present."

Outside the building, the air was fresh and the weather was mild for the end of March. Traffic in the city was light. The pair of them walked toward the pool car.

"This won't go down well," Reilly said to Gardener.

"You don't need to tell *me*, Sean."

The drive to the Harringtons' took a little over forty-five minutes. Roxanne answered the front door and invited them in. She made tea. Gardener felt guilty because he suspected Roxanne thought it was a call to update them with positive news. Once everyone was seated, Gardener explained the purpose of the visit.

Michael Harrington's expression was thunderous. His eyes – not to mention his lips – had narrowed. He clenched his fists and cleared his throat loudly.

"You're doing what?" he asked.

Gardener glanced at Roxanne, who was in tears.

"We've done everything we can, Mr Harrington," replied Gardener. "But the powers that be have summoned us back to Leeds Central."

"Oh," he shouted. "Something more important than our daughter, is it?"

"I wouldn't say 'more important', Mr Harrington," replied Gardener. "We realize how important the case is to you, *and* to us, but there are cases building up on a daily basis that need our attention."

"So, you've done everything you can," said Michael, his sneer cutting through the words. "Which basically means nothing; you have nothing to go on."

"You're partly correct in what you say," replied Gardener. "After everything we *have* done, we have nothing more to go on; nothing more that will give us another positive lead. I understand your loss and your grief."

Roxanne was still crying into a tissue.

"*Really?*" shouted Michael, rising from his chair and walking a few paces, physically shaking. He suddenly turned and glared stony-faced at Gardener. "Do you really have any idea what it's like to lose a loved one, cut down before their time? To have your life ripped away in an instant? Have *you* lost someone you love, *Officer* Gardener?"

"How about his wife?" shouted Reilly, staring fiercely at Harrington, obviously not prepared to listen to any more. "She was shot in the centre of Leeds and died in his arms whilst he was waiting for the ambulance. Does that qualify, *Doctor* Harrington?"

"It's okay, Sean," said Gardener, waving it away.

"No it isn't, boss," replied his partner, still facing Michael Harrington. "I realize you're grieving, believe me I do, but taking it out on us will not help your cause. You are not the first person to lose someone you've loved, and you won't be the last. Right now, your best bet of finding the person who did this and bringing them to justice is us…"

"I beg to differ," shouted Michael. "We've tried it your way, officer, and look where that's got us" – Michael Harrington was fuming, his eyes blazing – "nowhere. From now on, we'll do things my way. I have the money."

"Your money won't help you, Mr Harrington," said Gardener, trying to diffuse the situation.

"Well, let's put it to the test, shall we? Let me tell you something about me, officer. I am not used to losing control, of any situation. And seeing as you have washed your hands of it, from now on, we'll be doing things my way. *I* will find my daughter's killer."

Michael stepped closer, squaring up to both officers. "And let me tell you both now: what I want, I get."

Chapter Twenty-three

The Bramfield Community Hospital is a health facility in Bramfield, managed by York and Scarborough Teaching Hospitals NHS Foundation Trust, founded in 1905. It became part of the National Health Service in 1948.

Monday, the first week of May; a beautiful spring day, thought Ann Traves, as she locked her front door, strolled down the path and turned left onto Middlecave Road for the short walk to the hospital.

She was on her way to A&E for them to remove the pot she'd had on her arm for weeks; a fracture caused from a fall. When she'd fallen from the ladder and felt a jolt, strangely enough she had felt no pain.

That came afterwards, once they had finished prodding and poking in casualty. The X-ray had revealed the fracture. *That* was when she felt pain. Ann had been unable to work out whether or not it was in the mind; that once she had been told, she had a *reason* to feel pain. Though she doubted it. Logic told her she would have felt it at some point, even if she had not gone to the hospital.

She turned left onto Hospital Road, thinking of how she'd somehow coped, living on her own. She couldn't believe all the little things you took for granted: going to the toilet, making tea, preparing your food, washing and drying the pots. You accepted it readily because you had two arms and two hands, all of those jobs you could perform without a problem.

There had been times, in the beginning, when Ann had had to rely on neighbours. But how could you ask one to take you to the toilet? She'd have died of embarrassment. The first visit took her nearly half an hour to complete the cycle but she was damned if she was going to ask for help.

Sleeping was a joke, even if you *could* sleep. Many a night she had woken herself up, in pain, because she'd tossed and turned. Once awake, she couldn't go back to sleep, so she would rise and make her way to the kitchen where she would try and make tea. In the beginning, by the time she'd made it, she no longer fancied it. But time eventually taught her she could cope with one hand.

Shopping was easy. It could be done online. Using the phone was easy. You only needed one hand, as you did with the TV remote. She had been thankful for small mercies.

Maybe it's time I had a window cleaner, thought Ann. At least he'd be more used to steps and ladders.

As she approached the bus stop on the left by the hospital, she noticed four people waiting, one of whom was the lady who lived opposite her.

"Is it today?" asked Mabel Grayson.

"It certainly is, and it can't come quick enough."

Ann liked Mabel. Like herself, she was a widow. They often spent time together, and Mabel had been fantastic throughout Ann's ordeal.

"At least the pain has stopped," said Mabel.

"It's been replaced by the itching," said Ann. "It's driving me mad."

Mabel laughed.

The man standing behind Mabel piped up. "Drove me bloody mad when it happened to me, love."

He was well-built and appeared to be a factory worker of sorts, dressed in a boiler suit, with steel toecap boots and a flat black cap. A small amount of grey hair was showing down the sides of his head.

"I'll tell you what helped me," he continued. "The wife. She loves knitting. She gave me one of her needles to slide into the pot. Trouble was, I used it that often that by the time they took off the pot it looked as if I had a tropical disease."

"It had crossed my mind," said Ann, laughing.

"How did you do it?" asked another woman. "The arm, I mean."

Ann explained.

The fourth person at the bus stop added her wisdom. "You do right, love, you *wanna* get yourself a window cleaner. Let him take all the risk."

"Wouldn't be much of a risk, would it," said Ann. "They do it all day, every day."

"Yes, and they bounce easier and quicker," said the man.

They all laughed, and Ann left them in order to keep her appointment, slipping onto Maiden Grove.

She was very excited about meeting with her daughter and grandson for lunch at Botham's in Bursley Bridge later in the day. Nothing was going to stop or delay that meeting. She didn't care if her arm itched solid for the next twenty-four hours, she would still *be* there, and like as not she'd enjoy it more now that she'd be able to use both arms.

She hadn't seen anything of the family for three weeks because they'd all been on holiday to Benidorm. The holiday was only for two weeks but the week prior to going they flatly refused to leave the house in case one of them contracted Covid.

She could understand how people felt, and how protective they were over their first holiday in years. They must have felt like she did: nothing would stop them going on holiday, as nothing would stop her meeting them for lunch and hearing all about their trip.

At the junction with Spital Road, Ann suddenly noticed a pair shoes.

"What the devil?"

A bus crawled past her and she saw Mabel sitting in one of the seats near the window. She waved to Ann. The bus continued, driving past the hospital.

She peered a little more closely at the shoes. They were joined to a pair of legs, with the feet resting close to the nearby fire hydrant. The remainder of the body was hidden by the shrubs. The ironic thing was it was literally inside the grounds of the hospital.

"Oh my word, what's going on here?"

She glanced to her right. One side of the street had houses. The hospital side had more shrubs, and a fence bordering the grounds. She stared back at the bus stop, but the people she had spoken to had all gone, and no one else had appeared.

She glanced back at the legs and the shoes, wondering what on Earth was happening. She was reminded of how shocking the world was at the moment and how bad things in the UK were becoming.

People of all nationalities were turning up on our doorstep, thought Ann. She found it amazing that we appeared to be able to cater for everyone else: we brought in thousands of people every year; we put them up in hotels, fed them, paid them benefits so they didn't have to work, but we couldn't care for our own. Every night you turn on the news and people were struggling to make ends meet; most of them, our people.

She leaned in a little closer. "Hello?"

There was absolutely no reaction.

She stepped forward, as closely as she dared; you hear such funny stories about people now, the length to which they would go to attack people. But the person in the bushes didn't seem as though he would attack her, or anyone for that matter.

"Can I help you?" she asked. Though what use she would be with one arm was anyone's guess.

That question did not bring about a reaction.

She glanced around again. The street was still empty. Where the hell was everyone when you needed them? You could bet your last pound, if she didn't need any help, they'd be all over the place.

Ann blamed the government for all these problems; homeless, jobless people who had nowhere to go, and who relied on food banks. They never had food banks and benefits in her day. They never actually had anything. Everyone was poor. But they had community spirit. Everyone helped each other. Where were they now?

She wasn't on her own with that line of thinking; *everybody* blamed the government for losing control: the energy crisis, rising fuel costs, spiralling food prices – and shortages.

Where the hell will it all end? When we're all six feet under, no doubt, thought Ann. She was convinced it was one big conspiracy to reduce the population. There were too many people on the planet. Covid hadn't worked, now they'll price us out of existence.

Ann stepped closer, crouching down. "Are you hurt?" she asked.

No response.

"Would you like me to call someone?"

Still no response.

Christ, she thought, he must be in a deep sleep. She peered around, thinking it might be alcohol induced; something for which they could always find money, but she couldn't see any empty bottles.

After working up the nerve, Ann very quickly reached out and touched his feet, and withdrew her arm again immediately, quicker than she had reached out.

"Do you need any help?" she shouted.

Ann quickly glanced upwards, noticing a nurse walking toward her. She was still some distance away but at least it was a positive sign.

With still no response, Ann leaned in further and touched the man again, leaving her hand there a little longer.

The body was hard and cold.

Ann's scream started the nurse running.

Chapter Twenty-four

Gardener and Reilly were on the scene within the hour. The Irishman pulled the pool car to a halt on the road outside the grounds of the hospital, parking opposite Atherton's car, pretty much creating a crime scene barrier.

Gardener jumped out of the car and surveyed the scene. Two cars within the hospital grounds had formed an obstruction on the other side, and any staff watching were standing behind them. A crowd had gathered across the road, which Gardener suspected were some of the people who lived in the houses opposite the hospital.

Atherton and Dulux were talking to a mature lady whose grey hair was tied in a bun. She was wearing a two-piece, navy trouser suit, with a jacket over one arm, which was in a pot.

The pair of them approached.

"This is Ann Traves," said Dulux. "She found the body."

Gardener noticed the lady was well and truly shocked. Her complexion was a similar colour to her hair. She had obviously been crying because mascara had run down her cheeks. He displayed his warrant card and introduced himself and Reilly.

"Are you okay, Mrs Traves?" he asked.

"I've been better. But thank you for asking."

"I realize it must have been a shock for you," he said, "but can you take me through what happened?"

She did. Reilly took notes, Dulux and Atherton waited patiently.

When she'd finished, Gardener asked, "So you've not moved the body, only touched it?"

"Yes," she replied, "on his left leg."

"The people at the bus stop," said Gardener. "Did you know any of them?"

"Yes, my neighbour, Mabel Grayson." Ann Traves started crying again. "My word, I don't think I'll ever forget this."

"Thank you, Mrs Traves, you've done very well."

Gardener pulled Atherton to one side. "I'm going to call out my team. Once they arrive, can you take the lady home and take a statement from her? And can you also find out who the neighbour is and where exactly she lives? With a bit of luck, she might know the other people at the stop. We need to know if they saw anything."

"Yes, sir. Have you seen the body yet?"

"No," said Gardener. "We're going to have a look now. I assume he is definitely dead?"

"Yes, sir. I managed to reach in further and noticed a hand. There was no pulse. I couldn't see his face, so I don't know who it is."

"Okay, thank you."

Gardener turned and approached his partner, who had finished talking to the crowd that had gathered near their houses.

"Anyone see anything?" Gardener asked, opening the boot of the car.

"No," said Reilly. "I suppose it all depends on when this happened." As he replied he extracted a scene suit and started to put it on.

Gardener did the same. "When we've had a look and called the team, I think we'd better see if any of the staff at the hospital saw anything."

"Or if the CCTV is working, and where the cameras are."

"Good point, Sean."

Gardener finished off with boots and gloves. "Are you ready?"

Reilly nodded.

Gardener approached the shrubs hiding the body. He saw the shoes; they were not cheap. The man was wearing trousers, not jeans, and as he leaned in further, he noticed a jacket to match, indicating a reasonably expensive suit. The man was laid on his stomach, with his head buried a little way into the soil.

"Whoever he is," said Gardener. "He's not homeless."

Reilly nodded. "I can't remember the last time I saw a tramp wearing a suit and high-end shoes."

Gardener studied the area under the shrub. There were no empty pill bottles, or any alcohol. He knew the SOCOs would do a proper job, but he couldn't see anything at all out of place.

"He's been carefully placed here," said Reilly.

"Just what I was thinking, Sean. Whoever did this knew exactly what they were doing."

"And you can bet they picked their moment. Middle of the night when most people are in bed."

Before doing anything else, Gardener called Leeds Central, requesting the presence of his team as soon as possible. He also asked for SOCOs and PolSA, and the Home Office pathologist, Fitz.

When he'd finished, he placed his phone back in his pocket and turned to his partner. "I'm going to turn him over, Sean. Let's have a look at his face, and we'll check his pockets for ID."

Reilly nodded.

Gardener did as he said he would, immediately recoiling and stepping backwards, out of the shrubbery.

"Jesus Christ!" said Reilly, doing the same. "Is that who I think it is?"

"Yes," said Gardener.

Atherton suddenly appeared at Gardener's side, as if he had seen the sudden movement. "Are you okay, sir?"

Gardener nodded. "Yes, thank you."

"What's wrong?" asked the young PC.

"That was going to be my first question."

Gardener whirled around quickly and came face to face with Fitz. "Where the hell did you spring from?"

The pathologist was wearing a grey suit, with white shirt and grey tie. He pointed to the hospital. "In there."

"What were you doing in there?"

"Attending a meeting."

Gardener took Fitz to one side. "We have a very serious problem on our hands."

"Why?" asked Fitz.

Gardener told him.

"Oh, dear."

"Can you please do an immediate post-mortem?" asked Gardener, glancing at the hospital. "In there, if necessary. I need the results of this one straight away, if not sooner."

Reilly appeared and passed Fitz a scene suit. The pathologist donned it and crept into the bushes. Gardener knew that Fitz had the authority to move the body and he would do so quickly. What he didn't know was whether or not he could do a post-mortem here, in the Bramfield Community hospital – but he couldn't see why not. If he couldn't, Gardener would override whoever said so.

"You'd better phone old Maurice," Reilly said to Gardener.

"You read my mind again," said Gardener, raising his phone.

"Doesn't take much," said Reilly, smiling.

"I take that to mean because it's a crime scene and the procedure is standard," laughed Gardener, "and not that I have a small mind."

"You take it how you want, boss."

Gardener smiled and phoned Cragg. He updated the desk sergeant on the situation and stipulated that he wanted a crime scene tent erected immediately, and a police photographer found as soon as possible.

Fitz backed out of the shrubbery and called over a nurse. In order to prevent her contaminating the crime scene, he walked out to meet her.

When he returned to Gardener, he said, "I've asked for a gurney and sheets and a couple of hospital porters. I realize it's not standard procedure but then this crime is anything but. I'll take him into the hospital and do as you asked. Are you joining me?"

"As soon as I have the team here and I've set some actions."

Gardener glanced around. Fortunately, no further people had gathered.

Atherton approached Gardener. "Do you know who that is in there?" he asked, staring at the shrubbery.

"I'm afraid we do," said Gardener.

Chapter Twenty-five

Four hours later, Gardener and Reilly were sitting in an office waiting for Fitz to return. The SIO was drinking bottled water, and Reilly had a coffee in his hand. Gardener had set his own team off on the house-to-house inquiries – though he doubted anyone would have anything to report. The SOCOs were analysing the crime scene, and PolSA were conducting a fingertip search. Quite what anyone would find he had no idea, because he suspected that whoever was responsible would have been very careful.

Fitz suddenly opened the door of the office and took a seat behind the desk, facing both officers. He had now dumped his surgical scrubs in favour of his grey suit. He had no files with him, but he did have a cup of tea.

"I can tell you," said Fitz, "that Kyle Harrington was murdered, and died as a result of his liver having been removed."

"His liver?" repeated Reilly.

"I don't believe this," said Gardener.

"Have you any idea when this might have happened?" asked Reilly.

"It was definitely sometime last night," said Fitz. "I think you'd be looking at four hours minimum for a liver transplant. Though, in this case it was a simple removal and nothing else. Whoever did this would want to do so after dark, so I suspect he will have been dumped sometime in the early hours of the morning."

"Told you," said Reilly to Gardener. "He's picked a time when everyone's in bed and he's less likely to be seen."

"What about the arteries?" asked Gardener. "Have they been sealed off like they were with Chloe's kidneys?"

"A couple were," said Fitz.

"What does that mean?" asked Reilly.

"Others were left open, which is why he bled to death."

"This is pretty much the same MO as his sister," said Gardener. "She had her kidneys removed and was sent back out onto the street, and managed to live for a while. Could this have happened with Kyle?"

"No," said Fitz. "Not a chance. He would have bled to death almost immediately."

"Which means," said Gardener, "that he was dropped here, at the hospital, and not somewhere else."

"Almost certainly," said Fitz.

"Who would do this?" asked Reilly.

"For what it's worth," said Fitz, "I don't think you're looking for an organised crime gang. I believe this is personal."

Gardener nodded. That thought had already run through his mind. He turned to his partner. "We need to see the hospital CCTV before we leave, Sean."

The Irishman nodded.

Gardener turned back to Fitz. "I know this is probably a stupid question, but is it the work of the same person? I mean, I don't know how surgeons work; do different doctors specialise in different areas?"

Fitz nodded. "Generally speaking, surgeons tend to work within a broad area: for example, ear, nose and throat; orthopaedics; vascular; trauma, etc. There are also general surgeons who would tackle straightforward stuff, especially in an emergency admission.

"Transplant surgeons are very specialised and often tend to work with just one organ i.e., either the kidney, or the heart, or the liver, but they would understand the principles of transplanting organs in general. It's a very intricate procedure, which is the reason they specialise. They have to know where all the blood vessels and nerves are and when to avoid which ones, and those which need to be reconnected for the organ to work."

"But does this follow the same pattern as Chloe's removal?" insisted Gardener. "Given that a couple of arteries had been sealed?"

"I would say so, yes," replied Fitz. "The small tubes are in situ again."

"Why the hell would you seal two of the arteries and leave the others?" asked Reilly. "Why not leave them all, or seal them all?"

Fitz shook his head. "I'm only guessing, but maybe it was a pain thing. If whoever did this, did not use the correct amount of anaesthetic, Kyle would have been partially awake, and perhaps able to feel some pain."

"Jesus," said Reilly.

Gardener shook his head. "We asked Brian Chesterton if the person responsible for such a macabre practice could perhaps do it in a mobile operating theatre. He said it was possible but unlikely because it would be the size of a National Express coach and would cost thousands. What's your opinion, Fitz?"

"I'm liable to agree with him," replied the pathologist. "For a start, you wouldn't want a mobile operating theatre because it would be too difficult to move around, which means you would almost certainly draw attention to yourself. And secondly, why would you spend that kind of money when all you're doing is removing organs in order to cause the maximum pain, resulting in death?"

"Which once again suggests that whoever is responsible is local," said Gardener. "He or she is living within a small radius."

"It might also bring into question the cleanliness of the operation," said Fitz. "Perhaps the organs are being removed in a makeshift operating theatre. The risk of contamination is greater, but our surgeon doesn't care. Maybe he's not part of an OCG and he's not removing them for resale."

"Would you say the person responsible knows what they are doing?" asked Gardener.

"Almost certainly," replied Fitz. "I've examined both victims. There is no evidence to suggest they had been killed first and the organs removed later. The job is too neat. If you'd killed them first, you'd have hacked at them. But you can't go into a body and remove kidneys and the liver without knowing what you're doing, or what you're looking for. In both instances here, that person knew exactly what they were doing, and showed a high level of anatomical knowledge. And they were intending to inflict pain on their victims."

"Which makes it personal," said Gardener.

Fitz simply nodded.

"That brings three possible people to mind," said Reilly.

Gardener nodded.

"Who are the three?" asked Fitz.

"Edward White would have to be one," said Reilly. "We already know he operated on Chloe when she had the kidney transplant."

"And the second?"

"A young medical student by the name of Sam Sheppardson," said Gardener. "Do you know the name?"

Fitz shook his head. "Who's the third?"

"The man we now have to go and see," said Gardener, rising from his seat.

Chapter Twenty-six

"We have three people who know what they are doing, and more than capable of carrying it out," said Gardener.

They were in the pool car on the way to Thornton le Dale with Reilly driving. "Two have alibis for the first murder."

"Sam Sheppardson has one, but it's not strong enough," said Gardener. "The bus driver confirmed he was on the bus, but he can't say where he went after he left the bus."

They were approximately five minutes away from the Harrington residence. "He would only need the money if he was *running* the mobile operating theatre," replied Reilly.

"Where would he keep it?" asked Gardener. "It's not as if he lives in a palatial residence with plenty of ground to hide it."

"I think we can discount a mobile unit," said Reilly. "Too big, too cumbersome. No way could that thing get in and out of Bramfield without being seen or picked up on CCTV."

"Unless whoever was responsible was picking them up in another vehicle and taking them to the operating theatre," said Gardener. "But if that was the case, why would you bother with the mobile unit?"

"Precisely," said Reilly. "I suppose it could be White. We haven't seen where he lives."

"But he had an alibi for Chloe's murder. He was in Harrogate."

"As did Harrington," said Reilly, pulling off the road and into the grounds of the house. He came to a stop and killed the engine.

"Jesus, Sean," said Gardener. "I've actually got butterflies."

"If it's any consolation I'm not looking forward to this either," replied his partner.

Gardener opened the car door and stepped out. Nothing had changed, apart from the weather. It was overcast but warm. The front door opened and Michael Harrington approached them, wearing a blue T-shirt, black chinos and, once again, very expensive shoes. His complexion was reasonably healthy but then three months had passed since the death of his daughter. Time in which to grieve and try to come to terms with it.

Gardener wondered how Roxanne was coping, or how she would once he'd said what he had to say. Losing one child was bad, really bad. Losing two... Gardener had no idea what that was going to do to them.

Michael Harrington came down the concrete steps toward the drive. "Oh, what brings you here? Realized you were wrong and decided to reopen the case again, have we?"

Gardener figured that whatever Michael threw at him, he probably had every right and no matter what he and Reilly felt or thought, they were simply going to have to take it.

"Mr Harrington," said Gardener.

Michael's expression immediately changed. There was no smile. The expression in his eyes died and his colour drained. "That's a tone I recognize. No, no it can't be." He stepped back, retreating to the steps. "Please tell me you haven't come with more bad news."

Gardener noticed Roxanne appear at the front door. Her expression of optimism was soon replaced by fear. He doubted she could hear what was being said but her body language spoke volumes. She put her hands to her face, immediately turned and ran back into the house.

"You have, haven't you?" asked Michael Harrington.

Gardener stepped forward.

"Have you come about Kyle? He was out last night." For some reason, he turned and pointed to the house, and then faced Gardener again. "He hasn't come home. Is he okay?"

"Can we go inside, please, Mr Harrington?" asked Gardener.

"Oh my God." Harrington brought his hands to his head and ran them down his face. As if he had resigned himself to the fact that he wouldn't be able to stop them or do anything about what they were going to say, he suddenly turned, ran up the steps and into the house, shouting his wife's name.

Gardener had to go after him. He found them both in the kitchen. Roxanne was taking tablets, washing them down with a glass of water. Michael held her. She was already in tears, staring out of the window; maybe if she couldn't see Gardener, he wouldn't actually be there. He wouldn't tell them anything she didn't want to hear.

Michael Harrington turned to face them. "It is, isn't it? You've come to tell me that we've lost our son. Because if it was anything else, you'd have said so by now."

Gardener asked them to take a seat.

Roxanne fainted. She never even made it to the chair.

Reilly rushed over, with his phone in his hand. "Should we call an ambulance?"

Michael faced Reilly with red-rimmed eyes, and in a choking voice, replied, "Not unless you want a fatality on your hands."

Reilly turned to face Gardener with a perplexed expression. Gardener hadn't understood what he meant either.

Michael Harrington tried to lift his wife but failed miserably. "Please," he implored Gardener.

Reilly immediately helped him. They shuffled out of the kitchen and the surgeon nodded to a door off the panelled hall. Gardener opened it and found a guest bedroom, exquisitely furnished with a king-size bed and thick carpets. They put her on the bed. Michael kissed Roxanne's forehead and lifted her eyelids.

"She may be like this for some time," he said, leaving the room, heading for the living room, moving very swiftly.

Once all three were in the living room and Michael had poured himself a drink, he coughed very loudly and let rip, his mood nuclear.

"I blame you lot for this," he shouted. "It's all your fault!"

"Mr Harrington," said Gardener.

"Don't you bloody well Mr Harrington me. How dare you come into my house with more bad news; to tell me I have lost my son to some psychopath who killed my daughter, and you did nothing? You should have caught the person responsible – not given in."

"We didn't give in, Michael," said Reilly.

"Yes, you did," shouted Michael, his face red. The glass left his hand and Gardener wasn't sure whether he had dropped it or thrown it.

"If it wasn't for you lot, Yorkshire's finest," he shouted, spittle from his mouth flying in all directions, "we'd still have our son. My God, what the hell have you been doing for the last three months? Because you sure as hell haven't caught the bastard that took our daughter."

"Please, Mr Harrington," said Gardener. "Try to calm down–"

"Calm down," repeated Michael. "Calm down!" He stepped toward Gardener in a threatening manner; his fists clenched, his eyes narrowed and his body shaking.

"You tell me to calm down?"

But that was as far as the rant went. Michael dropped to his knees, covered his face with his hands and shook uncontrollably. Great big heaving sobs racked his body, and within seconds he ended up on the floor in the foetal position.

Gardener glanced at Reilly, and then nodded toward the drinks cabinet.

Reilly slipped over and fixed Michael Harrington a stiff brandy. Before returning, he noticed bottles of water, and grabbed a couple. By the time he had turned, Gardener had physically lifted Michael into one of the armchairs.

Reilly passed the surgeon the drink. "Please, Michael, drink this and let us all talk."

Michael took the glass but said nothing. Gardener took his water, unscrewed the cap and took a long swig, before taking a seat.

The detectives allowed him a few minutes. At the end of the silence, Michael fished a handkerchief out of his pocket and apologised.

"You have nothing to apologise for, Mr Harrington," said Gardener.

"I think I do. I've just said some awful things to you."

"With good cause," said Reilly, "in your mind."

"Nevertheless, I'm not stupid enough to think you had any say in the matter before, when you were told to concentrate on something else."

"Mr Harrington," said Gardener. "Is your wife going to be okay?"

After a drink and a pause, he replied. "Yes, she will be. Though God only knows how she... we, should I say, are going to deal with this."

Gardener leaned forward. "What did you mean about not calling for an ambulance?"

Michael Harrington appeared as if he didn't want to say anything, but after taking a drink, he spoke. "Roxanne suffers with anxiety, really badly."

"I'm not surprised after what happened to Chloe," said Reilly.

"Oh, no," said Michael. "It wasn't Chloe's death that caused it. The incident goes way back."

"Is that what the tablets are for, Mr Harrington?" asked Gardener.

"You were very quick to see that. She usually manages to hide it from everyone."

"To be honest with you," said Gardener, "I knew about it through a previous visit from my officers. They thought she was taking them to cope with Chloe's death, but she said it was another condition."

"Yes, Mr Gardener. She suffers from something called jiuhuphobia."

"Pardon?" said Reilly.

"It's a fear of ambulances."

"I didn't know such a thing existed," said Reilly. "Or that there was even a word for it."

"There's a phobia for everything, Mr Reilly," said Michael. "There are a large variety of reasons that cause or trigger the fear of ambulances, which is a branch of ochophobia.

"The most prominent ones are upbringing – people who are raised by people that either are afraid, or have transmitted a sense of uncertainty or danger related to ambulances.

"Or genetics – a person's ancestors that have been fearful of ambulances were probably more likely to survive and pass down these fearful genes to their children and so on. And the other possible cause, which is the category my wife falls into, is a past experience."

Now Gardener had him talking, he wanted to keep it that way for a few minutes, especially because he might learn something else. "What happened?"

Michael Harrington took another sip of the brandy. "Roxanne was six years old when the problem affected her. It didn't only cause a fear of ambulances but a general anxiety.

"She was playing with her brother, Leo. The pair of them had ventured further away from home than they should have done. They found an ambulance parked at the entrance to the hospital grounds in Harrogate, which is where they lived. The rear doors were open. They saw a great chance to play doctors and nurses with an added touch of reality. Time passed, and though no one could explain why, Roxanne ended up locked inside, hiding."

Gardener could see where the story was heading, but he simply nodded, believing that Michael needed to talk.

"Leo had somehow forgotten and went off to join friends, playing somewhere else. The next time anyone noticed that Roxanne was not around was at teatime. Shocked and panicking, Leo suddenly remembered where she was. Their father took him in the car but the ambulance had gone. After a frantic effort, the hospital reception finally found someone who could tell them that the vehicle had been taken to the scrapyard. In the days of no mobile phones, this created a real problem. A search went underway to find the whereabouts of the ambulance.

"When the police pulled into the scrapyard the vehicle was on the point of being dropped into the crusher. Roxanne was trapped inside, terrified and unable to shout for help. She was saved with seconds to go. She never spoke for five days, and ate very little. Her parents were almost as distraught as she was. She has lived with that fear, and the anxiety it caused ever since. Almost anything bad can set it off."

"I'm sorry to hear that, Mr Harrington," said Gardener. "It can't have been easy. And to lose Chloe must have been devastating to her, perhaps increasing her problems."

"You can say that again," said Michael, his head down, staring at the carpet.

But suddenly, he lifted his face and the expression in his eyes had darkened so much that Gardener wondered if they had a split personality on their hands.

"What happened to my son?"

Chapter Twenty-seven

Gardener thought carefully, but no matter what words he chose, there was no easy way of saying what had happened, so he would simply have to tell Michael Harrington and hope for the best.

"He what?" asked Michael, squeezing his hands so tight around his glass that Gardener feared it would crack, or smash.

"I'm really sorry, Mr Harrington, but whoever was responsible for your son's murder, removed Kyle's liver."

Michael's eyes scanned the room, as if in search of salvation. "His liver? What the hell is going on here? They took my daughter's kidneys, and now they take my son's liver. Who the hell is doing this to me?"

Gardener wished he could answer that question.

"Why?" shouted Michael. "Why are they doing it? Who is targeting me?"

"Someone clearly is, Mr Harrington."

Before Gardener could continue, Michael started again. "What have I ever done to deserve this?"

He left his chair and paced the room, strolling over to the window, staring out into the grounds. He suddenly let out an awful wailing sound and covered his face with his hands, sinking to the floor again.

Reilly stood up and joined him at the window. "Come on, Michael, old son, let it all out."

The man was sobbing again. "What the hell am I going to do?"

"Don't you worry yourself, none, Michael. We're here to get justice for you, and this time around we're not letting anyone remove us from this case."

Gardener came over to help his partner. Together they lifted Michael Harrington and helped him back to his chair.

"How the hell am I going to tell Roxanne? Oh my God, this will kill her."

Gardener suspected it might kill him as well. He remembered when his own son, Chris was kidnapped some time back. He couldn't sleep, he couldn't eat, he couldn't think; all of that had remained until he had Chris back. But Kyle wasn't coming back. Neither was Chloe. How do you live with that?

Gardener and Reilly sat back down, and Gardener was trying to work out what question to ask him first, when Michael suddenly said, "This is karma."

Gardener glanced at Reilly, and then at the surgeon. "I'm sorry, Mr Harrington, what do you mean by that?"

The surgeon stared blankly ahead without replying.

"Mr Harrington," said Gardener. "We concentrated our efforts on trying to find an organised crime gang. In light of what's happened to Kyle, we have to consider this as personal."

"We're now left with the question of who will be next – you, or your wife?" said Reilly.

Harrington sobbed. "Do you really think one of us will still be a target, after this?"

"We have to consider it, Michael," said Reilly.

"Mr Harrington," said Gardener. "Have you told us everything?"

Michael Harrington buried his head in his hands, shaking. "Oh, God, what have I done?"

"What do you mean?" asked Reilly.

After a pause, he said, "What have I done to deserve this? Because I can't think of anything. All I have done is help people, save their lives. And now the lives of the people who are closest to me are being taken. Why?"

"Do you have any idea who is responsible?" asked Gardener.

"I haven't a bloody clue," he shouted. "Who the hell would want to punish me so badly?"

"Can you think of anything from your past that may have created this problem?"

Michael sipped some of his brandy. "I can't," he replied. "I really can't."

Gardener remained silent for a few moments. His gut instinct told him that he was holding back, but at such a heart-rending moment, he couldn't force the issue.

"I do hope so, Mr Harrington," said Gardener. He didn't say as much, but he certainly thought, *I really hope you have told us everything, for the sake of you and your wife.*

Gardener knew now that they would have to repeat the whole performance all over again; like they did with Chloe, they would have to go over Kyle's life with a fine-tooth comb.

Before leaving, he arranged for a family liaison officer to once again pay a visit. He asked for the details of the people they needed to speak to in order to follow up the investigation; and once again, a recent photo. It felt like *Groundhog Day.*

He needed access to Kyle's room. He wanted any electronic devices, and diaries, if he had one, though Gardener doubted it. Boys didn't really do that. He needed to distribute everything around his team, who would have to check and contact friends, acquaintances, work colleagues, and a partner or girlfriend.

CCTV had to be watched, and if he was really lucky, he might have better luck tracing Kyle's final movements than he did with Chloe's.

But with a killer as careful as the one they were searching for, he doubted there would be much that he or she had done wrong.

Chapter Twenty-eight

It was late evening before Gardener and Reilly made it into Bramfield and the meeting of the first incident room for Kyle Harrington's murder.

The whole team was in attendance, including Maurice Cragg, and PCs Atherton and Mulson. The back of the room was laid out as usual, with a tea urn and plenty of tea, sugar and coffee, as well as a kettle. A couple of trays of snacks had been donated by one of the local bakeries – or perhaps more than one, judging by the amount. Maurice Cragg regularly tapped them for the end-of-the-day products that would otherwise go to waste.

While Gardener started, Cragg made both him and Reilly a drink. The SIO knew that the team knew who the victim was, and instead of updating them with what he had discovered, he first asked about the people at the bus stop.

House-to-house had brought nothing. Most of the people in the street had gone to bed around eleven and no one had seen anything up until that time of night.

"It's a really quiet hospital," said Sharp. "There aren't many ambulances flying in and out of there at night, waking people up."

"I didn't hold out a lot of hope on that one, Colin," said Gardener. "Whoever is responsible for this will have chosen their time well."

Anderson and Thornton had spoken to Mabel Grayson. "She knew everyone at the bus stop," said Anderson.

"Have we spoken to them?" asked Gardener. "Did *they* see anything?"

"No," said Thornton. "She'd been there all of five minutes before Ann Traves turned up. Alf Cottingley was already waiting at the stop. He works at an engineering plant in the town and was on a late start."

"The other two women turned up after she did, but before Ann Traves," said Anderson. "We've spoken to all the women, and we finally caught up with Cottingley after his shift."

"Everyone told the same story," said Thornton. "They didn't see anything. None of them had actually walked past the hospital entrance, otherwise they might have spotted the victim."

Gardener sighed, and sipped some water. Truth be told, he had not expected anything. He then updated them on his conversation with Fitz.

"His liver?" shouted three different officers, all at the same time.

"The young lad had his bloody liver taken?" said Anderson.

"This has to be personal," said Rawson.

"Too right," added Thornton. "First his daughter has her kidneys taken, and then his son has his liver removed."

"It wasn't stuffed in his mouth with his lips sewn up, was it?" asked Rawson.

"You should write books with that imagination," said Reilly.

"Why is someone having a go at Harrington like this?" asked Edwards.

"That's what we'd like to know, son," said Reilly.

"Can *he* actually think of anyone?" asked Maurice Cragg.

"No," said Gardener.

"Can he think of anything in his past that could have caused this?" asked Thornton.

"Apparently not," said Reilly.

"But you think otherwise," said Cragg.

"Stands to reason there must be something, Maurice," replied Gardener. "One child, you could be forgiven for thinking an OCG may have stumbled across them. But not two."

"Three months ago, he lost his daughter. Now he's lost his son. I'm surprised he could talk at all."

"What about Roxanne?" asked Longstaff. "How did she take it?"

"She fainted," said Reilly.

"Bloody hell," said Sharp. "Poor woman. She's certainly been through something, hasn't she?"

"And now she has all of this to cope with," added Benson.

"You haven't spoken to his wife?" asked Longstaff.

"We have," said Reilly. "But she wasn't up to answering many questions."

"And Michael Harrington absolutely, definitely does not know of anything or anyone who could have done this?" asked Gates.

"Are you taking night classes in law?" Reilly asked Gates. "That was a well-structured question."

"I'm surprised you got it," said Rawson to Reilly.

"*You'll* get something in a minute, sunshine."

Having let the banter die, Gardener replied that Harrington didn't. He then continued. "Bearing all this in mind, I would like to set up some actions here. We need to follow a similar procedure for Kyle as we did for Chloe. Sean and I scoured his room, which is why we're late tonight."

He glanced at Gates and Longstaff. "We took all of his electronic devices, apart from his phone. As yet, we have not found that. Michael Harrington gave us the number. We did ring it a couple of times, but it must be switched off somewhere. But if you ladies can trawl through his electronic history, including all social media sites, and try and get a call history for his phone, I would appreciate it."

He turned to the rest of the team. "As soon as the ladies have found anything of any use, we need to check and contact all his friends, his acquaintances, his work colleagues, and a partner or a girlfriend if he had one."

He made notes on the whiteboard and turned and addressed the team again. "But I'm certainly more inclined to think that someone has it in for Harrington and is getting to him by removing his children. This takes the investigation in a new direction. Someone knows this family very well. I'm certainly leaning towards someone with medical skills."

"And not just medical skills," added Reilly. "It's someone who wants to cause maximum suffering to their victims, and the family."

"So now it's a case of trying to find connections between the victims, and a common link towards a suspect," said Gardener.

"There was certainly a difference of opinion on what people thought about Michael Harrington the last time we spoke to some of the hospital staff," said Anderson.

"Maybe he *has* crossed someone," said Thornton. "It might have been something small at the time; not even considered significant."

"Well, whoever it is and whatever it was," said Gates, "they haven't forgotten."

Gardener nodded. "I certainly want to keep the actions going to trace all surgeons and medical staff with the skills to perform these types of operations, particularly those closest to this situation. Removing organs and keeping people alive without immediately bleeding out does have a certain skill to it.

"I think the time has now also come for Michael Harrington to be fully investigated. We seriously have to consider a potential revenge motive here.

"I'm still of the opinion it has to be someone living close by, who probably had a means of transport to carry out such a stunt. I think we all need to review the files from three months ago, particularly witness statements. Maurice, we could do with another press appeal for witnesses. Let's see if there is any common ground from that investigation."

He glanced at his watch. "I realize it's been a long day and it's getting late, but I would like to tie down some further actions."

Chapter Twenty-nine

"Sean and I will go and speak to Kyle's closest friend, Jeremy Rawlins. It seems that Jeremy was one of the last people to see Kyle alive as he spent the day with him. As we did with Chloe, we need to build up a picture of Kyle's last movements, and utilise any CCTV in order to try to confirm those movements."

"Was Harrington able to tell you *anything* about Kyle's last day?" asked Bob Anderson.

"Yes," said Gardener. "He'd made plans with Jeremy Rawlins to attend a car rally in Leeds."

"Where was that?" asked Thornton.

"Harewood House," said Reilly.

Gardener continued. "Kyle was up early, had breakfast with his parents. Michael talked about his week ahead, which would be spent in London. Roxanne was trying to arrange a holiday for them; apparently they haven't had one for about three years, which resulted in a discussion about Covid.

"Michael remembers asking Kyle what he was up to. He told them that it was very likely he was going to stay over at Jeremy's after the rally, and go into work early from there."

"Where does Jeremy live?" asked Sharp.

"He rents a house in Cawcliffe Lane in Wilton, a few miles east of Thornton le Dale," said Gardener. "He's a cashier for the Yorkshire Building Society in Bursley Bridge, which is handy because the house he lives in, is owned by the building society manager."

"Can't fault that one," said Rawson.

"Whoever is responsible for this probably knew every movement Kyle was making," said Gates. "Does that suggest he or she is someone close to Kyle, or the family?"

"It's certainly someone who can blend in," said Longstaff. "Maybe it isn't anyone connected to the family, but he or she can blend into the background without being noticed."

"Very possible," said Gardener. "When you check Kyle's social media, look closely at any photographs and see if we can spot someone we think might fit that bill."

Gates and Longstaff nodded in unison.

Gardener turned to Benson and Edwards. "Whilst we're doing that, I'd like you guys to speak to all of *Chloe's* friends again. Let's see how many really knew Kyle: have any of them seen him since his sister's death?"

"I wonder if any of them had heard anything at all, any gossip going around," said Benson.

"You mean anything further since Chloe's death?" asked Cragg.

"Well, that was one thought," replied Benson.

"Surely they would have come to see us," said Reilly.

"Unless they're being threatened," suggested Patrick Edwards.

"I wouldn't discount it, Patrick," said Gardener, "but I would see that more as OCG territory. If people cross *them,* they might use threats, because they would do anything to protect their position. I still don't see this as organised crime. Whoever this is, they're small, and I suspect they want to keep in the background. Given that we've found little or no evidence to support what they've been doing, I'd say they're succeeding."

Gardener updated the actions on the board and turned to Thornton and Anderson. "We definitely need to speak to Sam Sheppardson again; check his movements."

"Was he a friend of Kyle's?" asked Thornton.

"According to him he was friends with both Kyle and Chloe," said Bob Anderson.

"If it was him that murdered Chloe," said Colin Sharp, "maybe Kyle found something out and Sheppardson felt he had to silence him as well."

Gardener nodded. "I think it might be a little too drastic for that young man. However, we can't rule anything out, so we need to check up on him.

"I would also like someone speaking to Edward White. We know he had an alibi at the time of Chloe's abduction and murder. Where was he when Kyle was abducted and murdered? And in view of everything that went on earlier, I made a schoolboy error and didn't think to ask the Harringtons where they were the night before."

"Do you still think Michael Harrington could have done this, sir?" asked Cragg.

"Honestly, Maurice? I don't. But it is possible that there could be some kind of twisted logic going on in his brain that we have yet to uncover. Maybe all three are involved: Harrington, White and Sheppardson."

"I'd love to know the reason why, if they are," added Rawson.

"Wouldn't we all," said Gardener. "Bearing that in mind, we must continue to keep an eye out for OCGs. When we looked at this three months ago, we couldn't find anything. That's not to say it isn't going on, but it may be very well covered, especially if surgeons are involved.

"For now, our full concentration should be on what Kyle did in the final hour of his life – where was he? Dave, Colin, can you pop over to Porter and Preston in Thornton le Dale and interview Kyle's boss, Mr Porter, see what he knows? This time, we leave no stones unturned."

Chapter Thirty

Kerry Bolton was standing behind the counter of the newsagent when she noticed the old man she knew only as Edgar, shuffle through the front door and down the first aisle. Even though it had been about a month since her first encounter with him, he was still scruffily dressed in his old macintosh, the same trousers, and the same sandals with probably even the same socks, but she hadn't noticed.

Kerry was talking to two of her friends – Sophie Thomas, and Rosie Foster – who had popped in; not to buy anything, but to pass the time of day and perhaps talk about where they were going later.

Kerry heard the rattle of cups in the back room and glanced at the clock on the wall; late afternoon meant tea. Betty Miller was in today. Kerry liked her because Betty always brought cakes in from one of the local bakeries, who did a mega vanilla slice.

Sophie, a slim blue-eyed blonde who was currently chewing gum, blowing bubbles and smacking her lips, leaned forward and said, "Did you hear about that lad who was killed and left near the hospital?"

"What do you mean, did I hear?" said Kerry. "I work in a bloody newsagent; I could hardly miss it."

"What happened?" asked Rosie, glancing around her. For what, Kerry had no idea. Rosie was short and stumpy and wouldn't know fashion if it hit her in the face; clearly, something *had* done because she always had an expression like a bulldog chewing a wasp.

"What happened?" repeated Kerry. "Sophie's just told us: he was killed and his body dumped near the hospital."

"I know that," said Rosie, testily, "I mean, what happened, does anybody know?"

"Stabbed, I heard," said Sophie, quickly turning and staring behind her when the loud crash from the middle aisle suddenly startled her. "What was that?"

"He wasn't stabbed," said Kerry. "Word on the grapevine is: he was missing his liver."

"Oh my God," said Rosie. "A liver? Was he all cut up like, bits missing, blood all over?"

"Oh, don't worry about him," said Kerry to Sophie, who had her back to Kerry, still staring down the aisle, "it's only Edgar."

"Who the bloody hell is Edgar?" she asked; then blew the biggest bubble from the gum, which nearly covered her face. When it burst, it made nearly as much noise as Edgar had, with whatever he had dropped today.

"No," said Kerry. "He wasn't cut up with bits missing and blood all over. Not from what I heard anyway."

"Who did you hear it from?" asked Rosie.

"Edgar?" said Kerry. "He's harmless. Lovely old chap. Looks a bit scruffy but he's okay, you'll like him."

As she said it, Edgar appeared to have dropped something else.

Sophie turned and glanced behind her. "What the hell's wrong with him? Why's he keep dropping things?" She was still chewing the gum. She blew a series of small bubbles and made a number of cracking sounds.

"I have my sources," said Kerry to Rosie.

"Tea's nearly ready," shouted Betty Miller.

"I heard the man who was cut up was related to that girl who had her kidneys removed a few months back," said Sophie. "Chloe Harrington, wasn't it?"

"It was her brother," said Kerry. "And there's nowt wrong with Edgar, he's just old."

"Oh my God," said Rosie. "Brother and sister killed and both missing organs. What the bloody hell is going on around here? It's getting like London, not bloody safe to go out. We better watch it tonight, Soph. Are you coming with us tonight, Kerry?"

Kerry's answer was lost by another gum bubble bursting, and Edgar's outburst.

"Do you mind, young lady?" Edgar said. "And if you don't, will you kindly go and make those disgusting animal noises somewhere else?"

Edgar appeared quite angry, thought Kerry. Though why, she had no idea.

"Excuse me?" said Sophie, staring at Edgar.

"Did your parents teach you any manners?" he asked.

Sophie – a merry shade of pink – stared at Kerry and then back at Edgar. "What the hell are you on about?" She chewed the gum very quickly and blew a bubble in Edgar's direction.

Edgar's expression of pinched face and staring eyes would have halted electricity in a cable immediately.

Rosie and Sophie both glanced at Kerry, as Edgar dropped his shopping basket and brought his hands to his ears. The basket hit the floor and his goods rolled out: one bottle of rum, one of whisky. Both rolled toward the chiller stand, but fortunately, neither smashed. There were other items, but Kerry didn't notice what.

But she did notice that Edgar's complexion was quite yellow. He hadn't appeared to be in the best of health the last time she saw him, but she thought he was worse now.

"You, young girls, no manners, dress like tarts, swear like troopers, too much make-up. You're an absolute disgrace to society. You should have been given a good slap when you were younger, perhaps then you'd have more respect for people."

"Do you mind?" shouted Sophie.

"Come on, Soph," said Rosie. "Let's get out of here." She grabbed her friend by the arm. "It's not even safe *inside*, these days."

"It's you who needs a good slap," said Sophie, backing toward the front door. She glanced at Kerry. "Do I have to take this abuse?"

"Look, I'm sorry," said Kerry. "Might be better if you *do* leave, let things calm down."

"It's him who wants to leave," shouted Sophie, as her and Rosie disappeared through the front door.

Edgar glanced at Kerry.

"I think she might be right, Edgar, love. I don't know what's got into you today but you're not yourself. I think a trip to the doctor might be a good idea."

Edgar bent down and picked up the stuff from his basket and laid it on the counter. He threw fifty pounds down, collected his stuff, and left.

"I'm sorry," he said. "And a doctor is of no use to me." He made for the door. Kerry shouted him back, but he was too quick.

She had the fifty pounds in her hand, waving it after him, when Betty Miller appeared with a tray containing two teas and two vanillas, which she placed on the countertop. "Whatever's going on?"

"I had to ask him to leave," said Kerry, still waving the money around.

"Who?"

"That Edgar bloke."

"Edgar Crowther?" said Betty. "Leave? Whatever for?"

"Do you know him?" asked Kerry.

"I certainly do," replied Betty, placing the tea tray on a shelf under the counter. "And I have to say, he's one of the nicest people you'll ever meet."

"Well, he wasn't just then. He kicked off, big style, with a couple of customers."

"Why?" asked Betty. "What were they doing?"

"Nothing."

"They must have been doing something," said Betty.

"I tell you, Betty," said Kerry, "they weren't. They were just eating."

"Eating?" questioned Betty. "Well, that explains it."

"Explains what?" said Kerry. "They were eating, for God's sake. Everybody eats, apart from Edgar, by the look of it. What's his problem?"

"It's a medical complaint," said Betty, taking a sip of tea.

Kerry stared at Betty, wondering what the hell it was. "What medical complaint? How well do you know him?"

Betty nodded. "Very."

"Oh," said Kerry, taking a bit of the vanilla, as if that explained everything and it was time to move on.

"He suffers from misophonia," said Betty.

"Miss what? What the hell is that?"

"It's a condition where people experience intense anger and disgust if they see or hear someone else eating. Particularly sounds, like people chewing, or lips smacking; even breathing can set them off."

"I've never even heard of it," said Kerry, licking her lips for the bits of custard from the slice, suddenly aware that if Edgar was still here, he'd probably have turned homicidal.

"He gets very irritable and short with people," said Betty. "And there are times when he simply has to leave before he throws up."

"Oh, God. How do you know all this?"

Betty took another sip of her tea, and a small bite out of the vanilla. As always, the custard squashed and fell out of the side of the pastry.

"If it hadn't been for Edgar, my Harold would have died."

"No," said Kerry, quite startled. "What happened?"

Betty took another bite and then placed the bun back on the plate. "Our Edgar is a bit of a problem solver, he likes to get to the bottom of something and he likes to be able to help people – at least, that's how he used to be."

"Used to be?" asked Kerry. "What was he?"

"A chemist. A very good one," said Betty. "My Harold was a patient at the Bramfield Community Hospital. He was suffering from a very serious skin condition following an operation to treat a urinary tract infection."

"Was that here, in Bramfield?" asked Kerry.

"No, the operation was in Manchester. We'd been visiting his sister. He'd been home three days when I noticed a problem. Harold had been bed-bound: no energy, and he struggled to eat or drink, or even open his eyes. I didn't know what the hell to do and I suggested a shower might help, if I could move him.

"It was a hell of a job, but I managed to get him up. He immediately collapsed. Then I noticed that the skin covering his body had all blistered, mostly around his private parts. And when I took more notice, his mouth and his eyes were getting that way."

"Oh, bloody hell," said Kerry. "Poor Harold."

"We got him into hospital, and a couple of days later, there was little or no improvement. A doctor consulted the pharmacist, who happened to be Mr Crowther, Edgar, and asked him to have a look; had he ever seen such a condition?

"Edgar studied Harold's notes and found that he'd been prescribed a couple of what he called sulfa drugs: Gantanol and Azulfidine."

"What are they?" asked Kerry.

"Edgar explained that they were a group of medicines used to treat bacterial infections. Sulfa drugs kill bacteria and fungi by interfering with cell metabolism. Don't ask me any more, because that's the only bit I remember. Anyway, following every test Edgar could think of, he

177

suspected that Harold had developed something called Stevens-Johnson syndrome. The blisters caused by Stevens-Johnson syndrome affect the top layers of skin and are very shallow.

"By the time Edgar returned to treat him, Harold's skin was breaking, and starting to ooze fluid. Edgar was worried; he'd been reading that if the condition progressed to affect more than ten to thirty percent of Harold's body, it might have to be considered a toxic epidermal necrolysis, TEN."

"Christ," said Kerry, noticing from her friend's vacant gaze that she was reliving the events in her head. "That sounds a barrel of laughs."

"That's a condition where large areas of skin actually separate from the body, forming open wounds that are at risk of becoming infected without treatment. Edgar realized it may lead to permanent scarring, or even Harold going blind.

"Anyway, Edgar needed to act fast. His choices were limited. Firstly, he chose to stop all medications that could be triggering TEN. He then suggested the nursing staff replaced lost body fluids through an IV. And in order to prevent a skin infection, he prescribed an antibacterial cream of his own making, which he called GME 3HX. I've no idea what was in it. Apparently, only Edgar knew that."

"How the hell can you remember all this technical stuff?" asked Kerry.

"It's amazing what you *do* remember when your husband is dying," replied Betty.

Kerry realized she had not touched her tea or her slice since Betty had started relaying her story. "Is your Harold okay now?"

"Within three days, Harold had made an amazing recovery and his skin was almost back to normal," said Betty. "Basically, Edgar Crowther saved Harold's life, when no one else had any idea how to treat him."

Kerry put her cup down. "I feel awful now."

"Why?"

"Because of how I treated him."

"You weren't to know, Kerry, love."

"Maybe not, but I could tell he wasn't having a good day to start with."

"Why?"

"He looked shocking," replied Kerry. "He didn't look so good the other day, but today he was all yellow."

"Yellow?"

"Yes, not quite as bad as a banana but he was getting there; looked really unhealthy. What do you think it is?"

"Sounds like liver problems," said Betty.

"Oh my God," said Kerry.

"What's up?" asked Betty.

"Isn't that what happened to that Kyle Harrington? He had his liver stolen." Kerry stopped and put her hands to her mouth. "Hey, you don't think one of them gangs is ripping Edgar off, do you?"

"What do you mean?"

"Well," said Kerry, "he must be worth a bob or two if he was a chemist. Do you reckon someone's taking advantage of him? Someone stealing body parts and selling them? If Edgar needs a liver and they have one…"

Chapter Thirty-one

Two days had passed since Gardener and Reilly had been to see the Harringtons to inform them of what had happened to their son; two days of sheer hell as far as they were concerned.

It was almost ten in the evening and Michael was in the kitchen. The room was basically a large square on the back of the house; the walls and the floor were tiled. An island stood in the middle, containing all the domestic appliances: cooker, washer, drier and anything else electrical, each of which had matching doors to the cupboard units positioned around the outside of the room. Pans and utensils hung from beams on the ceiling.

In the corner of the room a radio was tuned to Classic FM but despite Michael's interest in classical music he had no idea what it was, nor did he care. The kettle boiled and he made tea. Roxanne's was something herbal to help relax her, but it wasn't working; nothing was. He poured the drinks and placed everything on a tray, including some cereal bars; an effort to make her eat something. He picked up everything and left the kitchen for the downstairs bedroom.

As he entered, he found his wife stretched across the bed. She was still clothed in a white tracksuit. She wore no make-up and resembled only a shadow of her former self. That was only to be expected. In the corner of the room, the ITV news was on the TV. He had no idea what had been happening in their part of the world. Nor did Roxanne. It was meant to be a distraction, but it wasn't working.

Michael placed the tea tray on a small table to the left of the bed. He pulled up a chair.

"I've brought you some tea," he said. She glanced at it. "And some cereal bars. Roxanne, you really should try to eat something."

"Why?"

"You know why, my love. You need to keep your strength up."

"For what?" she asked, without turning to face him.

"Roxanne," said Michael. "You must try. This is not what the children would have wanted."

She turned to face him. "What about what *we* want, Michael? Does that count for anything? What we wanted was not to lose our children, but we did. What would they have wanted?"

Michael was at a loss to answer. He knew she made good points, but so did he.

"They wouldn't want us to give in, Roxanne."

After some time, she replied. "Well, we'll never know, will we?"

He held her hand. "Please, darling, don't do this to yourself. Chloe and Kyle would not want us to give up on life, or on each other, or on finding out who did this to them. They would want us to fight all of this and get some justice for them. Find the person who did it."

Tears ran down Roxanne's face. "Maybe they would, Michael, but none of that will bring them back."

He couldn't argue with that logic either. All he could say was, "Maybe not, but I'll never give up on bringing their killer to justice. Whoever did this will be caught and punished, whether it's me or the police who get to the bottom of things."

Roxanne's expression deepened and she stared into his eyes. "You're a good man, Michael, but I really believe we're out of our depth here. Whoever this is, they are way ahead of us, not to mention the police. But I know what's going on here…"

"What do you mean?"

"It's an eye for an eye," said Roxanne. "Someone out there believes our children were not entitled to those organs."

Michael blanched and his stomach turned. "That's ridiculous. Why were they not entitled?"

"You tell me. Do you know something I don't?"

"Are you serious?" asked Michael, wondering where the hell the conversation was going. "What could it possibly have to do with me?"

She took her hand away from his. "If you don't mind, Michael, I think I'd like to try for some sleep now." Once again, her eyes penetrated his, as if they were reaching deep inside his body to see what reserves he had, and whether or not it would be enough for both of them.

"Okay," he said. "At least sleeping is good for you."

"That isn't why I sleep, Michael."

"What do you mean?"

She turned away, staring at the TV. "Sleeping is the only time I see my children, and it's the only time I will ever see them again."

That sent a shiver down Michael's spine. If he lived to be a thousand, he would not have an answer for that one.

"But before I do," said Roxanne. "We both know what's coming next, don't we? I just hope you've told the police everything."

The doorbell suddenly took his attention. He glanced at his watch. "Who the hell is that at this time?"

Roxanne never answered. She continued to stare at the TV.

Michael left the bedroom and walked down the hall to the front door. He couldn't see anyone through the frosted glass but he thought he could hear a vehicle – perhaps a motorbike – leaving.

When Michael opened the front door however, there *was* no motorbike, no vehicle of any description. The porch lights were on, penetrating the darkness a little. As he glanced around, he couldn't see anyone. There were outside lights on most of the outbuildings and stables, but all was well in that direction.

As he was about to go back in and shut the door, he noticed the parcel in the porch, to the right. The box was cardboard, cube shaped, and small enough to perhaps sit on the palm of his hand. As he reached down, he noticed it was addressed to him.

Michael couldn't remember ordering anything and found it very odd that a courier would be working at such a late hour, but then, he had known Amazon drop shipments off late in the evening. He picked it up and studied it. There was no weight to the box. He shook it very slightly but there was no movement on the inside. Puzzled, Michael closed the door and went back to the bedroom Roxanne was in. She was now sitting on the edge of the bed, more alert than he had seen her since the news of Kyle's death.

"Was it the police?"

"No," replied Michael.

"Who was it, then? And what's that in your hand?"

"That's what was at the door, in the porch."

Roxanne frowned. "Who is it from?"

"I don't know," said Michael, staring at it.

"Didn't you have to sign for it?"

"No, it was on the porch when I opened the door."

"Who delivered it?"

"I don't know that either," said Michael, spinning the box around in his hands. "But I did hear a motorcycle, so it must have been a courier."

"What kind of a courier leaves a parcel without asking for a signature at this time of night?"

"One who's in a hurry."

Roxanne shrank back on the bed, wrapping her arms around herself. "I don't like this, Michael."

He didn't answer. He unwrapped the tape around the box and opened it. Whatever was inside was wrapped in a felt packaging. Michael put the box on the bed and opened up the felt, immediately recoiling in horror, dropping the contents.

Roxanne screamed loud enough to wake the dead.

Chapter Thirty-two

When the front door opened, Gardener and Reilly faced a man whose grim expression said he had been to hell and back more than once. The SIO knew that to be true, because of what had recently happened. Michael Harrington's grey complexion was that of the walking dead. His eyes were once again red-rimmed and his hair was very unkempt; even his clothes were not of the meticulous standard they normally were.

Michael held the door wider and beckoned both officers in, before closing it behind them. He led them to the bedroom. Gardener noticed the room was unoccupied. The bed was made, but a little rumpled on the top, as though someone had been there.

The only thing on the bed was a small brown cardboard box. Some inches from that was a layer of velvet cloth. Next to that was a human liver, dark and dry.

"I haven't touched it," said Michael. "Only the box and the velvet."

"When did you get this?" asked Gardener.

He checked his watch. "About an hour ago."

"Where?" asked Reilly.

Michael turned to face him. "A courier dropped it off. Left it on the front porch."

"Did you see the courier?" asked Gardener.

"No," he said. "The doorbell sounded. As I approached the front door, I did hear what I thought was a motorbike pulling away. But when I opened it, the bike had gone."

"You didn't see anything?" asked Reilly.

"Only the package."

Gardener took a pair of gloves out of his pocket and leaned forward. He picked up the cardboard box. It bore a white label with the Harringtons' address. There was also a stamp mark.

Reilly leaned over. "Someone's been brave, using a courier for this. It's traceable."

"That's just what I was thinking, Sean."

"Surely the person responsible for my children's death wouldn't be so stupid as to do something that would trace back to them?"

"You wouldn't think so," said Reilly. "But maybe he or she hasn't."

"What do you mean?" asked Michael.

"This could have gone through a number of different people, Mr Harrington," said Gardener. "And all we'll be left with is a dead end. But I can assure you it will not stop us trying. We'll check everything for prints, but it may not help. Do you have CCTV, Mr Harrington?"

Michael nodded. "Of course."

"We will need access," said Gardener. "We have a couple of ladies at the station who are experts. If we can see the registration of the courier's motorbike, we're halfway there."

He turned back and examined the liver. He was pretty sure that whatever had happened here, the offal before him was not shop bought; it was not the liver of an animal, which could only mean one thing.

"I'd like to take it with me, please," said Gardener. "I want a DNA sample taken as soon as possible."

"To see if it's Kyle's?" questioned Michael.

Gardener nodded.

"Not much point in it belonging to anyone else, is there?" said Michael. "Would you excuse me for a moment?"

He left the room.

Gardener turned to his partner. "We're going to have to scrutinise Mr Harrington more closely."

"I agree," said Reilly. "I'm left wondering something; whoever has it in for Michael Harrington, are they local, or are they from London?"

"I'm still not convinced that it's anything to do with London," said Gardener. "It's unlikely because they would not know the layout of everything up here. And if you think of the timing of everything that's happened, it really does suggest someone with a local background and knowledge."

"Which brings us back to three people," said Reilly. "One of whom is Harrington himself."

"I can assure you, gentlemen, I am not behind any of this," said Michael Harrington, who had entered the room.

"You'll have to forgive us, Mr Harrington," said Gardener. "When a person is killed, we have to look very closely at family members, because in a significant number of cases, it is family."

"You can go through my life with a fine-tooth comb, Mr Gardener," said Michael. "I have absolutely nothing to hide."

"That's a very brave statement, Michael," said Roxanne, who had now also appeared in the doorway.

Gardener and Reilly stared at Roxanne. She was equally as grey as Michael Harrington but her clothes appeared fresher.

"Would you like to tell us what you mean by that statement?" said Gardener.

She stared at her husband. "Have you told them everything?"

"Everything?" asked Reilly, staring at Michael, who remained silent.

Gardener allowed him the chance to speak but nothing came out.

"Mr Harrington, we previously asked if you could think of anyone who could be responsible. We also asked if you had upset anyone recently, or in the past, that you may consider bearing a serious grudge. You said no to both answers. Your wife is suggesting otherwise. Would you care to explain what she means?"

Michael Harrington was caught between a rock and a hard place, and Gardener could tell that he was extremely unhappy with his wife.

"You'd better come through to the living room," he said.

Once there, Harrington poured a drink for himself but he noticed that the small table nestled near the chairs had a tray with cups, a teapot, sugar and milk.

Roxanne took a seat and poured everyone one whether they wanted it or not.

Michael sat and took a sip of whatever he had poured.

"The last time we were here," said Gardener, "we asked you if you'd told us everything."

"And to be honest, Michael, old son," said Reilly, "you never actually answered. But now you're going to tell us, aren't you?"

"Yes," said Michael.

"I'm sensing this is a pretty big revelation. Which one of you does it involve?" asked Gardener.

"Roxanne."

Gardener glanced at her. She nodded and took a sip of tea.

"Why didn't you tell us the other day?" asked Gardener, feeling pretty ruffled, wondering how far he could actually trust Michael Harrington now.

"It happened a long time ago. I didn't think it relevant."

Reilly shook his head. "With all due respect, Michael, what you think is relevant will be very different to the way we think. You should have told us everything in the beginning."

"He's right, Mr Harrington," said Gardener. "I'm not saying we *would* have saved your son but it's possible.

Would you like to elaborate on what you know? And would you please tell us everything, no matter how trivial?"

Michael took another drink.

"Roxanne was twenty-five when her health started to deteriorate. She had a variety of symptoms that she managed to keep from me for some time because I was always in London: sporadic chest pains, palpitations causing irregular heartbeats that led to a feeling of fatigue, shortness of breath and eventually dizziness, before succumbing to serious abdominal pain due to an enlarging liver."

"How did you find out?" asked Reilly.

"She passed out in from of me in the kitchen one Sunday. I grabbed a stethoscope and started listening. The sounds were abnormal, which shocked me. As I said, I knew nothing about her symptoms. I suspected a possible heart valve disease because she had a characteristic heart murmur; abnormal sounds in the heart due to turbulent blood flow across the valve can often mean valve regurgitation or stenosis.

"In order to define just which type of valve disease, and the extent of the valve damage, I needed to take her to the hospital to undergo a number of tests: an echocardiogram, a chest X-ray and an MRI."

"Lucky you were here," said Reilly.

Michael nodded. "I came to the conclusion that Roxanne had a bicuspid aortic valve defect. The aortic valve had only two leaflets instead of three. It had narrowed, so it was harder for the blood to flow through, causing it to leak backwards. If untreated, a bicuspid aortic valve would eventually lead to symptoms of heart failure, and I felt that given the symptoms she had already described to me as having, Roxanne was very close to that. Also, if untreated, an aortic aneurysm might develop downstream from the aortic valve, leading to bleeding or rupture."

"What happened?" asked Gardener.

"Initially, I had no choice but to revert to medicines, because Roxanne has a very unusual blood type: AB negative. I had to use a variety of drugs until a heart could be found."

"Was there nothing else that could be done?" asked Gardener, suddenly remembering the fateful night in Leeds when he had lost Sarah. He wished now he could have been of more use to her.

"I considered a heart valve repair, and even a replacement," said Michael. "Another option would have been balloon valvuloplasty. This is a non-surgical procedure in which a special catheter is threaded into a blood vessel in the groin and guided into the heart. At the tip of the catheter is a deflated balloon that is inserted into the narrowed heart valve. Once in place, the balloon is inflated to stretch the valve open, and then removed. This procedure is sometimes used to treat pulmonary stenosis and, in some cases, aortic stenosis.

"However, none of these, I felt would help. What I needed was a donor, and quickly."

"And you found one?" asked Reilly.

"Luckily, yes."

Gardener wasn't surprised by the confession. He knew now that it was personal, and that he would have to investigate both transplants much further. He needed to know the common thread running through them if he had any chance of catching the person responsible.

"Where was it done?" asked Gardener.

Michael hesitated. "Here, in Bramfield." He glanced at Roxanne. She remained silent.

"Can you remember who the heart came from?"

"I can't, Mr Gardener. Patient confidentiality forbids us from knowing anything about it."

Gardener would like to believe Harrington. But he wasn't happy. He decided he was going to have to go through the surgeon's life with a microscope.

"Did you never try to check yourself?" asked Reilly.

He shook his head. "No, I had my wife back. I didn't need to know."

"And you really cannot think of who could be responsible for causing you so much upset?" asked Gardener.

Michael thought and then said, "No. But I can tell you that I am not responsible for what happened to Chloe and Kyle, and nor is Edward White."

Chapter Thirty-three

Frustrated, Gardener had called an incident room meeting early the following morning. He started by explaining the liver incident at the Harringtons.

"The liver was delivered by courier?" asked Rawson, struggling to believe it; though why, Gardener wasn't sure. They had dealt with a fair number of psychopaths over the years.

"Don't suppose we have the courier's details?" said Sharp.

Gardener shook his head and told them everything he and Reilly had found out. He confirmed they did have the CCTV footage from the Harringtons' residence. He asked if Gates and Longstaff could make a start, to see what they came up with.

"Do you think it's Kyle's liver?" asked Bob Anderson.

"I can't imagine why it wouldn't be," said Gardener. "There'd be little point in sending something the killer had bought from a shop."

"Does seem a little pointless," said Thornton.

"Hopefully," said Gardener, "Sarah and Julie will find something on the CCTV. That will point us to the courier who might be able to direct us to the killer."

"I doubt it will be that simple," said Reilly.

"You're probably right, Sean," replied Gardener. "But we can hope."

After updating the whiteboard, Gardener decided to drop the bombshell about Roxanne's heart transplant.

The room grew silent, until Cragg broke it. "You said you didn't believe him, sir."

"I wish I'd been wrong, Maurice," said Gardener. "This puts a whole new perspective on things."

"It certainly puts him in the frame," said Anderson.

"If not as a killer," added Rawson, "definitely the common denominator. He must be the reason it's all kicked off."

"He's obviously done something in his past to anger *someone*," said Benson.

"But where do you start?" asked Edwards. "This man's been a surgeon all his life. He works all over the place. How are we going to start figuring out what he's done?"

"It won't be easy," replied Gardener. "However, the fact that he *is* a surgeon is ringing alarm bells. I want everything we can find on Harrington. I want to know all about the operations he's performed."

"All of them?" asked Sharp.

"That could literally be thousands," said Rawson.

"Let's start with his family," said Gardener. "We need to concentrate on them: a list of people he has worked on personally may have to follow depending on what we find out from the three people closest to him."

"The last time we were in this room," said Cragg, "we were considering that he may not have been personally involved in the operations, but he might have been pulling the strings."

"Very likely, Maurice," said Gardener. "Every industry must be the same. If one of our own is burgled, or is involved with the police, don't we always try and pull out all the stops, give them some preferential treatment?"

"Stands to reason," said Longstaff.

"I realize what I'm saying here," said Gardener. "It sounds like we help our own more than we help the public."

"Doesn't sound like that at all, sir," said Cragg. "It's a good comparison. I agree with Julie, it stands to reason that with inside knowledge, you're in a better position to help. As *we* are with family, so must he be. Who's to say he hasn't pulled some strings to get his daughter and his wife an organ much quicker than anyone else would get one?"

"I can see the point," said Reilly. "We're talking life and limb here. He probably moved mountains, bounced Chloe and his wife up the list and in doing so, he's really pissed someone off."

"Sounds like it, Sean," said Gardener. "Which is why we want him scrutinised. He may not have actually done anything illegal, or immoral, but someone has it in for him. And they're not going to stop. Chloe was first, Kyle second; it's obvious Roxanne is next. In which case, it's imperative we nip this in the bud now."

Gardener had a thought. "We are also going to have to press him on potential illegal work or working abroad."

"That's a point," said Rawson. "Working abroad. That could take ages."

"It's going to take a lot of hours and a lot of people. It's a hard slog – but the answer will be in there somewhere, so it needs doing."

"Which is all well and good," said Reilly. "But how much time do we have?"

"How much time does his wife have?" said Gates. "We could work around the clock but whatever we find out might not be quick enough."

Gardener nodded. "I agree, and that's on top of everything else we're already investigating. Did anyone find out where Sam Sheppardson was the night Kyle was killed?"

Bob Anderson raised his arm. "Sheppardson has an alibi, boss. He was in his student accommodation all night with friends. So any thoughts of him being involved are not stacking up."

"I take it he told us who the friends were and we've checked?" asked Gardener.

"Yes, sir," said Thornton. "He was with another three people. They'd all had quite a bit to drink and passed out in the same room."

"The first one to wake up confirmed the other three were still there," said Anderson. "CCTV in the corridor also confirmed that no one left the rooms during the hours it happened."

Gardener nodded. "Has he seen anything of Kyle Harrington since Chloe's death?"

"Only once," said Thornton. "They bumped into each other in Leeds a couple of weeks ago. Didn't speak much. They asked how each other was but Sheppardson said it was very strained."

"It can't have been Edward White either," said Sharp. "He was attending a lecture and dinner at The Queens Hotel in Leeds."

"Not looking good for us, is it?" said Reilly.

"No," said Gardener. "All the main players have alibis. Doesn't mean to say they are not involved but it's looking very unlikely. Someone else is controlling this, which is why we need to find out as much information on Michael Harrington as we can."

Gardener turned to Benson and Edwards and asked about Chloe's friends, and whether or not *they* had seen or heard anything from Kyle Harrington.

The answer was negative. They'd all been living their lives without Chloe, and really missing her. None of them had seen or heard anything of Kyle, apart from the odd social media comment.

"We've spoken to Jeremy Rawlings," said Gardener. "He didn't have a lot to say but we did manage to find out something of Kyle's last movements, so it might help point us in another direction."

Gardener nodded to Reilly who produced his notepad and took the team through what they knew.

"It isn't much," said Reilly. "Jeremy picked Kyle up at nine on the Sunday morning, and they drove to Harewood House in Leeds for the show to start at ten. It was a vintage car display, with a game fair sharing the field.

"They met with two more friends: a Peter Watson, and a Callum Ross, kids they knew from school, who all had similar interests. After some time walking around the vintage car display, talking to the owners, they slipped into one of the tents for a bite to eat. After dinner, more walking and talking. Everyone was upbeat, happy to be spending the day relaxing. By four o'clock, they all went their separate ways."

"So," said Gardener, "two more people to interview. From what Sean has just said, there is probably nothing they can tell us, but it's possible that one of them may have seen someone hanging around. They may have seen someone more than once, someone who looked out of place. That alone is worth following up."

"What happened when they went their separate ways?" asked Longstaff. "Did Jeremy know?"

"He dropped Kyle in Thornton le Dale at five o'clock," said Reilly. "Kyle said he had wanted to stop in at the office."

"The office?" questioned Gates. "Five o'clock on a Sunday night and he wanted to drop into the office after a day out? There's dedication for you."

"Did he say *why* he wanted to go to the office?" asked Longstaff.

"Just reckoned that he had needed an hour to prepare for a meeting he had with clients the following week," said Reilly. "Sunday night was probably his last chance."

"Which brings us to you two," said Gardener, glancing at Sharp and Rawson. "You guys called on Porter, Kyle's manager. What did he have to say?"

Rawson consulted his notes. "Porter was quite shocked. He knew Kyle to be pretty dedicated but he hadn't known about him going into the office on the Sunday evening. Not that he had a problem with it. The staff all had keys and they could come and go as they pleased. He appreciates the team he has."

"The office alarm recorded Kyle as entering a couple of minutes after five o'clock," said Sharp. "But there was no record of him leaving."

"Which could mean he was literally abducted from the office," said Gardener. "Any CCTV in there?"

"No," said Sharp. "Small office, small team. Porter didn't see the need."

"But something did happen outside," said Rawson. "I think the girls have something on that."

Gardener glanced at Gates. She nodded confirmation. "Okay, we'll come back to that." He turned to Sharp. "Who were the clients, do we know?"

"An old established firm called Hughes Engineering in York. They were looking at buying out another company and Porter felt Kyle was more than capable of offering the advice. Had it turned out okay, Kyle would have had a bit of a promotion and a pay increase."

"Oh, dear," said Gardener. "We will have to call at Hughes Engineering and check the story out with them. See if they can add anything to this mystery." He nodded for them to continue.

"The office computer confirmed he logged on at seven minutes past five, and he was still logged on the following morning," said Rawson. "The office was still unlocked as Porter arrived for work, but there was no sign of Kyle."

"He tried Kyle's mobile," said Sharp, "and he was quite surprised to find the ringing tone actually came from Kyle's desk. His phone was underneath some paperwork.

He checked the entire building, but Kyle was nowhere to be found."

"He then called Kyle's parents to ask if they knew where he might be," said Rawson. "They didn't pick up, so Porter called the police."

"So there must be a record of that local police visit," said Gardener. "Can we find out who went and check their statements?"

He turned to Gates and Longstaff, asking if they could inquire about that.

Chapter Thirty-four

Gates went over to the laptop and screen set up on another table to the right of the whiteboard.

"We can do that," said Gates, "but before we go any further, we have a confession to make."

"Okay," said Gardener.

"Some CCTV evidence has appeared from the night Chloe was abducted."

"Appeared? From the night Chloe was abducted?" questioned Gardener, as if he couldn't believe it, considering how much time had passed.

"It's my fault," admitted Longstaff.

"What is?" asked Gardener.

"*Our* fault," corrected Gates.

Gardener didn't say anything. The girls had obviously made a mistake during Chloe's investigation, and these things happened. He wasn't going to berate them until he knew what it was, and how important it might be; and even then, maybe he wouldn't say too much anyway, because these girls were good, rarely made mistakes.

"In view of something that's come to light with Kyle's investigation," said Gates, "we went back over the CCTV footage of the town, particularly outside the restaurant."

"We missed something," said Longstaff.

"Something important," said Gates.

"Whoops," said Rawson.

Gardener nodded. "Go on."

Gates pressed a button and the camera had picked up Chloe standing outside of the restaurant. She waved her friends off. Shortly after that, Sam Sheppardson appeared. They talked for around ten minutes before he left. It was another five before the vehicle came into view.

"That's quite a big vehicle for a taxi," said Sharp. "Especially for one person."

"Is it private?" asked Rawson. "I can't see any name on the side."

"We think it might be," said Longstaff. "The vehicle is an eight-seater Peugeot minibus. As you can see, it's silver, in good condition, but it's not as new as it looks."

"Camera angle is a bit awkward," said Gardener. "We can't actually see the driver from here."

"Maybe she knows him, boss," said Reilly. "Her body language tells me she's happy about it."

As Reilly said that, Chloe jumped in and closed the door. As the vehicle drove off, it was still difficult to place the registration or the taxi plate number.

"Can we do anything with that?" asked Gardener. "Change the angle, blow it up, make it clearer?"

Longstaff stepped up and fiddled around with the software. After five minutes they managed enough of the plate to perhaps try and figure it out. The number 15 was present and clearly in view, and the preceding letters were *FT*.

"We can't see all of it," said Gardener, "but we have enough to go on. From what we have, we should be able to narrow it down to vehicles in the area and see where we can go from there. We should also check the rest of the CCTV in the area, now we know what we're looking for."

"Can we see the taxi plate?" asked Anderson.

Despite more fiddling around, they couldn't. Gardener was happy they had part of the registration. "Is there also something from Kyle's abduction that ties in with this?"

"It appears that the same minibus was also present when Kyle was abducted," said Gates.

"From what we've picked up," said Longstaff. "The driver took Kyle from outside the office, at the back door area, but there was no CCTV."

"No CCTV?" questioned Gardener. "So how do we know this?"

"We have a witness," said Cragg. He consulted notes from a file. "A Mrs Brenda Middleton of Thornton le Dale claims she saw something amusing at the time Kyle was picked up."

"Amusing," said Rawson. "What's amusing about an abduction?"

"Well, it didn't look like an abduction to her at the time," said Cragg. "It's only when she read the papers that she realized what had happened."

"What did happen?" asked Gardener.

"What looked like a taxi was at the rear of the building. We now know it was the same Peugeot minibus," said Cragg. "The driver were struggling to put his passenger into the seat of the vehicle, as if the man were drunk, which she found quite shameful at that time of night.

"She shouted and asked the driver if everything were okay, and did he need any help? He waved her away, said he were fine, and to be fair, he had the man almost inside."

"Bloody hell," said Anderson. "That's a pity. Looks like we would have had our man banged to rights."

"Did she get a good look at the driver?" asked Thornton.

"No," said Cragg. "Apparently, she wasn't close enough. The best description she could give were average height and build but he were wearing a baseball cap, and what might have been leather driving gloves."

"Not stupid, is he?" said Sharp.

"She noticed the vehicle enough to describe it as a taxi, a minibus. But she doesn't know make of vehicles well enough to tell them apart; she reckons they all look the same nowadays; in all fairness, she didn't think it were British, and she thinks it were a 15-plate vehicle, and it were silver."

"That corresponds with what we've just seen," said Gardener.

"Did she see it leave?" asked Reilly.

"No," said Cragg. "So, it could have gone anywhere."

Gardener made a note on the whiteboard and then said, "I wonder if this was the vehicle used to take him to the hospital. Is there any CCTV of that?"

"We don't think so," said Gates. "However, we may have something else we can help with on that one."

Gardener was all ears. "Don't tell me a witness has come forward for the dumping of Kyle's body?"

"No," said Longstaff. "It was far too early in the morning for people to be around, and the bush where the body was dropped was just out of view of the CCTV."

"But," said Gates, raising her hand and pointing her index finger, "a homeless man *has* actually come forward."

"A homeless man," repeated Reilly. "What the hell was he doing hanging around the hospital in the wee hours?"

"Scrapping around for food," said Longstaff. "He hadn't eaten all day. He said he definitely saw an ambulance approach the hospital from Middlecave Road."

"Did you speak to him personally?" asked Edwards.

"As a matter of fact, we did," said Gates. "From a distance." She waved her hand under her nose.

"And he maintains he saw an ambulance?" said Gardener, eager to move things along. "What kind of an ambulance?"

"The one we might be looking for," said Gates.

"He thought it odd because it was driving very slowly, with no lights flashing," said Longstaff. "It pulled into the entrance at about three-thirty in the morning. He never saw it leave because by then he *had* found the discarded remains of a McDonald's happy meal, which certainly made him happy."

"Shit," said Reilly. "A few minutes longer and a bit more detail and we might have been singing a different tune."

"To be fair," said Gates, "he didn't do that bad. He left with his meal, heading in the opposite direction to the hospital."

"Away from the ambulance?" asked Sharp.

"Yes," said Longstaff, "but he saw enough to help us. The ambulance was white, and very old."

"Go on," said Gardener.

"The only thing he could remember seeing was some letters but he's not sure of the order," replied Gates.

"What do you mean, not sure of the order?" asked Gardener.

"There were two letter *C*s and an *L*, which he thinks was on the door."

"Bloody hell," said Rawson. "He certainly wasn't inebriated at the time, was he?"

"And there was another number on the side with a letter *A*," said Longstaff.

"Was the number in front of the letter, or behind?" asked Gardener.

"We asked that," said Gates. "The number was in front, and there was an emblem or a flag or something above it."

"Get in," said Rawson. "Well done, that man. I hope you gave him a big kiss."

"No," said Longstaff, "but we bought him the biggest hot meal he'd ever had from the nearest café."

"And then gave him your number for the kiss," said Gates.

Everybody laughed, and when the laughter died down, Cragg drew their attention.

"We have something else on the white ambulance," he said.

"Go on," said Gardener.

"It just shows you that some people have their wits about them and they do keep their eyes open," said Cragg. "We now have a third witness. One Joseph Chandler of Bramfield actually has evidence on his phone of said ambulance, with a registration."

"With a registration?" repeated Reilly. "Well now, Maurice, old son, when you've finished with your information you know where to go for *your* kiss." The Irishman glanced at Rawson.

"If it's all the same to you," said Cragg, "I'll settle for the hot meal."

More laughter.

Cragg continued.

"He's a bit of a classic car freak who knows what it is, and all about the London Ambulance Service."

"The London Ambulance Service," said Gardener. "Is that what it is?" He was fearful of the answer. The investigation may take them down south, which was something he would like to avoid.

"He reckons it were part of the London Ambulance Service's historic collection. He said, this style of 'plastic' ambulance, based on a Morris LD chassis, was unique to London."

"Christ," said Reilly. "Our Joseph knows his stuff, so he does."

Cragg nodded. "Certainly does. It were designed in-house, and constructed in the council's workshops at Wandsworth. Dating from 1962, he also said, the model replaced London's classic, Daimler ambulances. The giveaway here are the letters LCC on the door. London County Council."

"And what's the registration?" asked Gardener.

"371 LDN," said Cragg.

"Have we checked it?"

"Not yet," said Cragg. "This information is fresh off the press, so to speak. Anyway, there's a bit more from this ambulance buff. He says the Wandsworth Ambulance was built by the London County Council in their Wandsworth workshops in London in the 1960s.

"It were one of the first ever GRP fibreglass bodied ambulances to be produced in the country. The warning system was originally the Julius-Sax 6" electric bell which sat on the front nose faring, later upgraded to an amplified bell by a microphone and a box amplifier, amplified through an ice cream cornet shape speaker on the roof over the driver's head.

"Apparently," said Cragg, "one or two still survive in the London Ambulance Historic Fleet and regularly attend social functions and shows throughout the London area."

"This is positive," said Gardener. "But now I'm really concerned because what you've just said may take us down to London. Maurice, can you follow this up? Trace the registration we have. If we're really lucky, it might belong to someone up here. Maybe you can also try that Bangers & Cash outfit. See if they found out anything about the one they sold years ago, and does it correspond with the information we have?"

Gardener updated the whiteboard and turned back to face everyone. As always with any investigation, you could stale mate for long enough, but when something finally started to show positive signs, the atmosphere changed considerably.

"So we have possibly a taxi and an ambulance involved. Does two vehicles mean we have two people working in unison?" said Gardener. "Or is it the same person?"

Chapter Thirty-five

Edgar picked up the poker, prodded the coals, igniting the sparks, which flew up the chimney breast. He laid the poker back on the hearth, grabbed three large logs and threw them all on. They caught hold very quickly, producing bright orange flames.

He felt the cold much more these days. Edgar felt a lot of things much more now than he used to. Leaving his bed took a lot longer, and when he did, he felt more pain, for more prolonged periods. His whole body appeared to have a new ache or pain each day.

Food didn't taste or smell the same; and when he did eat, he couldn't always guarantee to keep it down. He relied on his glasses much more because he couldn't bloody well see as well as he used to. His hands were nowhere near as steady as they should be. Good job he wasn't still working in the pharmacy. He'd have probably killed people through incorrectly weighed doses. There were many days that Edgar felt completely useless. And it wasn't old age. Everyone grew old but they didn't have what Edgar had.

One thing he did feel was sorrow, for the girl in the shop. It had prayed on his mind for a couple of days. He had been nasty to her, and he shouldn't have. It wasn't really her fault.

But he did apologise to the shop assistant. Not that it made *him* feel any better. He could see how embarrassed she was; didn't know what to do about it.

Edgar sat back in his seat, studying the room. He'd let the place go to rack and ruin since Milly had died. She would have been horrified if she could see it now. Every corner housed cobwebs: in fact, they were all over the bloody place, never mind the corners. Newspapers and magazines littered his table, which had only one chair to accompany it, because there was only one occupant in the house. What would be the point of having more?

The room was very old-fashioned, and Edgar still had gas mantle lighting on the walls, which were now on a low setting. The carpet had been down for more years than he cared to remember, and was now threadbare in places.

The crackling of the logs on the fire filled him with comfort, which was about the only thing that did these days. That and drinking a glass of something. Next to him on a small table to the right of his chair were the remains of a bowl of soup, the only thing he'd eaten all day; something else Milly would scold him for. She used to cook the most delicious meals, have them ready when he came home. After which, they cleaned up together, then caught some TV, or sat and talked. They were happy in each other's company. They didn't really need anyone else.

Edgar glanced at the table, to the half-empty bottle of Havana Club rum, and a tumbler. He reached out and poured another. Behind the bottle was a photo frame of Milly.

He picked it up, smiling. "What happened, my love?"

She couldn't reply, of course, only inside his head.

"We had everything, and it was all taken away in an instant." He turned and stared at the fire. "How disappointed you must be to see me now."

He suddenly stopped staring at the fire and turned back to the photo. "But without you, my dear, I'm nothing." He put the photo back on the table, and then said, "Still, not be long now, we'll meet again. And I'm sure you'll have something to say, but at least we'll be talking again."

Edgar finished his drink and then poured another. He sat back into his chair, reliving the worst night of his life.

Milly had felt nauseous for nearly a week, and for no reason that she could think of. Toward the end of that period, she was sick, more than she should have been. A loss of appetite quickly became apparent, with a high temperature and a flushed face.

Edgar had been working late but when he arrived home, he recognized the symptoms and immediately called for an ambulance. The manifestations quickly grew worse, and Edgar felt that time was of the essence, so he took Milly himself to the Bramfield Community Hospital.

She was diagnosed with an enlarged appendix, and A&E decided that the only treatment to cure the problem was an appendectomy, and quickly. But there was a drastic staff shortage, and they were struggling. Milly's condition meant she could not wait too long for the operation.

Edgar hadn't expected them to find a doctor.

But they did.

As things were improving, and the mood was hopeful, Edgar had not expected Milly to die.

But she did.

Chapter Thirty-six

Roxanne was sitting in the living room on a chair she had dragged across to the bay, allowing her the chance of some peace and quiet, and to simply stare out of the window.

What the hell had happened to their lives? How do you go from being a very successful couple with a loving family to the opposite end of the spectrum in such a short space of time?

Roxanne remembered the crater-sized hole that had appeared in her life when the police had told them that Chloe had died.

Died? How could she have died? She was twenty-two years old with everything to live for: a good job; a lovely partner; a trip to Africa. She had the world at her feet.

As if that hadn't been the end of Roxanne's world, they had now lost Kyle, their son; another one in the same position as Chloe.

Everything she and Michael had worked for, built up: the house, the children, their life, had all gone. Roxanne felt as if she had nothing left. Nothing left to live for: no children, no life; everyday was the same – a huge empty space. She felt as if she was living in a time-sealed bubble, and every movement, every breath, was a fight. How much longer could she go on without her family?

She had Michael, she knew that. How long would that last? The pair of them were being tested to the limit. Could they survive what was happening? Even if they did, they wouldn't be the same people again. It wasn't possible. Roxanne felt they had drifted already.

What was coming next?

She reached out for the tumbler and sipped some water.

If she was being honest, she knew what was coming next. Someone was coming for her, if she had worked out correctly what it was all about.

Or was it Michael? Had he done something to upset someone so badly that they figured the best way to teach him a lesson was to remove everyone around him?

Who was after them? Who was punishing them?

That was a question she really couldn't answer. Michael might be able to but if that was the case, he wasn't prepared to do so yet, or in fact do anything about it.

Unless it *was* him?

Roxanne shuddered. Surely to God, Michael wouldn't have any direct responsibility for what had happened? He couldn't have, thought Roxanne. On the occasions that their children had been killed, Michael had either been in London, or at home with her.

That thought was irrational. Michael may have had many faults but he was a loving, caring father, who had only ever wanted the best for his family.

He suddenly walked in. "Are you okay?"

Roxanne didn't even turn to face him when she answered. "What kind of a question is that? When will I ever be okay after what's happened?"

She put the glass back on the table, continuing to stare out of the window.

"That wasn't what I meant," said Michael. "Believe it or not, I *am* trying to help."

"And what are you doing; to help, I mean?"

"I've been thinking that maybe we should move down to the penthouse in Notting Hill. For our safety, until all this has blown over."

Roxanne's stomach curdled. "Blown over?" she repeated. Now she did turn to face him. "We've lost our children, Michael. We haven't been caught speeding. This isn't something that will blow over. Our children won't be returned to us like a driving licence in a few months' time."

"I'm just trying…"

"I know, Michael," she retorted – not nastily. "You're trying to help. But that suggestion *isn't* helping. I will not hear of it."

"Why not?" asked Michael, folding his arms, defensively.

"The children were born in the house. Here, in Thornton le Dale, and this is our family home, despite having very little family left to inhabit it."

"That's another reason to move away for a while, darling. Put some space between us and what's happened.

Eventually, whoever has done this will be caught. When they are, we can come back and rebuild our lives."

"It sounds so easy," countered Roxanne.

"Of course it isn't. Not as easy as I've made it sound, but eventually, we must try to resume some kind of normality."

"No one is going anywhere, Michael," said Roxanne. "No one is running away. No one is forcing us out of our house."

He opened his mouth to speak but she cut him off before he said anything.

"I don't know anyone down in London. The penthouse, your job, it's all your world, not mine."

Roxanne wrapped her arms around herself, suddenly feeling cold, but mostly insecure.

"Anyone could get to me there. At least here no one can approach without me seeing. I will make sure of that." She turned to meet Michael's glare again. "Because I am not going to move from this seat."

"You'll have to at some point, Roxanne, if only to go to the toilet."

"Don't be churlish. It doesn't suit you."

"I'm just saying you can't sit here all your life."

"I don't intend to," she replied. "Just long enough to protect myself. It doesn't look like you can protect me. So I'll have to protect myself, Michael."

He sighed. "And how do you plan to do that, Roxanne?"

She turned back to the window. "Whoever is responsible will have to show themselves eventually. When they do, I would like to be ready for them. I would like to look the person who killed my children in the eye. Hopefully then, they will be punished accordingly."

"I don't think that's a good idea, Roxanne."

Roxanne broke down in tears, sobbing, wiping her face with her hands. Michael ran to her side, putting his hands on her legs.

"What the hell is going on?" she asked.

"I don't know."

She grabbed a tissue and blew her nose and wiped her eyes and turned to face him.

"Please, tell me now, have you been involved in anything in your past that is catching up with us?"

Michael didn't answer, he simply stared at her as if she'd lost her mind.

"Have you?" she asked again.

"I've told both you and the police that I have not. I keep telling you, over and over."

"I know what you *keep* telling me, Michael. But I *keep* struggling to believe it."

Chapter Thirty-seven

Gardener had called another incident room meeting for the team to swap information. After the last one, he believed they were making progress and he was hoping to hear something confirming that. The only two missing at the moment were Sharp and Rawson, but he figured they would turn up soon.

As soon as everyone had coffee, he picked up the report from Fitz. It didn't reveal anything they hadn't already suspected.

"Fitz has confirmed that the liver sent to the Harrington's *was* Kyle's."

"We figured it might be, boss," said Reilly, sipping his coffee, holding on to a sausage roll as if his life depended on it.

Gardener nodded. "I know, Sean. I'm not disappointed but it doesn't get us any further. Does anyone have anything that might?"

Benson nodded. "We have something but it's not that good."

Gardener nodded. "Okay."

"We've spent a couple of days flat out with the DVLA on the Peugeot minibus."

"We think they're stolen plates, sir," said Edwards. "There is no combination of those letters and numbers on a Peugeot, so we think whoever has that vehicle has swapped them with something else."

"Okay," said Gardener. "Keep on it. Can we get a list of Peugeots in the area and cross reference them?"

"Done that," said Benson. "Now we have to look out of the area, and you know how time consuming that could be."

Gardener realized that. "What about the taxi plate?"

"Pretty much the same," said Edwards. "It's not registered with any of the local firms, so now we have to check further afield."

Gardener was disappointed but he thanked them for what they were doing. He turned to Gates and Longstaff.

"We had a bit more luck, sir," said Gates. "We've been through Harrington's CCTV and we've found the motorbike courier; we managed to speak to him about an hour ago."

Longstaff took over. "His name's Steve Marriott and he pretty much operates a company called A2B Couriers. It's easy to keep a track because they only have three drivers at the moment."

"But," said Gates, "it was Marriott himself who collected the package. Or the liver, as we now know it to be."

"Where did he pick it up from?" asked Gardener.

"Here, in Bramfield," said Longstaff. "From the Community Hospital."

"You're joking," said Anderson. "It came from the bloody hospital?"

"Well, what does that tell us?" asked Thornton.

"That we may have been right all along, but it all depends on who he collected it from," said Gardener. "It wasn't the reception desk, was it?"

"No," said Gates. "It was actually from a doctor."

"A doctor?" questioned Gardener.

"Yes," said Longstaff, "but don't get excited, because he doesn't technically exist. We've checked."

"Technically," said Gardener. "I can't wait to hear that one."

"The doctor met him outside with the package," said Longstaff. "He had all the gear on: the white coat and the stethoscope. Said it was extremely urgent, which is why he didn't want the courier walking all the way around the hospital, wasting time trying to find him."

"That was well thought out," said Reilly.

"Did he give his name?" asked Gardener.

"Yes," said Gates. "You're going to love this. He said he was Doctor George Fitzgerald."

"Are you serious?" asked Reilly.

"Has to be some kind of joke," said Gardener. "There's no way Fitz is involved in anything like this."

"How did this so-called doctor pay?" asked Benson.

"Cash," said Longstaff.

Gardener shook his head. "How much?"

"He said the bloke shoved a hundred pounds in his hands," Gates replied. "Marriott said it was too much, but the doctor said it didn't matter, he just wanted it there, pronto."

"Have we any idea how he booked this parcel to be taken?" asked Gardener.

"Phone call," said Longstaff. "But we can't trace it because the number was withheld. We *are* still working on it."

"Did the courier not question that? A withheld number, offering to pay cash?" asked Anderson.

"As it was a hospital, he didn't feel the need," said Gates.

"I suppose that would carry some weight," said Gardener.

"How does someone *posing* as a doctor get into the place unnoticed?" asked Reilly.

"I imagine he wasn't questioned if he looked like one of them," said Longstaff. "How many times have we heard about the building site scam? You wear a hard hat, safety footwear, a high-vis jacket and carry a clipboard and no one will question you. Maybe it's the same here. Hurry into the reception area with a white coat and a stethoscope, ask no questions, look as though you know where you're going; who's going to stop you?"

"Surely it can't be that easy," said Thornton.

"That suggests it could have been any one of the people we suspect," said Gardener. "Harrington and White are well known, they wouldn't be questioned. It could have been Sheppardson. Did the courier describe him?"

"Pretty bad by all accounts," said Longstaff.

"What does that mean?" asked Reilly.

"The courier's words were, the doctor actually looked as if he needed one himself. The bloke was middle-aged, short of breath, a bit thin and a rather funny colour."

"What funny colour?" asked Reilly.

"Yellow," said Gates.

"That's interesting," said Cragg.

"Why?" asked Gardener.

"I bumped into Betty Miller yesterday. She works part-time in the newsagents."

"Isn't she the lady you met up with at midnight when Chloe was killed?" asked Gardener.

"Aye," said Cragg. "As a matter of fact, she was."

"Is there something you're not telling us, Maurice, you old goat?" said Reilly, laughing.

"Chance'd be a fine thing," replied Cragg. He continued before it went any further. "I reckon the description sounds a bit like a man called Edgar Crowther. Betty Miller said he were in the newsagent yesterday. He looked awful. Kicked off big style." Cragg told the team about the incident in the shop as Betty had described it.

"You would have to be very brave to be so brazen if that's how you looked," said Gardener. "It almost sounds like he wants to be caught. Who is this Edgar Crowther, anyway?"

"I've been doing a bit of digging, because I thought his name sounded familiar. Edgar used to run the hospital pharmacy at the Bramfield Community Hospital."

That bristled the hairs on Gardener's neck but he didn't say anything.

"He was struck off following the death of his wife."

"His wife died, and *he* was struck off?" questioned Reilly.

"That doesn't sound right," said Gardener. "What happened?"

"I can't tell you at the moment," replied Cragg. "Information is thin on the ground, because it all happened fifteen years ago. I'm still trying to get hold of some records, or at least someone who will speak to me about what happened. The only thing anyone really knows is that for about five years after the event, maybe even longer, no one saw anything of him."

"Nothing?" asked Reilly. "Why?"

Cragg shook his head. "No idea. Some say he'd left the country, so grief stricken was he; others reckoned he had gone to live with relatives; not that they ever met or had heard of any. Others say they thought he'd died."

"He obviously hasn't," said Anderson.

"This is a very interesting bit of information, Maurice," said Gardener. "Sounds like he has the pedigree to be our man but there are questions we need to answer first. We've uncovered a lot of things in the investigation, but we have no idea if they would tie up to this Mr Crowther. Do we know *how* his wife died?"

"No," said Cragg. "Not yet."

"Do we know *where*?" asked Gardener.

"According to what I've found out, we think it might have been here, in Bramfield," said Cragg.

"And you don't know about it, Maurice?" said Reilly. "I thought you knew everything."

"I never seem to have the time to learn everything," laughed Cragg. "But I know most things."

Sharp and Rawson quietly slipped into the room. As they did so, Rawson's phone rang. He glanced at it, apologised to Gardener, saying that he had to take it, and left.

Gardener asked Sharp how they were doing. Before Sharp could reply, Rawson shot back in. "That was our man from Bangers & Cash."

"Really?" said Gardener. "What did he have to say?"

"Only that he's managed to find the paperwork relating to the old white ambulance they sold. It was someone local."

"Who?" asked Gardener.

"A bloke called Edgar Crowther."

"I don't believe it," said Gardener. "We've been investigating this case for months and he's never been mentioned. Now, his name crops up twice in as many minutes."

Gardener informed Sharp and Rawson of what Cragg had told them. "As I see it, there are two things we need to do urgently here. Firstly, I'd like Colin and Dave down at Bramfield Community Hospital. I want you to find out everything you can on Edgar Crowther and what happened to his wife."

"Do you think they'll tell us?" asked Sharp. "Patient confidentiality and all that."

Gardener thought about it. He had a point. Medical records are usually prohibited. He couldn't apply for a blanket warrant, something known as a 'lift and sift', which would allow them to take high volume material.

"I'll call DCI Briggs and we'll have to go for a standard search warrant. We're in normal hours so we can contact the court and speak to the clerk." He glanced at his watch. "I imagine the first available slot will be PM. You'll have to swear the warrant out in front of the judge. Job done."

The pair of them left quickly.

Gardener turned to Cragg. "I think that just about seals things. Maurice, can we have Edgar Crowther's address? It's time we paid him a visit. I'd like to know what happened with his wife, why he was struck off and, more importantly, where the hell has he been for fifteen years?"

Chapter Thirty-eight

Reilly eventually brought the car to a halt outside Edgar's house and killed the engine. Both men jumped out. Gardener surveyed the building facing him.

The old York stone house was tall, imposing, with a red pantile roof and two chimneys, all in need of repair. There were two large rooms on the ground floor, both having huge bay windows; each had nets and curtains, neither of which had seen a washing machine for years.

It was the same with the upstairs rooms but the brickwork above the windows had been shaped to form turrets. The front door, though solid, needed a lick of paint. Above that was another window frame but Gardener didn't know if it was a room or part of the hall, stairs and landing.

The place was detached, desolate, and situated on a lonely stretch of road known as Bean Sheaf Lane, between Bramfield and Bursley Bridge on the A169. Around the back, Gardener noticed a number of odd-shaped rooms connected to the main building, each with nets and curtains in the same condition as the front rooms.

He turned and counted at least eight outbuildings. The nearest one to him had wooden doors, both open wide. When he stepped inside, he was met by the biggest collection of logs he had ever seen, filling the small barn. The smell of pine was prominent.

Scurrying round the others with Reilly following, he found that five of them were locked with large hasps and padlocks, the type designed to keep people out; the other two unlocked sheds or buildings housed piles of random rubbish, stuff that Edgar had probably hoarded over the years.

But if that was the case, thought Gardener, how had he built it all up if he had been missing? Had he actually been missing, or simply keeping out of people's way?

As Gardener exited the last outbuilding they had checked, he walked back and stared at the house. There was literally no sign of life, and both front and back doors were locked. A quick peek through the letter box revealed no action whatsoever. From what Gardener could see of the hallway, it was as cluttered as everywhere else he'd seen.

"This is all very mysterious," said Reilly, staring up at the bedroom windows. "Where has this guy been for years? And where is he now?"

"Plotting his revenge by the look of things," said Gardener. "Assuming he is our man."

Reilly turned and stared out across the surrounding fields, most of which were barren. "Sounds like he fits the criteria. He's in the right place. It's miles from anywhere. And look at the size of it."

In the distance, Gardener noticed a clump of trees. "I have to agree, Sean, it does seem to fit. If you think about it, we need someone who knows his way around a body. How the medical service works. We're looking for a person who has the resources and the money to carry things off. This place doesn't look cheap. It's big, a bit run-down; there are ramshackle buildings all over the place but if you wanted to buy it, your bank account would have a fair-size dent in it."

"Any one of these could be a makeshift surgery," said Reilly, studying the outbuildings.

"And the area is big enough to hide a mobile operating theatre," said Gardener. "Though I'm still not sure about that one."

"Do you not get the feeling it's all rather convenient?" asked Reilly.

"What do you mean?"

"We've hit nothing but dead ends all the way through, and now, suddenly in the last day or so we have a suspect who fits the bill, who's been missing for years and is then suddenly spotted in the town."

Gardener nodded. "It's the stuff of fiction, isn't it? But sometimes that's how it goes. After hours and hours of hard work, you need a break. You can't say we haven't put the man hours into this one."

Reilly nodded. "Maybe you're right. You've maintained all along that Harrington has held something back. Maybe this is where we'll find it. Maybe he's crossed this Edgar one, who's clearly waited for the heat to die down and now he's evening up the score."

Gardener peered through the letter box again, but he saw nothing to suggest any movement within.

"Maybe," replied Gardener, standing back. "But it's a long time to wait. I'd like to know where Edgar's been and what he's been up to in all that time. We also need to know more about Harrington's involvement. If he is responsible for the death of Edgar's wife, how is he? What happened?"

"With a bit of luck," said Reilly, "Colin might find out for us. Meanwhile, let's do what we came here to do, have another snoop around. Guy's obviously not home."

"Or he's refusing to answer. Let's be honest, he could be anywhere in this place. That said, I can't see any CCTV, can you?"

The pair of them stared up at the building, which revealed nothing. They both strolled around the perimeter once more, checking every nook and cranny. There were no cameras that they could see, but it didn't mean there weren't any.

They checked all the outbuildings once more. Gardener had to admit there was no sign of life. It wasn't as if he could seek information from the neighbours. There were none.

The pair of them jumped back in the car.

"Where now?" asked Reilly.

Gardener's ringing phone stopped him from answering. He fished it out of his pocket, saw that it was Sharp, and slipped it into a cradle on the dash before putting it on speakerphone.

"Colin. What can I do for you?"

"We've uncovered something you might want to hear," said Sharp. "We're just at the community hospital. Luckily, with the warrant we didn't have too much of a problem and the receptionist led us into the office of a consultant who remembers Edgar."

"Did he remember what happened with Edgar's wife?" asked Gardener.

"He does," said Sharp. "She went in for a routine operation, an appendectomy."

"That *can* kill you if you don't get it done in time," said Reilly. "Especially if it ruptures and bursts. Is that what happened?"

"To be honest, whether or not anyone really knows what happened, or they do but they're not saying, I have no idea," said Sharp. "But the story on the ground is, they're not sure what went wrong. Something did. Milly was in surgery for quite some time but the result was, she died."

"She died, but they don't know why?" questioned Reilly.

"Like I said, *I* think they do, but for some reason they're not saying."

"Sounds like a cover-up to me," said Reilly.

"Here's the interesting bit," said Sharp. "Turns out that she carried a donor card."

Gardener shivered. "I can't wait to hear the next bit, Colin."

"The appendectomy was performed by Michael Harrington."

Gardener and Reilly stared at each other.

"Finally," said Reilly. "Is this the link we've been looking for?"

"I'd say so," said Sharp. "Especially when we discovered that Roxanne Harrington received the heart only two hours after Milly Crowther had been pronounced dead."

"Two hours?" questioned Gardener.

"And Harrington was in charge of the appendectomy?" asked Reilly. "It doesn't take a genius to work out what's happened here."

Gardener glanced at his partner. "If Harrington is as good as everyone says he is, and he performed the appendectomy on Milly Crowther and she died, what the hell went wrong?"

"That's what we need to ask Harrington," said Reilly. He glanced at Gardener. "You've said all along he's been holding something back."

Gardener nodded. "I had hoped I'd be wrong." He turned and addressed his phone. "And you can't find out any more about it, Colin?"

"Not so far, sir. Would you like us to keep digging?"

"Yes, please," said Gardener. "I'm not sure what we'll have to get in the way of warrants to obtain that information but it would be nice if you continued asking questions and someone volunteered it."

Sharp acknowledged and cut the connection.

"What now?" asked Reilly.

"It's time we paid another visit to Michael Harrington."

Chapter Thirty-nine

Roxanne was walking down the staircase when she heard the doorbell chime. She stopped at the bottom of the stairs wondering who it was. It could be Michael. Their earlier conversation had started mildly but finished up angry. He left in a hurry, probably without his keys. Serves him right, thought Roxanne, turning toward the kitchen. She switched on the kettle and took a mug from another part of the worktop, slipping in a herbal tea bag.

The bell chimed again, twice. That sounded like Michael. He'd always been a touch impatient. Wanted everything now, or at the very least, his own way.

The kettle boiled and she poured the water into the cup.

The bell rang again; three times. If she waited another hour, Roxanne wondered how many times it would be ringing by then.

But she didn't. She left the kitchen and walked through the hall. As she reached out, anxiety kicked in and she suddenly wondered what the hell she was doing. It may not *be* Michael; could be anyone.

She stared through the small diamond-pattern piece of glass in the door but it was so thick and wavy she couldn't see anything with any clarity.

"Who is it?" she shouted.

The answer was muffled. She never caught it.

"Sorry," she shouted. "Can't hear you."

"Delivery for you," shouted the disembodied voice.

Roxanne tried to think. It might be Amazon. She had placed an order yesterday.

"Who is it from?" she asked.

"I'm not sure," came the reply. "There are so many labels on that it's difficult to tell."

How odd, thought Roxanne. What kind of a courier driver couldn't tell you where it was from?

"Well, what is it?"

"I don't know that either," shouted the voice.

"You must have some idea."

"Look, I don't mean to be awkward, love, but if I could tell you what it was without opening it, I wouldn't be a courier driver. I'd be making money and having fun because I'd be the only person in the world with X-ray eyes."

Perhaps you shouldn't be a driver anyway, thought Roxanne. You'd make a lot more money on the comedy circuit.

"Do you have identification with you?" she asked, growing more restless by the minute. All she really wanted was to sit in the bay window and sip her herbal tea and think about her children.

"I do, yes."

"Can I see it?"

"How would you like to do that without opening the door? You don't have X-ray eyes as well, do you?"

221

She glanced downwards, realizing the door had no letter box. When they had bought the place, Michael had always wanted one of the American style mailboxes on a pole. It stood to the left of the front door, down a couple of steps.

"Can you leave it on the floor, or in the mailbox?"

"I can't, I'm afraid. It needs a signature."

Roxanne wondered if Michael had ordered something.

She stood back. She didn't know what to do. Should she call Michael and ask him to come home? But he could be anywhere. He'd been annoyed when he left, so he'd probably be even more annoyed if she disturbed him. Perhaps best if she let him cool off.

"Okay, love, I understand," said the voice from beyond the door. "You're probably in on your own and you're a bit anxious about opening the door to a stranger."

You can bloody well say that again, thought Roxanne. If only you knew *how* anxious.

"I'll have to take it back and I'll leave you a card and you can call the company and rearrange a new delivery."

Roxanne's mind was a jumbled mess. If it was something important for Michael and she'd turned it away he wouldn't be happy.

She walked toward the front door, unlocked it but left the safety chain in place. She opened the door as far as the chain would allow. Everything outside seemed natural. The man was side on and wore a helmet and gloves.

"Do you have your ID handy?"

He pushed his hand forward and slipped the card through the gap. She noticed an iPad in his other hand. She couldn't see a motorbike but then the gap wasn't very wide.

She took the card and studied it. Steve Marriott A2B Couriers. It certainly seemed genuine enough. There was an address and a phone number.

"And are you Mr Marriott?"

"Yes, love, I am."

Roxanne quickly stepped back out of sight and pulled her mobile out of her pocket. She called the office number on the card and inquired about Marriott. The receptionist said he was out delivering in Bramfield; then one in Bursley Bridge, and two in Thornton le Dale. Satisfied, Roxanne cut the connection.

"Would you hang on just one more minute, please?"

She left the door on the chain and ran into the living room to check the CCTV, but decided it would be better if she simply peeked through the right-hand side of the window. She saw the courier, still dressed for the occasion; his iPad in one hand, a brown box in the other.

Further satisfied, she turned back to go to the front door and her world diminished rather quickly, as her vision closed in. The bay window was quite large and she had only seen what was on the right-hand side. To the left of the window was the stuff of nightmares. It was large and white, with letters on the side, and a number, and an odd-shaped bell on the front.

A bloody ambulance. Why was it there? She was sure it wasn't there before. Why would a courier want an ambulance?

Roxanne was on the brink of a meltdown. In a blind panic she turned and suddenly came face to face with the courier.

"How did you?" She put her hands to her face.

"These," said the courier, holding out the bolt croppers.

"Oh... my... God!" said Roxanne. Her stomach somersaulted, and she suddenly felt very sick.

She glanced at the ambulance. "What is that doing there?"

"It's for you."

"Me?" shouted Roxanne, backing away, her mind in overdrive. She rambled very quickly. "What the hell are you talking about? I never called for any ambulance. Why the hell would I? No one here has been injured."

"I'm sorry, you misunderstand me," said the courier.

"How can I misunderstand you?" questioned Roxanne, glancing everywhere for an escape. "I never called a bloody ambulance."

Roxanne needed to sit down before she fell down.

The courier removed his helmet and smiled at her.

"Just a minute," she said, "don't I know you?"

"When I said it's for you," replied the courier. "That is exactly what I meant. It's for *you*."

"Oh, God, please tell me this isn't happening. Please tell me I am in the middle of a bad dream and that any second now I am going to wake up."

Roxanne grabbed her mobile out of her pocket, fumbled, and dropped it. The phone hit the floor, the screen cracked, the back came away from the front and both halves landed in front of the courier.

"Oh, dear, me. What have you done?"

Roxanne stared at him, moving her hands in all directions because she had no idea what else to do with them. "I'm sure I know you."

"You do. Nice to see you again, Roxanne. I'm pleased you're looking so well. Milly's heart must be suiting you."

Her world suddenly went black.

Chapter Forty

Reilly pulled the car onto the drive and the scene that met Gardener's eyes was not what he was expecting to see.

Gardener jumped out, followed closely by Reilly. The drive was empty, no vehicles. Staring across the grounds, there were no people either. The doors to the outbuildings were shut and locked, leaving only the house to study.

The house with an open front door.

"This doesn't look good," said Reilly.

"God only knows what we're walking into but we'll have to check," said Gardener.

Before doing so, he pulled his mobile out, made a call and requested backup from Anderson and Thornton.

"Right," said Gardener. "Let's go."

The pair of them climbed the steps, entering cautiously through the front door. The building was silent, not even the sound of a radio. Gardener took a few tentative steps forward and glanced into the living room.

No one home.

Reilly took a few more, peeking into the ground-floor bedroom that Roxanne had been in when he'd last been to the house.

"Nothing doing, boss."

"Where the hell are they?"

The pair of them slipped into the kitchen. On the worktop, Gardener saw one cup with a kettle next to it. He strolled forward and felt the cup, noticing water and a tea bag inside.

"Gone cold," he said to Reilly. "Someone's left in a hurry."

"Or been made to."

They then checked the rest of the rooms upstairs, all of which they found the same – empty.

Gardener went back outside, studying the drive, in the hope he may see some tyre tracks, but there was nothing that would help him.

"Where have they gone, Sean?"

Reilly glanced around. "They can't have gone far, because the doors are open. But they're not in the grounds and those buildings opposite are locked."

"Which comes back to your earlier point. Has someone beaten us here and taken them?"

"That could only be the killer."

"Why the hell couldn't Michael Harrington have been straight with us from the off?" asked Gardener.

"He obviously has something to hide."

"Have we misread the situation?" asked Gardener. "Is Michael Harrington our killer? Is whatever he's done so bad, that he's had to remove everyone?"

"But he has alibis," said Reilly. "And where does Edgar fit in? He owns the strange white ambulance that's been seen around the town, and his wife died in the hospital in Bramfield."

"Which leads you to believe he must have a part in it somewhere," replied Gardener.

"Is he working *with* Harrington?" asked Reilly.

"You wouldn't think so if Harrington had something to do with Milly's death."

The pair of them slipped back into the house. As they did so, Reilly called Gardener's attention. When he turned back, the sergeant was holding a small business card in his hand.

"Where did you find that?"

"On the floor, behind the door. That's a name we've heard before."

Gardener read the details of the A2B business card. "Isn't this the courier who collected Kyle's liver from the bogus doctor in Bramfield?"

"Allegedly," said Reilly.

Gardener glanced at Reilly. "You mean there might not have been a bogus doctor, and Marriott simply spun us a line?"

"Possible," said Reilly. "He's a courier, knows his way around town, has transport."

"But is he a doctor?" asked Gardener.

"Is he a courier?" asked Reilly. "Or is Edgar posing as Marriott?"

"Not likely, Sean," said Gardener. "Julie and Sarah interviewed the man."

Gardener was back on the phone, calling the courier's office to ask about Marriott.

"God, he's popular today," said the receptionist. She informed Gardener that he had finished his deliveries and was now on his way to Leeds Bradford airport to collect a package for a timed delivery in Leeds. Gardener asked where. She replied and named one of the banks on Bond Street.

"Can you track him?" asked Gardener.

"Yes. Is it important?"

"Very," replied Gardener.

After a small break she said he was now at the airport. Gardener thanked her, cut the call and then phoned Gates. When she answered he put her on speakerphone, told her where he was, and what had happened, and then asked her about the interview with Marriott.

When she'd finished, he said, "Can you describe him?"

"He was around six feet tall, stockily built, with short black hair."

"Nothing like the man we believe is Edgar Crowther?"

"The complete opposite," said Gates.

Gardener still wasn't happy. Marriott may not be responsible, but he could be working with the person who was. He told Gates where Marriott was going to be very shortly and asked her and Longstaff to pick him up and bring him back to the station for questioning.

"Have you checked the Harringtons' CCTV?" asked Gates.

"We were just about to," said Gardener.

"We?" said Gates.

Gardener heard Longstaff sniggering in the background.

"You're going to check the CCTV, with the Neanderthal?" asked Gates.

"He can hear you, you know," laughed Gardener. "Anyway, what's wrong with that? You think we're old school, not up to it?"

He heard muffled voices before Gates came back on the line. "What are you two talking about?" Gardener asked.

"Nothing," said Gates. "Just that me and Julie would love to see this."

"If I didn't know any better," said Gardener, "I'd say you were looking for a change of role. Fancy walking the beat again, do you?"

Gates laughed but then suggested she should talk them through the process.

Gardener agreed. They found the Harringtons' computer. Within minutes, the footage revealed an old white ambulance pulling into the drive, parking with only the front end in view, and that was from above.

The driver left the vehicle with his hands full: in one, a parcel; the other held what appeared to be an iPad. He was dressed as a courier, and to be fair, did not resemble the man Gates had described. The driver had a slight stoop and walked more slowly and determinedly.

"What would a courier need with a white ambulance?" asked Reilly.

As the scene unfolded, Gardener and Reilly could see very little of what was happening but it ended with Roxanne being carried outside. From what they could see, Roxanne had either been drugged or passed out – the latter being more likely – because she offered no resistance.

Gardener had to assume that she had been placed in the back of the vehicle because the pair of them could only see the front from the viewing angle.

Minutes later, the ambulance left.

"We're still none the wiser," said Reilly. "That courier could have been anyone."

"True," said Gardener. "It didn't look like Edward White, or Sam Sheppardson."

"Or Michael Harrington for that matter."

Gardener grabbed his phone, but Reilly touched his arm. "Hold your horses, boss."

Gardener's attention was diverted back to the screen. What could only have been a minute later, Michael Harrington's black Range Rover pulled up. He jumped out and ran into the house. He then ran back out almost immediately, jumped back in his car and took off.

"Where the hell is he going?" asked Reilly.

"Judging by the look on his face and his actions," said Gardener, "it's hard to believe he's involved. He looked worried, he was running, and he didn't stay very long."

"He must have done what we've just done, found his wife is missing, and he's gone to find her."

"Or join someone else who has found her," added Gardener. "All of which shows a degree of him knowing what's happened in the past and keeping it quiet."

Gardener was back on the phone to update Cragg.

"That's interesting," replied the desk sergeant. "We've just had a report of the old-fashioned white ambulance, spotted outside Thornton le Dale."

"Where?" asked Gardener.

"On the A169, between Bramfield and Bursley Bridge."

"It must be Edgar," said Gardener.

"That's what I was thinking," said Cragg. "He's on his way home. Do you want me to send your lads out there?"

"Anderson and Thornton are already on their way here," said Gardener. "I have Gates and Longstaff picking up Steve Marriott, so you'll only have Benson and Edwards."

As Gardener cut the connection he walked outside in time to see Anderson and Thornton pulling into the drive.

"Follow us."

Chapter Forty-one

As darkness approached, visibility was lessening because an early summer mist had descended upon the community. Whether you had an old three-wheel Reliant Robin, or an up-to-date, state-of-the-art Range Rover, made little difference, if you couldn't really see a lot.

But Michael Harrington was in no mood for the weather; he was in fact, in no mood for anything. Besides, he knew exactly where Edgar Crowther lived. Bean Sheaf Lane was reasonably straight and Michael floored the Range Rover, which responded with frightening accuracy. Within a minute he arrived at a pair of gates that led into Edgar's drive, which were, thankfully, open.

Michael glanced at the outbuildings and as he tore into the place he noticed most of them had closed doors. Swivelling his head to the front of the building, Michael quickly stamped on the brake pedal and turned the steering wheel to a sharp left. The Range Rover spun violently and went into a skid, heading for the front of the house.

"Jesus," shouted Michael, as an involuntary spurt of urine left his body.

As the car came to a grinding halt, he finished up inches from one of the front bay windows. The engine was screaming at high revs, and Michael realized he had somehow knocked it into neutral but his foot was hard to the floor. He removed his foot from the accelerator and killed the engine, shaking, as he sat there in the dark.

"Christ. That was close."

Whilst the adrenaline was still rushing, he jumped out of the car and left the driver's door open, listening intently.

There was nothing to be heard: no conversation, no raised voices, no screams.

Were they even here?

They had to be, decided Michael.

He was livid, not only with Edgar, but himself. It was now pretty obvious to Michael that a past misdemeanour had come back to haunt him. But he had believed all of the rumours – that Edgar had either died or gone missing. Once a month for years he came to check on the empty house, hoping he wouldn't find the pharmacist; but if he did, to see what was going on inside his head. Well, now he knew.

Where the hell had he been? What had he been up to that would give him so much knowledge to do what he had done? Edgar Crowther was a chemist, not a bloody surgeon. How would he know how to remove organs, with such accuracy that in the case of Chloe, she had been left alive for some half an hour?

Michael searched for his phone but he didn't have it; nor did he have time to work out where it might be. Roxanne's life depended on his actions, the speed of them anyway.

He stepped through the front door into a cluttered hallway. The carpet had, at some time, been removed, leaving stained floorboards. The walls had lots of paintings, and every corner was filled with junk. Rooms led off left and right, and a majestic staircase led to the upper levels. He didn't believe Edgar would be up there. In fact, he wasn't even sure Edgar was actually here. He believed the place was deserted.

Until he heard a noise.

Michael stopped dead, his heart pounding. He held his breath in order to listen harder.

To his right, it sounded like someone whimpering.

He had a mind to rush into the room, but he didn't think that would help him, or anyone else.

Michael stepped cautiously across the hall, and peeked in, where he believed the sound to be coming from. Once again, it was a mess. A number of chairs appeared to have been hurriedly placed anywhere. Cobwebs hung in all corners. The curtains at the windows were closed. Michael figured if he tried to open them, they would simply fall apart.

As he slowly advanced, he heard the whimpering sound again.

Behind him.

Michael spun round quickly, fearing he would be attacked at any second. He had nothing with which to defend himself.

He was shocked however, to see a modern television fastened to the wall. But not as shocked as what he saw playing out on it.

On the screen, Roxanne was desperately trying to free herself from a steel gurney in what appeared to be a sterile room.

Michael shot forward, touching the screen, as if it might somehow help.

His only consolation was that she was still alive. She was breathing, she was whimpering, she was moving. That had to mean something.

But where in God's name was she? The room was in a complete contrast to the house, so it couldn't be here.

With renewed enthusiasm, he lunged out of the room, into the hall, and took the steps on the staircase two at a time.

Fuck the noise he was making. If Edgar was here, perhaps it was time he knew who had arrived.

All upstairs rooms were empty, and the mess in them equal to the downstairs rooms.

Back on ground level he checked more rooms, stopping once again to make sure that Roxanne was still trying to free herself. Finally, he ended up in the kitchen – which was also empty.

There was no one home.

Michael put his head in his hands. "Where the fuck are you, Crowther?" he shouted.

As Michael turned, he suddenly noticed another door, in the corner of the kitchen.

He crossed the room and tried the handle. The door opened, revealing a wooden staircase, leading to what could only be a basement.

And it was lit.

Caution had now returned, and he took the steps slowly, one at a time. Halfway down, the room started to come into view, but one of the stairs creaked loudly, causing him to lose his balance. As he fell forward, he grabbed the banister, but it didn't help and he took the rest of the stairs two at a time and landed up in a dusty heap on the basement floor, coughing and choking and covering his eyes with his hands.

As the dust settled, a voice said, "Hello, Michael. Good of you to join us."

Pulling himself together, Michael rubbed and cleared his eyes, stopped coughing, and studied the view.

It did not meet with his approval.

The room was one large square with a concrete floor and brick walls. In contrast to the other rooms, it was reasonably clean, lacking in cobwebs and not so cluttered. Shelving was stacked up against one wall with a variety of goods – mostly tins of food as far he could make out. On one, he saw an old-fashioned radio, the big wooden type with a glass front, which people listened to during the war.

Another wall held wine in a rack. Another had a TV similar to the one upstairs – Roxanne was still trying to free herself. The final wall had a large steel door in it. Michael could see no handles, or windows; no way in or out but he figured that's where Roxanne might be. It was obviously operated remotely, which led him to the object to the right of the door.

A protected cage, the type you saw in a fairground. The bottom section had wooden sides, whereas the top half was steel mesh, with a window for what he could only describe as the ringmaster; Edgar fucking Crowther. His head and face were dangerously yellow, and his complexion sallow. Michael had seen better in the morgue.

He quickly jumped up, wincing at a shooting pain that ran through his shoulder.

"What have you done with my wife?" he shouted.

"All in good time, Michael," replied Edgar, in that irritatingly smug tone that only someone who has the upper hand could use.

Michael lunged forward and grabbed the sides of the steel mesh, screaming into Edgar's face, but unable to reach him.

"What have you done with my wife, you bastard?"

Edgar stood up swiftly, grabbing his own side of the mesh, and shouting equally as loud. "Why don't you start by telling me what you did to mine?"

Chapter Forty-two

Surprisingly, as Gardener and Reilly approached Edgar's house, the mist had lifted, leaving the SIO a clear view of Michael Harrington's Range Rover, inches from one of the bay windows, as if it had been airlifted in. The driver's door was open.

Both downstairs rooms in the house were lit.

"What the hell's happened here?" asked Reilly.

Gardener jumped out of the car. "I'm not worried about what's happened here, more about what might have happened either somewhere else, or inside that place."

Thornton and Anderson pulled up behind the lead car, with Benson and Edwards following up at the rear. All officers jumped out bearing confused expressions.

Gardener walked toward the front door and slipped into the hall. He stood and listened but couldn't hear anything.

He turned. "Bob, Frank, can you check upstairs, please? Patrick, Paul, can you stay with us and scour the downstairs?"

All of them nodded. Anderson and Thornton took the staircase. As they neared the top, Gardener suddenly heard a whimpering sound coming from the room on his right.

He raised his right hand, pointing to the room. Reilly walked in and called the others. A TV fixed to the wall showed Roxanne struggling to free herself from a gurney.

"What the hell's going on here?" asked Patrick Edwards.

"If it *is* happening here," said Gardener, "it's a bonus. At least she's still alive."

"But where?" asked Reilly.

"Judging by the cleanliness of the room in the picture, it isn't in this house," said Benson, staring around at the mess.

Anderson and Thornton ran into the room. "Empty upstairs, boss," said Anderson.

Staring at the screen, Anderson said. "What's going on here?"

"Let's split up," said Gardener, without explaining. "Attack the ground floor."

They all finally ended up in the kitchen. Gardener halted them and crept toward an open door, leading into a basement. He peered downwards when he suddenly heard shouting. Two voices. One was Michael Harrington's. He didn't recognize the other, but it didn't take a genius to work out who it would be.

Gardener rushed down the stairs, followed by the others.

"Where's my wife?" shouted Michael.

"Not until you tell me," shouted the other man.

Gardener reached the bottom. "Edgar Crowther?" he shouted.

"Police?" replied Edgar.

Gardener nodded, displaying his warrant card, studying the man in the cage. His hair and body were thin, his complexion was awful, his voice raspy.

"Good," said Edgar. "I want you all to hear this. It should be worth it."

"What have you done with Mrs Harrington?" asked Gardener.

"He won't tell us," said Michael.

"I want an explanation for what happened to my wife," said Edgar. "I know something did because one of the surgeons present on the team told me he'd seen this" – Edgar pointed to Michael – "so-called, eminent surgeon make a serious mistake, which he then tried to cover up."

"Who told you that?" said Michael.

"Peter Marsh," said Edgar. "Remember him, do you? He left your team and he then left the profession because he couldn't live with himself after the lies you told."

"He's talking rubbish," said Michael.

"Is he?" asked Reilly.

"Of course he is," said Michael. "And so is this man."

"Why don't you try us, Michael, old son?" said Reilly. "If this man was talking such rubbish, why did he kill your son and your daughter and kidnap your wife?"

Michael Harrington held steadfast, said nothing.

"That expression and your silence tells me there is a lot more to the story than you've told us, Mr Harrington," said Gardener. "So I suggest you come clean with us now, while you have the chance."

"Especially if you want to see anything of your wife again," added Edgar.

Tense seconds passed before the atmosphere changed, a point when Michael must have realized he was all out of options.

He suddenly aged years in a matter of seconds. He leaned back against the wall.

"I'm so sorry."

But he didn't say anything else.

Edgar rose up from his seat in the cage. "Sorry for what?"

Gardener was about to intervene, but Michael started to answer Edgar Crowther.

"I'd been in London for the entire week. I actually had to carry out three heart transplants: one on Monday, Wednesday and Friday. They went well but I had to be up at four on the Friday morning in order to perform the surgery at six sharp at The Royal Brompton and Harefield Hospitals in Uxbridge. The operation went well but was not without complication, and it took six hours to complete."

"Get on with it," said Edgar. "We don't need all the details."

"Do you want this story, or don't you?" replied Michael.

The silence spoke volumes.

"I met with someone for lunch at The Savoy near Covent Garden, before going to the St Bartholomew's Hospital in West Smithfield for an afternoon lecture on cardiology. The lecture was scheduled from four till five, but I didn't leave London until seven in the evening, by which time I was already very tired.

"I arrived home at nine-thirty. Fifteen minutes later, my phone went and I was called into Bramfield Community for an emergency treatment. I didn't want to go because Roxanne was very pale. She had no energy, but she told me to go because she said she was going to bed. She also said that I was, first and foremost, a surgeon. Despite my reservations, if it meant saving a life, I had to go, especially as there was no one else. The nearest surgeon was at least two hours away."

"You didn't, though, did you?" said Edgar, as if trying to rile him.

"Didn't what?" asked the surgeon.

"Save her life, you imbecile."

"Mr Crowther," said Gardener. "I don't think that is helping. You wanted an explanation." Gardener glanced at the screen, to Roxanne, who was still trapped.

He turned back to Edgar. "My concern is for that lady. Is she okay?"

"You can see she's okay," said Edgar.

"I can see she's alive," countered Gardener. "But I don't know if she's okay. None of this is helping you, Mr Crowther. Why don't you let her go, and then we can talk? I need to know she's okay."

Edgar sat back. "I want the remainder of the story first."

Gardener could see the man would not budge, and he had no idea what to do, other than to let it play out, but he would be extremely annoyed if Roxanne didn't make it and he could have saved her.

Michael continued, as if he suspected the Mexican stand-off would not be resolved unless he did. "When I arrived and checked the patient, I suspected there was more to it than a simple appendectomy."

Edgar suddenly sat forward but remained silent.

"I quickly established that Milly had a large tumour of the appendix, which would require more aggressive surgery, with possibly the removal of part of the colon. I favoured the traditional technique of one large cut.

"Following the operation, I suggested Milly would need close monitoring, and possibly medication with antibiotics. Ibuprofen, acetaminophen, and ice to treat the pain from surgery. I also said only to use narcotic pain medication if that didn't work."

"So what happened?" asked Edgar, clearly losing patience.

"Things did not go according to plan, I'm afraid," said Michael. "Whether or not I was too tired, I really don't know." He suddenly stepped forward, very frustrated. "Look, do I really need to go through all of this? My wife is in there." He nodded to the steel door in the wall. "Can't we at least get her out?"

"When I'm ready."

Gardener stepped forward, but Edgar stopped him. "It will do you no good, officer. Both this cage and that door are security protected, operated by me."

"Okay," shouted Michael. "We get it! On removing the tumour, I ended up nicking the colon, which cut the middle colic artery."

"So you admit it!" shouted Edgar.

Harrington ignored him. "Which tore the inside of the artery that carried blood to the heart, causing the inner layers to separate from the outer layers. Blood quickly pooled in between those layers. The pressure of the pooling blood made the short tear much longer, which in turn caused serious internal bleeding.

"I was very aware that the complication could weaken the heart muscle, which could result in a heart attack. But I couldn't stop the bleeding."

"Did you try?" asked Reilly.

"Of course I tried. What do you take me for?"

"According to Peter Marsh, you didn't try at all," said Edgar. "Oh, you made it look like you were trying but I suspect you were thinking more about your own wife; how my Milly was probably a perfect recipient for her. Your choices were very limited, were they not, Michael? Do you save Milly, or Roxanne?"

"It wasn't like that," shouted Michael. "By the time I knew what was going on, Milly had in fact, bled out. It's no consolation, I know, but she died very quickly."

"And you lot closed ranks, didn't you?" asked Edgar. "The official story was that Milly's surgery was needed, but the complications that arose could not have been foreseen. That was the terminology used, was it not?"

Michael Harrington never answered.

"I could not accept that official explanation," said Edgar. "I demanded an inquiry. I also said I would sue the hospital, and whoever had carried out the operation. You closed ranks again. I was told it was my right, but they would not disclose the surgeon in charge. I only found out through Peter Marsh. I tracked him down and the story came out."

"Right," shouted Michael, lurching toward the cage. "Now you know. You know everything. So maybe I can have an explanation."

Gardener joined Michael at the cage. "Do we really have time for all of this?" He stared at Edgar. "I want you out of this cage now, and I want to see Roxanne Harrington for myself."

"How the hell did you know what to do with my children?" demanded Michael. "You were only a bloody pharmacist, not a surgeon."

A tense stand-off still persisted. Gardener could tell that whatever demands he was making, everything would go at Edgar Crowther's pace. He turned to the cage again.

"I'll play your game, Mr Crowther," said Gardener, "but if anything has happened to Roxanne Harrington, I'll throw the book at you."

Edgar simply smiled.

Chapter Forty-three

"Who are you working with?" asked Gardener.

"No one," replied Edgar.

Gardener's phone rang. It was Gates. He answered. "Sarah?"

"Just thought you'd like an update, sir. We've interviewed Marriott again. He is definitely not involved in this."

"What did he say?"

"He confirmed the addresses in Thornton le Dale that he'd delivered to and they backed him up. We downloaded his tracker and he went straight from there to the airport and then straight back to the bank where we picked him up. He wasn't at the Harringtons this afternoon."

"Okay, Sarah, thank you."

Gardener cut the connection.

Harrington suddenly screamed and lurched at the cage, hanging from it like an ape. "Come on, you bastard. We're wasting time."

The cage didn't move.

"Mr Harrington," shouted Gardener.

Anderson stepped forward. "Do you want me to get some bolt croppers, boss?"

Gardener studied the cage. He could see how well fastened it was to the walls. The steel mesh door at the side had a complicated locking system attached that simply had to be remote-controlled. Edgar was going nowhere till he was ready.

"Thanks for the offer, Bob, but it won't help."

"What about burning gear?" asked Thornton, stepping forward, staring at the cage.

"By the time we have that, Frank, I'm pretty sure this situation will be over." He glanced at Edgar. "Won't it, Mr Crowther?"

"Tell him, not me," said Edgar, like a petulant child.

"Mr Harrington," said Gardener. "Calm down, this is not helping."

"Neither are you."

"What do you mean by that?" asked Gardener.

"Arrest him."

"What good will that do?"

"It'll prove to him that he is facing some serious charges and that he can't get away with this," retorted Michael.

"He is and he won't anyway," said Gardener. "But reading him his rights now will do nothing at all for you or your wife. And he's not the only one facing serious charges. You might be."

"Me?" shouted Michael. "What have I done?"

"Your operation on Milly Crowther and the relevant accusations will be taken seriously, Mr Harrington. It will have to be fully investigated following the accusation."

Michael stepped back, thoroughly ruffled. "Do what you like. But I'm warning you now, if I don't get my wife back, I'll be pressing charges against you lot."

"That's your right, Mr Harrington," said Gardener. "You'd do well to remember that none of us would be here in the first place if you had levelled with me."

As Michael had nothing more to say, Gardener turned to Edgar. "You have five minutes or I'm going to rip this place apart brick by brick."

Gardener realized it was an empty threat but he was eager to move things along.

Edgar stared at Michael. "You really want it, do you?"

"I want to know how you've been able to kill my children the way you have."

"Following the death of my wife," said Edgar, "I was beside myself. I studied all the relevant paperwork, including the death certificate. I believed something was not right. The pathologist had remarked on a possible problem that I knew could have arisen due to negligence in the operating theatre. He *said* there was a small tear in the colon that was difficult to ascertain the reason for.

"Of course," continued Edgar, "proving negligence would be another matter. I sought a meeting, which did little to alleviate my mood. As I said, I felt you were closing ranks. Although I suspected I knew what had happened, I couldn't prove anything, nor could I find out who had actually performed the operation. A showdown in the hospital lost me my job and I ended up in court due to the slanderous accusations I was making."

Gardener noticed Michael's expression. He was almost squirming.

"You even spoke up for me," Edgar said to Michael. "Pressing upon the court that I'd had a very traumatic time following the death of my wife, Milly. It seems that held some power. The hospital and the trustees felt it wouldn't be in anyone's interests to take any further action, providing I underwent therapy, which they were happy to provide, still seeing me as one of their own."

Edgar snorted with derision. "I agreed, but I had no intention of sticking to it. I retreated, became a hermit, rarely seen around the town, and if I was, I was usually drunk and dishevelled. I knew what people were saying.

"Finally," said Edgar. "It was you, Michael, who visited me here. You even told me that I had to go on with life, that Milly had gone, nothing would bring her back, and she would not want me to shut myself away, and kill myself on drink.

"Later however, I met up with Peter Marsh. That's when he told me he had left the medical profession, unable to live with what had happened. I asked him what the hell he was on about. Marsh told me that it was you who had performed the operation on Milly, and you who had made a terrible mistake, which you tried to cover up.

"He said *you* had nicked the colon; he'd seen you do it. Marsh didn't actually know at the time whether it was a mistake, or if you had done it on purpose, knowing that your wife needed a heart, and having seen Milly's file, that she would be a perfect donor. Shortly after Milly had died, he had heard on the grapevine that your wife had become the recipient of a new heart.

"It had to have been Milly's heart, as she had carried a donor card, and I remembered being asked if they could use it. I asked why Peter had not said anything before. He said he couldn't find me. No one could. I had gone missing, and some people even assumed that I had died."

Gardener stepped forward. "Mr Crowther, can you please open the door to the other room? Let us see Mrs Harrington is alive and well?"

Edgar ignored him. "I despair of your negligence whilst caring for my wife; and at what followed. The matter went unpunished because you all looked after one another, closed ranks, kept it a secret. Your impunity was the motive for my vengeance."

"Do you want me to open that cage, boss?" said Reilly.

"How do you plan on doing that, Sean?"

"Simple, I'll drag *him* through the small gap."

Edgar suddenly spoke up. "I felt very bitter in the following months. I decided retribution was my only option."

Harrington stepped forward, fists clenched.

"I flew to Romania where I retrained as a surgeon – illegally, of course, using Milly's life insurance money. It cost me quite a considerable amount, and seven years of my life, but I still had the house."

"Right, Mr Crowther," said Gardener. "We've heard enough. If you don't open the door, I will call for backup and use the necessary force to remove you."

Gardener then read Edgar Crowther his rights.

When he'd finished, Edgar said, "You don't think I will stand trial, do you?"

"Why wouldn't you?" asked Gardener.

Edgar rose from his seat in the cage. "Because I too have impunity."

"Impunity?" repeated Gardener. "What are you talking about? There's no way you can escape punishment for what you've done, despite your reasoning."

Edgar pressed a button. The door on the cage opened and he stepped outside. "My work is done here."

Michael ran forward but Gardener stopped him in his tracks. "We'll deal with this, Mr Harrington."

"Why won't you stand trial?" Gardener asked Edgar.

"Ask *him*." Edgar stared at Michael.

"I'd say he has liver cancer."

"Correct," said Edgar.

"How long?" asked Michael.

"Not long enough to stand trial."

"There are treatments available," said Michael.

"Don't you think I know that?"

"You've refused them, haven't you?"

Edgar smiled. "Like I said, impunity."

"There's something not right about this," said Reilly.

Gardener glanced over. He had not realized that his sergeant was now in front of the TV.

"There's nothing right about this situation," said Anderson. "We're all holed up in a basement with a madman who's controlling everything."

"No," said Reilly. "I meant the TV."

"What about it?" asked Gardener, joining him.

"It's a recording."

"What?" screamed Michael, turning to stare at the TV.

"That picture is on a loop," said Reilly. "I've been watching it for ages."

Michael turned to Edgar. "You bastard. You've had us here all this time and she isn't even in there."

Gardener turned to Edgar. "I suggest you give us access to that room right now, Mr Crowther, or so help me God, when I've finished tearing down this place it will look like a nuclear bomb's gone off."

Reilly approached Edgar. "I would if I was you, Edgar, old son. He means it."

Edgar leaned into the cage, pressed a button, and the door in the wall buzzed and opened.

Michael ran in. Reilly followed him.

All Gardener heard were the frantic screams of the surgeon.

Gardener ran into the room. It was exactly as they had seen it on the TV; impeccably clean with a gurney in the middle of the floor.

But it was empty.

No Roxanne Harrington.

There was, however, a heart on the gurney.

Michael turned and ran out. Gardener and Reilly followed.

"Where's my wife?"

"Who?" said Edgar.

"What have you done with her?"

"Who are you talking about, Michael?"

"My wife."

"*Your* wife." Edgar smiled. "I thought she was my wife. After all, she has Milly's heart."

Harrington suddenly stood stock-still, clenching and unclenching his fists. "Wait a minute."

He went back into the room with the gurney and came back out clutching the organ. "This is not a human heart, it's a pig's."

"Well done, Michael," said Edgar. "I thought I'd fooled you for a minute."

Michael threw the heart at Edgar and lurched forward but Reilly held him in check. "It's not worth it, Michael, old son."

"I'm going to kill him," shouted Michael, trying to fight the Irishman.

"No, you're not," said Reilly. "If you do, you will never find your wife."

"Where is she?" Michael demanded of Edgar.

"I suppose she *is* your wife, really," said Edgar, calmly. "If we think about it a bit more. In terms of percentage, she only has Milly's heart. Everything else is hers. I suppose you are right, Michael. She is your wife."

"So where is she?" asked Michael, his mouth open.

"You've no need to worry about her, Michael," said Edgar. "She's gone."

The room fell into silence.

"Gone," said Michael. "What do you mean, gone?"

"What I say," shouted Edgar. "You'll never see *her* again. Just like I'll never see Milly again."

Gardener stared at Thornton and Anderson. "Take him away, please," he said, pointing to Edgar.

The pair of them stepped forward and handcuffed Edgar before marching him out.

"My wife," said Michael. "We need to know where she is and he's the only person who knows."

"And we'll find her, Mr Harrington," said Gardener. "He's not being taken to a hotel. He's going to the police station and we will talk to him. You can quite clearly see your wife is not in this house and we need to find out exactly where she is. Now, if I can ask you to go with my officers." He glanced at Benson and Edwards.

"Me?" shouted Michael. "You're arresting me, now?"

"No, Mr Harrington, but we would like to speak to you under caution."

As he left with the two officers, Reilly glanced at Gardener. "What are we going to do?"

Gardener was calling Cragg. "We'll have a team of operational support officers come in and scour this place from top to bottom, Sean. I think we're wasting our time. I doubt she's here; and Edgar was never going to tell us where she was whilst Michael was still in the room."

Cragg answered the phone. Gardener explained everything that had happened and asked if the desk sergeant would release pictures of Roxanne to the press for information, asking if anyone had seen her. It was a matter of urgency.

"Jesus," said Reilly. "What a mess."

"Between you and I, Sean, I think it's only just started."

Epilogue

Early on the Monday morning, two weeks later, Gardener was sitting in his office at Leeds Central, sifting through his paperwork, when the phone on his desk rang. He reached over and answered it.

"Morning, sir."

"Morning, Maurice. How are you?"

"I'm okay. I have some news for you."

"Go on," said Gardener. He leaned back in his chair as Reilly walked into the office with a coffee and a doughnut and a bottle of water.

Gardener switched it on to speakerphone.

"It's a mixture of good and bad."

"It always is," said Gardener. "I'll leave it to you where you want to start first."

"I thought you might like to know that all your hard work catching Edgar Crowther wasn't for nothing."

"What do you mean?" asked Gardener.

"He doesn't have impunity. You will be able to take it to court."

Reilly pulled up a chair and listened more closely.

"Why?" asked Gardener, thinking about what had happened since then. The most important fact was that a thorough search of Edgar's house held no clues as to Roxanne Harrington's whereabouts. The only thing they found was the Peugeot minibus. There was no trace of the old white ambulance. "Has he somehow miraculously recovered?"

"You could say that," replied Cragg.

"What do you mean?" asked Reilly.

"Following his arrest," continued Cragg, "Edgar was brought to the station here. The police doctor immediately transferred him to Bramfield Community; Edgar had said that if he couldn't go there, he wasn't going anywhere. When he arrived, he was unconscious. Tests were done very quickly and a liver became available almost immediately."

"How?" asked Gardener.

"I've no idea," said Cragg. "All I do know is Edward White had something to do with it. He found the liver, he did the transplant, and now Edgar is recovering nicely."

"Good old Edward," said Reilly. "Looking after their own again."

"Executing Harrington's wish, possibly?" said Gardener.

"Definitely," said Cragg. "I'm afraid the easy way out is not an option for Edgar now. He'll be forced to live, in prison; after you've finished with him, I dare say."

Gardener couldn't believe what he was hearing. After everything that had happened. "Edgar Crowther must be fuming."

"Lawsuits have been mentioned," said Cragg.

Gardener glanced at Reilly, who broke out into a grin. "Never a dull moment, is there? You couldn't write this stuff."

"Thanks for letting us know," said Gardener. "I'll pass this on to DCI Briggs and we'll tie up the relevant paperwork. This should please Harrington, but it won't be enough to exonerate him."

"That's not going to matter, sir."

"Why not?" asked Gardener.

"That's where the bad news comes in."

"Go on," said Gardener, glancing at Reilly.

Cragg continued. "We found Michael Harrington this morning."

"When you say found, what do you mean exactly?"

"He was in his garage, sir. In his car. Everything were sealed and a pipe from the exhaust led into the car. He must have been there a while, judging the condition he were in."

Gardener ran that one through his mind. Michael Harrington had been questioned and released on bail pending inquiries. What had happened with Milly was fifteen years old and it would take another entire team to sort through that case.

"How did you find out about Michael?" asked Reilly.

"Because we've found his wife."

"What?" Gardener shot forward, the desk nearly overturning.

"Where?" asked Reilly.

"She were found wandering around in the grounds of her own house," said Cragg.

"She was at home?" questioned Gardener.

"Yes, sir, in a very distressed state. She had the same clothes on that we saw on the CCTV the day she were carried out of the house. She's lost some weight; her complexion is ashen and the Lord only knows where she's been."

"Where is she now?" asked Gardener.

"She's been taken to the hospital, sir. She's unable to speak to anyone. You get the odd whimper out of her but that's all. Once they've completed tests, they'll decide what's best for her. Wherever she goes, I doubt she will ever come out again. I doubt she'll ever talk again. What that poor woman has been through."

"Where has she been?" asked Gardener. "Have you any idea?"

"No one knows," replied Cragg. "Like I said, she hasn't spoken, and I don't think she will."

"I wonder if she's been locked in that bloody ambulance for two weeks," said Reilly.

"If she has," said Gardener, "where the hell is it?"

Everyone grew silent before Gardener said. "You don't think she might be responsible, do you, for Michael's death?"

"I don't think there's any chance of that sir, she's too far gone. And all the indications are there that it was suicide."

"Did he leave a note?" asked Gardener.

"We didn't find one."

"Why did you think Edgar let her live?" Reilly asked Cragg.

"There's only one reason I can think of."

"Which is?" asked Gardener.

"She has Milly's heart," replied Cragg.

If you enjoyed this book, please let others know by leaving a quick review on Amazon. Also, if you spot anything untoward in the paperback, get in touch. We strive for the best quality and appreciate reader feedback.

editor@thebookfolks.com

www.thebookfolks.com

ALSO AVAILABLE

If you enjoyed IMPUNITY, the tenth book, check out the others in the series:

IMPURITY – *Book 1*

Someone is out for revenge. A grotto worker is murdered in the lead up to Christmas. He won't be the first. Can DI Gardener stop the killer, or is he saving his biggest gift till last?

IMPERFECTION – *Book 2*

When theatre-goers are treated to the gruesome spectacle of an actor's lifeless body hanging on the stage, DI Stewart Gardener is called in to investigate. Is the killer still in the audience? A lockdown is set in motion but it is soon apparent that the murderer is able to come and go unnoticed. Identifying and capturing the culprit will mean establishing the motive for their crimes, but perhaps not before more victims meet their fate.

IMPLANT – *Book 3*

A small Yorkshire town is beset by a series of cruel murders. The victims are tortured in bizarre ways. The killer leaves a message with each crime – a playing card from an obscure board game. DI Gardener launches a manhunt but it will only be by figuring out the murderer's motive that they can bring him to justice.

IMPRESSION – *Book 4*

Police are stumped by the case of a missing five-year-old girl until her photograph turns up under the body of a murdered woman. It is the first lead they have and is quickly followed by the discovery of another body connected to the case. Can DI Stewart Gardener find the connection between the individuals before the abducted child becomes another statistic?

IMPOSITION – *Book 5*

When a woman's battered body is reported to police by her husband, it looks like a bungled robbery. But the investigation begins to turn up disturbing links with past crimes. They are dealing with a killer who is expert at concealing his identity. Will they get to him before a vigilante set on revenge?

IMPOSTURE – *Book 6*

When a hit and run claims the lives of two people, DI Gardener begins to realize it was not a random incident. But when he begins to track down the elusive suspects he discovers that a vigilante is getting to them first. Can the detective work out the mystery before more lives are lost?

IMPASSIVE – *Book 7*

A publisher racked with debts is found strung up in a ruined Yorkshire abbey. Has a disgruntled author taken their revenge? DI Stewart Gardener is on the case but maybe a hypnotist has the key to the puzzle. Can the cop muster his team to work some magic and catch a cunning killer?

IMPIOUS – *Book 8*

It could be detectives Gardener and Reilly's most disturbing case yet when a body with head, limbs and torso assembled from different victims is discovered. Alongside this grotesque being is a cryptic message and a chess piece. A killer wants to take the cops on a journey. And force their hand.

IMPLICATION – *Book 9*

When a body is found in a burned-out car, DI Stewart Gardener quickly establishes that a murder has been concealed. But with a missing person case and a spate of robberies occupying the force, he will struggle to identify the victim. When the investigations overlap, he'll have to work out which of the suspects is implicated in which crime.

IMPALED – *Book 11*

When Gardener is called to investigate a crime, he has no idea of the terrible scene that awaits him. The corpse of a man has been found with nails driven into his chest and no hands. There are no witnesses to the crime, just reports of a strangely dressed man seen nearby. Gardener feels a serial killer is at work, and the clock is ticking.

IMPROPER – *Book 12*

When a local actress is found dead in her luxury apartment, DI Stewart Gardener can't find any signs of foul play. Yet he is sure something is amiss. Investigating her last movements, he finds she associated with a known drug dealer, plus a mysterious man. Following his nose on what others see as a wild goose chase, has he lost the plot or will his hunch prove correct?

Other titles of interest

MURDER ON A YORKSHIRE MOOR by Ric Brady

Ex-detective Henry Ward is settling awkwardly into retirement in a quiet corner of Yorkshire when during a walk on the moor he stumbles upon the body of a young man. Suspecting foul play and somewhat relishing the return to a bit of detective work, he resolves to find out who killed him. But will the local force appreciate him sticking his nose in?

MURDER MOUNTAIN by Riall Nolan

Wanted by the FBI and hiding out on a remote island in
the Pacific, Peter Blake has an unwelcome visit. He's been
rumbled by a man who "trades in information" and the
price for not being handed over to the authorities is to use
his mountaineering experience to lead a team on a
dangerous mission to recover a fallen satellite. If he fails, it
will cost him his life.

YOUR COLD EYES by Denver Murphy

A serial killer is targeting women. He is dressing them up and discarding their bodies. Detectives become convinced that it is something about the way the victims look that is making them be selected. They need to find out just what that is, and why, to hunt down the killer.

All FREE with Kindle Unlimited and available in paperback!

www.thebookfolks.com

Printed in Dunstable, United Kingdom

64404002R10153